Raindrops

Lexington Justice

authorHOUSE®

AuthorHouse™
1663 Liberty Drive
Bloomington, IN 47403
www.authorhouse.com
Phone: 1 (800) 839-8640

© 2016 Lexington Justice. All rights reserved.

No part of this book may be reproduced, stored in a retrieval system, or transmitted by any means without the written permission of the author.

Published by AuthorHouse   07/11/2016

ISBN: 978-1-5246-1803-2 (sc)
ISBN: 978-1-5246-1802-5 (e)

Library of Congress Control Number: 2016911206

Print information available on the last page.

Any people depicted in stock imagery provided by Thinkstock are models, and such images are being used for illustrative purposes only. Certain stock imagery © Thinkstock.

This book is printed on acid-free paper.

Because of the dynamic nature of the Internet, any web addresses or links contained in this book may have changed since publication and may no longer be valid. The views expressed in this work are solely those of the author and do not necessarily reflect the views of the publisher, and the publisher hereby disclaims any responsibility for them.

Preface

Webster's dictionary defines the word *destiny* as the seemingly inevitable succession of events, or simply put, one's fate. Such an unsophisticated word, yet for ages its definition has challenged some of the greatest minds with the idea that our entire life has been predetermined, the possibility that no matter what we do, where we go, or what risks we take none will have any effect on our preprogrammed future and we will always end up where we were meant to be from day one.

However, what happens when the concept of "free will" is entered into the equation? What if each of our lives has been blueprinted and our future set but, by our very own doing, can be altered by the simplest of choices? What are the repercussions? What will the effects be? Will the results be negative? If so ... how extreme? Where does destiny play its role in the future then?

Wikipedia describes the Butterfly Effect as "the sensitive dependence on initial conditions, where a small change at one place in a deterministic, nonlinear system can result in large differences to a later state." The name of the effect, coined by Edward Lorenz, is derived from the theoretical example of a hurricane's formation being contingent on whether or not a distant butterfly had flapped its wings several weeks before.

This doesn't define destiny, but the idea that the smallest of events possibly causing tremendous influences in the future coincides with concept of minor events changing or affecting an individual's fate.

If you prefer not to believe in such notions, then life is what you make it. There are no preexisting influences, and you alone will dictate your fate. On the other hand, what if your future is prearranged and you begin on life's path but deviate from your course? Will destiny correct your trajectory? If so … how long will it take for this adjustment to take effect? Or will your shift be permanent and destiny no longer exist, leaving you on an unknown course?

Most never give this concept much thought, if any. Life is what they are going to make of it. They are in complete control of their existence, and with the exception of some minor influences, they command every action and decided how to deal with every reaction.

What if these individuals are wrong?

CHAPTER 1

The sun peeks over the top of the trees as Stefani Tanner turns onto Ardent Drive, the last stretch of her early morning run. Although once a competitive long-distance runner, she now runs to stay in shape but more importantly to prepare for the upcoming day. By the end of the week, her knees and ankles let her know that two days of rest are tremendously needed. Today being Monday, her legs are fully rested, and her pace is much faster than most would deem a typical jog.

As usual, her run began promptly at 5 a.m. The outing provides her with a much-needed opportunity to think without distractions and time to organize her thoughts and relieve stress. She never runs with the iPod she received as a Christmas gift three years ago simply because it would prevent her from concentrating, even though her husband has commented on many occasions what a waste of money it was. No, this time of the morning is quiet time. No kids complaining, no straightening up the house, no phone calls, no meetings, no interruptions… period. Her runs are totally for her and no one else.

As she nears the end of her run, her pace slows. Charlotte, North Carolina, in early June can be very warm and the humidity brutal, making breathing often an effort in itself. Physical activity at midday or during the late afternoon can be exhausting, not to mention outright dangerous. It is better to beat the heat early than to fight it at its peak. Many have suggested that Stefani invest in a treadmill or an elliptical, but she finds the time spent outside far too enjoyable.

Finally, she turns into her driveway and approaches the house. She never fails to remember how luck played a major part in finding this home seven years earlier. The wonderful, two-story colonial is tucked into a quiet neighborhood minutes from the chaos of the city. By chance, a simple afternoon drive led her and her family to this home that had been put on the market that very morning. There had been no doubt in her mind that this was to be home. She loves it as much now as she did then and has never second-guessed the decision to match the initial asking price; she never once considered negotiating a better deal.

After reaching the front steps, she walks in a circle repeatedly, her hands on her hips, catching her breath. Even at the age of forty-three her body quickly recovers from the five-mile run, and in no time her breathing is back to normal. She bends over, picks up the newspaper, and heads for the front door. As it does every morning, the run serves as a symbol for Stefani. Simply put, it marks the beginning of another frenzied day.

Quietly she closes the door behind her and makes her way through the darkness. Her husband, David and two sons, Blane and Jared, continue to sleep. She heads to the master bathroom, slips out of her running clothes and jumps into the shower. The warm water cascades through her silky, long, blond hair and down her well toned, petite body. Her dedication to keeping fit is evidenced by the definition of each muscle; hers is hardly the body of a middle-aged woman who carried two children and excels at a full-time job, not to mention all the responsibilities of keeping a house in order. Without question, her workload is one to make most individuals buckle at the knees.

Minutes later, Stefani is out of the shower, wrapped in a robe, and blow-drying her hair. There is no time to spend enjoying the sensation of the warm water; there is far too much to do and far too little time to do it in. Quickly, she is out of the bathroom and headed for her walk-in closet. As she passes the bed, she glances at David, who is snoring heavily, unaware that she is well into the beginning of her day.

Stefani exits the closet dressed in a formal business suit, the accepted attire for a senior marketing executive at AMERI-GEN, one of the largest electrical turbine manufacturing corporations in the country. It's not exactly the industry one would picture a beautiful woman thriving in, but Stefani has never been one to let gender or size influence her desire to succeed in anything. Her motivation and drive stem back to her days growing up in St. Michaels, Maryland. Her father, a waterman, and her mother, a dedicated homemaker, provided Stefani with a solid foundation and a strong moral fiber, creating an unparalleled work ethic. Being a straight-A student, valedictorian of her high school senior class, homecoming queen, and a superior athlete prepared her for her time spent at the University of NorthCarolina, where she received her BS in mechanical engineering and later her

MBA. As many have commented throughout her life, "Her level of energy is unchallenged."

Stefani makes her way to the kitchen. The scent of freshly brewed coffee fills the air. Although the coffee is ready it is solely for David. The one thing David manages to accomplish before going to bed is loading the automatic coffeemaker and confirming the timer is set to brew at exactly 6 a.m. Stefani reaches into the refrigerator and pulls out a container of green tea and a bowl of diced fruit. As she pours the tea into a glass, she hears the sound of an alarm clock. It is quickly silenced, and not long after, David staggers into the kitchen and grabs a coffee mug from the cupboard. Before he acknowledges Stefani's presence, he pours a cup and takes a sip. He sits at the bar, yawns, and scratches his head.

Stefani glances over and grins. "Good morning, sunshine."

David, two years older than Stefani, obviously doesn't possess the morning liveliness she does. Although he stays active by playing golf, his physical tone hardly compares to hers. Many times he has made the comment that Stefani is obsessed with her exercise routine, but she easily discounts his remarks as nothing more than his way of saying it's not for him.

He slowly looks up and groans. "It can't be Monday, can it?"

Stefani takes a sip of her tea and then pulls two cereal bowls from the cabinet. "I think it is, grumpy."

David sits and holds his coffee mug as he watches her prepare two bowls of cereal and place them on the breakfast-nook table. She pours two glasses of milk and places a Flintstone vitamin next to each glass. Both vitamins must be the same color to avoid a conflict between Blane and Jared. Only two years separate the boys, and the competitiveness between the two brothers is insanity. Blane, who is nine, clearly has a leg up on younger Jared. That being said, like his mother, Jared never backs away from a challenge.

Stefani wipes her hands on a towel and heads for the hallway. "Time to wake the sleeping beauties."

David continues to sit at the bar, sipping his coffee. "Knock yourself out."

Stefani enters the large bedroom that the boys share. There is a second bedroom across the hall that was originally intended to be Jared's, but scary noises in the dark and the occasional nightmare make sleeping in the same room with Blane much easier on everyone. The boys have managed to transform the other bedroom into a playroom that serves as a place to occupy themselves with video games as well as a battle zone when tempers flare.

The boys' bedroom is dark with the exception of the light illuminating a small fish tank sitting on a desk. Stefani walks over, glances at the two large goldfish, and sprinkles food into the water. "Hey, guys, how about some breakfast?"

She turns and stops for a moment to gaze at the boys, sleeping soundly in their bunk beds. Their angelic appearance warms Stefani's soul, but the innocent personas will soon disappear once they are disturbed. She smiles as she reaches up and softly shakes Blane's arm and then bends down and rubs Jared's head. "Okay, guys, it's time to get up."

The boy's final day of school was last Friday, which means they get to spend the weekdays of summer vacation at day care. This, in the boys' opinions, is punishment worse than death.

Stefani walks out of the room and heads back toward the kitchen. Moments later, Blane and Jared grudgingly stumble in. Both boys are wearing shorts, Carolina Panthers T-shirts, and hair that would frighten any hairstylist. As if on autopilot, both boys, with eyes half open, slide into their chairs and immediately slip a vitamin into their mouths. They eat their cereal, neither muttering a word. Stefani quickly slips back into their bedroom and lays out their clothes. She makes their beds, picks the dirty clothes off the floor, and tosses them into the hamper. She returns to the kitchen to find David thumbing through the newspaper and the boys finishing their cereal.

"Okay, guys, you need to jump in the shower. Your clothes are on your beds, and please remember to brush your teeth." She looks over at David, still sipping his coffee and reading the paper. "David, please remind Jared it's his turn to clean the fish tank when he gets home."

David nods without pulling his face out of the paper. Stefani scans the kitchen one last time. She walks over and kisses Blane and Jared on top of their heads. "Okay, guys, have a good day. I love you."

Each boy mumbles in return, "Love you, too, Mom."

Stefani turns and leans over to David. "Love you."

David tilts his head but does not turn to face her. Stefani kisses him on the cheek, grabs a leather shoulder bag off the counter, and heads for the front door. She reaches for the doorknob and then turns back. "David, don't forget about tonight."

David pops his head up from the paper and is suddenly alert. "Tonight? What's tonight?"

Stefani drops her head. "We're eating at Mallory and Jason's tonight ... remember?"

David slams the newspaper together and shakes his head. "Seriously ... that's tonight?"

Stefani lifts her head and stares at the front door. She pushes her tongue against the inside of her lower lip. "Yes, David ... it's tonight. I told you this a week ago. We're to be there at six ... remember?"

David shakes his head and then sarcastically chuckles. "Then I guess we'll be there at six."

Stefani opens the door. "Bye, guys."

When she walks out onto the landing the sun immediately warms her face. She momentarily stops, closes her eyes, and lifts her face toward the brightness. She smiles and takes a deep breath. "Let's do this."

Stefani makes her way down the walk and opens the door of her Volkswagen Touareg. As she slides in and carefully sets her bag on the passenger seat, she looks at the closed garage door in front of her. Inside sits David's BMW 550i. In her mind it's not that David doesn't deserve to drive such a nice vehicle—after all, he is a senior vice president in charge of production—but Stefani usually carts the boys around. Doing so in a vehicle that is nearly nine years old with over one hundred and fifty thousand miles on it doesn't instill a strong feeling of security. She occasionally drops hints to David about the vehicle, but for some reason her attempts always seem to fall on deaf ears.

She places her Bluetooth headset on her ear and then carefully backs out of the driveway. She turns on the local news and begins her thirty-minute trip. As she drives, she runs her morning activities through her head. Although she has a detailed calendar on her computer that is linked to her iPhone, her memory is as reliable and quicker to organize. Her ability to digest the news broadcast and review her schedule is a simple example of how well she can multitask with no confusion whatsoever.

Suddenly her concentration is interrupted by the ringing of her cell phone. She presses a button on the steering wheel, and the news is instantly muted. She glances over and sees "Office" displayed on her phone. She reaches up and taps the Bluetooth headset. "Hello."

After a brief pause, in a whispering voice, "Stef, it's Tonya."

Tonya Conner has been Stefani's administrative assistant and very close friend for nearly nine years. "Tonya, why are you whispering?"

Again there is a brief pause, and then Tonya says, "Stef, I'm freaking out! Something is going on in here this morning. I don't know what, but people are flying around the office, and you can cut the tension with a knife. To make matters worse, Mr. Roberts is up from Austin."

Stefani snaps her head back. "Mr. Roberts, as in Chairman of the Board Mr. Roberts, is in town? Was this announced?"

"No. I'm telling you, something is up. They have been behind closed doors and in Wendell Sander's office. Tracey has been racing files into them constantly."

Stefani looks at the clock on the dashboard. "Tonya, it's five after seven. Why is Wendell in the office now? He never gets there before eight. And Tracey? Are you kidding me? That girl has a hard time getting to work by eight, and she's there more than an hour early on a Monday?"

Stefani looks out the side window and shakes her head, totally mystified.

"Stef, I came in just before seven like I always do. I started to make coffee and grabbed the weekend reports when I noticed all the commotion. Stefani, you'd think it was eleven in the morning the way these people are flying around the office."

Stefani sits quietly as she processes everything. Soon, however, sounding anxious, Tonya blurts out, "Hello?"

"Sorry ... I'm still here."

Stefani is confused but knows priority one is to calm Tonya down. Tonya, although the absolute best person to have as an assistant and a friend, can let her emotions get the best of her.

"I'm sure it's nothing. I'll be there in about twenty minutes. Don't worry—we'll figure this out."

"Okay, girl ... just get here quick!"

"I'll be there in a few."

Stefani ends the call and places both hands on top of the steering wheel and taps the wheel with her thumbs. *Why would Roberts make an unannounced visit on a Monday? Why is Wendell in early? What are all the meetings about?*

Stefani looks over her left shoulder and merges onto the interstate. *And Tracey is early? Something is up.*

Stefani reaches over and picks up her phone. She scrolls to her calendar to check her schedule. "Phew, didn't miss a meeting."

She then runs through her emails. "Nothing out of the ordinary."

Before she picked up the phone she knew she hadn't missed anything. Many of her colleagues accuse her of having a photographic memory, and once it's in her head she never forgets. She sets the phone on the console and continues her drive. "Well, this week is starting off on the right foot."

Twenty minutes later Stefani pulls into the employee lot and slips into her parking spot, which is clearly identified with an AMERI-GEN sign displaying her name. She gathers her phone and bag and heads for the main entrance. As she walks through the revolving front door, she is greeted by the receptionist sitting at a large wooden desk.

"Good morning, Mrs. Tanner."

"Good morning, Lori. How was your weekend?"

"It was nice, thank you."

Stefani heads for the elevators but then pauses. She turns and looks back. "Lori, I hear things around the office are somewhat exciting this morning."

Lori nods. "I think you're right. Mr. Roberts arrived early this morning. Then a group of men dressed in very expensive suits came in shortly thereafter. I'm not sure what that's all about."

Stefani turns back to the elevators and then glances back at Lori. "Any of these suits work for us?"

Lori slowly shakes her head. "If they do I've never seen them before."

Stefani squints, puckers her lips, and tilts her head. "Interesting." She readjusts her shoulder bag and then walks to the elevator. "Thanks, Lori. Have a great day."

"You too, Mrs. Tanner."

Stefani reaches the elevator and presses the UP button. She looks up and patiently watches the illuminated numbers until the elevator finally reaches the ground floor. The door opens, and she steps inside. She presses the button for the executive level, the ninth floor. Rarely does she have the elevator to herself, but the few times she does allows her to drop her guard a bit and check her makeup in the refection of the mirrored walls. As she looks herself over, she shakes her head. *Why would Roberts be holding meetings early on a Monday morning and not tell everyone from the executive team?*

The elevator doors open, and Stefani steps out. Clearly she is on the executive floor. The walls are paneled in dark cherry, and the furniture would make Bill Gates proud. She walks down the long hallway and turns into an open area filled with individual cubicles surrounded by private offices on the perimeter.

As she makes her way to her office, she passes Tonya's workspace. Tonya isn't there, so she turns to her door and slides her key into the lock. The door opens, and she is greeted by a tidy and organized office. The morning sun shines through the slightly tinted plate glass windows, providing more than enough light to see everything is in its place. She walks around her desk, pulls the high-backed chair out, and sits down. She wiggles the mouse, and her large screen comes to life, displaying her desktop background picture of Blane and Jared in their Little League baseball uniforms. She clicks on the Outlook icon. "Okay, let's see what we have here."

There are seventeen new messages in her mailbox. She scrolls through the list and deletes the emails she knows are junk. "Eleven ... not bad for a Monday morning."

As she opens the first email, Tonya slips through her door and looks behind as though worried that someone may be watching her. Once satisfied, she closes the door and turns to Stefani. "Stef, I'm telling you something is going on, and I don't think it's a good thing."

Stefani leans back in her chair. "Okay, tell me what you think is going on."

"Girl, it's something big. People are walking around here like they have eggshells under their feet, and the entire H. R. department is in a closed-door meeting in the conference room."

Stefani immediately sits up. "The entire Human Resource department is in a meeting? Is Roberts in there?"

Tonya quickly nods. "I'm pretty sure he is."

Stefani flops back in her chair and leans her head back. "Certainly sounds like we may be caught up in a very serious legal issue."

Tonya folds her arms in front of her, leans forward, and tilts her head to the side. "A legal issue?"

Stefani slowly rocks forward and rests her elbows on her desk as she clasps her hands against her lips.

"Sounds like it to me. Evidently we either had a casualty at one of our facilities or have been cited for some kind of violation, either patent related or an EPA defiance. Why else would all these suits be here along with Mr. Roberts first thing on a Monday morning?"

Tonya turns, cracks the door open, and peers out. She then opens the door and walks out, but quickly turns back. "Stef, find out what's going on before I lose it."

Stefani snickers. "Okay … just don't flip out."

Tonya heads for her desk as Stefani gears up for the day. She responds to the emails and makes a few telephone calls. Unexpectedly, Amy Tyler from the Human Resources knocks on the open door. Stefani looks up. "Hello, Amy."

Amy walks in and stands at Stefani's desk. "Stefani, there's a meeting scheduled for twelve in the executive conference room."

Stefani sits up, concerned. "Okay. Do I need to prepare anything?"

Amy shakes her head. "No … just come as you are. Wendell Sanders will be heading the meeting."

"Any idea what the topic of discussion is?"

Amy smiles, though it looks forced, and turns to exit Stefani's office. "Nothing to get concerned about I'm sure."

Stefani, rattled, reaches for the phone as soon as Amy leaves. She dials David's cell number and anxiously waits for him to answer.

"Hello."

Stefani leans forward as if doing so will muffle her whispering. "Hey, it's me."

"What's up?"

"I don't know. Things around here are crazy. People are constantly walking in and out of meetings. Some of the people in the meetings no one has ever seen before. Everyone is clearly on edge. To top everything off Amy Tyler comes in my office and announces a meeting that is to take place at noon. She tells me I don't need anything for the meeting. I've never experienced anything like this before."

"What's your gut tell you?"

"Well, like I told Tonya, either we are in violation with someone like the EPA, or we are being cited for a patent infringement or possibly a casualty at one of our facilities." Stefani peeks out her door to see if anyone may be listening in on her conversation.

"Stef, it's probably nothing. Maybe the old man is stepping down and they're going to announce his replacement."

Stefani takes a deep breath. "I guess … if I don't call you back I'll fill you tonight before we head to Mallory and Jason's."

"Terrific."

Stefani quickly becomes irritated. "David, I know it's difficult for you to have fun, but do me a favor and try to look happy when we get there."

"Whatever you say."

"Okay, gotta go."

"Bye."

She hangs up the phone and leans back in her chair. *What the heck is going on?*

Stefani sits at her desk fumbling through files. She looks up at the clock on the wall every five minutes. Finally it's 11:50 a.m. She rises from her chair and grabs her leather bag. She tosses the strap over her shoulder and takes a deep breath. As she exits her office, she puts on a firm "corporate" face and heads for the conference room. When she reaches the huge wooden double doors she grabs the large brass handle and pulls. The heavy door opens revealing nearly fifty people all dressed in very formal attire and softly chatting in separate groups. Stefani scans the room, looking for a "friendly." Suddenly Wendell Sanders calls out to her. "Stefani, please find a seat … we'll be starting shortly."

Stefani nods and walks over to one of the many large, high-back leather chairs tucked under the enormous mahogany conference table. She rests her bag on the floor and slips into the chair. She pulls out a legal pad, pen, and cell phone. She checks to make sure her phone is on the silent setting. When she looks at the screen she sees a text message from Tonya: "Girl, let me know something ASAP! I am freaking out!"

Stefani snickers, confirms the phone is silenced, and slips it into her pocket. As she organizes her items in front of her, Sanders barks out, "Okay, people, let's get started."

Quickly everyone settles down, and the room is silent. Stefani looks around and recognizes many people from different departments, but no one makes any eye contact.

"All right, I'm quite sure everyone is interested in the activity that has taken place here this morning."

Without warning the conference room door opens and Roberts enters, followed by two other men. Sanders continues, "Everyone knows Mr. Roberts. These other gentlemen are Richard Manchester and Carl Adair of Aeron International."

Stefani notices the uncomfortable movements everyone is making. Manchester and Adair follow Roberts to the head of the table, each taking a seat. There is a painful silence that lasts only a few seconds but seems like an eternity.

In a raspy, deep voice, Roberts speaks. "Everyone … there's no need in sugar-coating what needs to be said, so let's keep from wasting everyone's time. For those of you who do not know, Richard Manchester and Carl Adair are the principal owners of Aeron International. Roughly three months ago these two men approached our board of directors and offered to purchase AMERI-GEN."

Groans can be heard throughout the room as everyone adjusts themselves in their chairs.

"After extensive consideration AMERI-GEN has decided to accept Aeron's offer and will transfer ownership of the entire AMERI-GEN operation to Aeron International effective midnight tonight."

Stefani's chin drops. Everyone is clearly in shock, and she's sure most are concerned about their future with the organization.

"With this being said I will now turn over the meeting to Richard Manchester."

Manchester sits up and quickly gazes at the group. "People, I am fully aware this has come as a shock to each and every one of you. I am also aware there is major concern pertaining to the security of your positions with the corporation. Yes, many people will be transferred or will be outright dismissed. This is the unfortunate result of a corporate acquisition. However, Aeron International didn't get to be where it is by making senseless mistakes. During the last few months we have reviewed each and every corporate executive's position and their importance to AMERI-GEN. Trust in the fact we would be unwise to remove anyone who has proven themselves a fundamental asset to the success of AMERI-GEN. Bottom line, we will keep the people who have made this company what it is."

Stefani hangs her head and stares at the blank legal pad sitting on the table in front of her. Does the empty page represent her future with Aeron International? A cold sensation suddenly shoots up her spine. She looks up and scans the room. With the exception of the administrators at the head of the table, she is surrounded by lifeless bodies.

Manchester continues, "Each one of you will meet with our staff to discuss your future and your role with the organization. Until then everyone needs to continue to perform as you did before the news of this acquisition was announced. In other words ... business as usual. If anyone outside of this room asks you anything, you are to tell them a formal announcement will be made tomorrow explaining everything ... that is all."

Everyone slowly stands and exits the room without saying a word. Stefani, rattled, makes her way back to her office. She sets her materials on her desk and slumps down into her office chair. Seconds later Tonya pops into her office and closes the door. "Okay, what the hell is going on?"

Stefani looks at Tonya and shakes her head. She knows she needs to tell Tonya something but is in a position where she can't reveal too much information.

"Well ... the only thing I know is there will be a meeting tomorrow explaining everything in detail. Beyond that I don't have much of a clue."

Tonya cross her arms and puckers her lips. "Seriously, that's all you know?

"Tonya, we just had a fifteen-minute meeting. How much can possibly be said in fifteen minutes? We should know more tomorrow."

Tonya turns and heads for the door. She pauses and looks back at Stefani. "Girl, this shit has me nervous as hell."

Stefani forces a smile. "Tonya, everything is going to be fine."

Tonya turns and leaves. Stefani tries to focus on her work, but she finds it impossible. Thoughts race through her head. *What if they let me go? What if they want me to relocate? Relocate? I can't move. What's David going to do? What about the boys? My God … this can't be happening.*

Stefani gets up and heads to the ladies' room. She walks over to the sink and looks down at her trembling hands as she turns the faucet on. Two women from accounting are standing together just down from her, and she can't help but hear their conversation. Obviously they, too, are concerned about their future. One goes as far to say she heard Aeron International is run by a group of "ruthless pricks" and are known for eliminating everyone at the corporate level when there is an acquisition. The two exit, leaving Stefani alone. As she reaches for a hand towel, she stares at herself in the mirror. Feeling lightheaded, her breathing becomes labored. *What am I going to do?*

She returns to her office and sits down. She stares at the image of Blane and Jared on her screen, takes a deep breath, and tries to focus on her work. As the day drags on, her pain intensifies. She leans back in her chair and rubs her eyes.

When she pulls her hands from her face, she finds Tonya standing in front of her desk. "Stef, are you okay?"

"Yeah, just a bit of a headache"

"I have some Aleve in my desk."

"No, that's okay … I'm good."

Tonya looks over her shoulder and then back at Stefani. "Stef … all bullshit aside, what's your gut tell you?"

Stefani takes a deep breath and blows out hard. She stares Tonya in the eye for a second and then says, "I honestly don't have a clue. I wish I had something to tell you, but at this point everything is speculation. I honestly don't know."

Tonya rests her hands on the desk and leans forward toward Stefani. "Like I asked earlier … what's your gut tell you?"

Stefani pinches her lips together and slowly shakes her head. "Tonya … I'm afraid."

Tonya drops her head and exhales hard. "Shit. I knew it." She raises her head, and Stefani is sure Tonya sees the concern on her face. "What the fuck are we going to do?"

Stefani shrugs her shoulders. "I guess what they told all of us in the meeting."

"Yeah? What the hell was that?"

"Business as usual."

Tonya blurts out a sarcastic laugh. "Oh, sure … that's like telling a guy on death row, who has hours to live, to act today like any other day."

Stefani runs her hand through her hair. "I know."

Tonya crosses her arms and turns to look out the window. Clearly she is fighting to hold back a tear. Stefani rests her elbows on her desk and rubs her forehead with her fingertips. "Tonya, as soon as I hear anything I'll let you know."

Tonya nods her head and sniffs. "I know you will."

"Hey, Tonya …"

"Yeah?"

"Not a word about any of this to anyone, okay?"

Tonya looks at Stefani and nods. "You got it."

CHAPTER 2

Stefani, David, and the boys head for dinner at Mallory and Jason Morgan's house. The ride is totally void of conversation. Stefani is stressed about her situation at work, and talking about it would do nothing more, at this point, than intensify the already existing anxiety. Besides, Stefani and David made a promise, years ago, to never discuss their business issues in front of the boys. Stefani turns and looks at the boys, who are snugly belted into their seats of the Touareg.

"Now, you guys know to be on your best behavior."

Both boys cut a disdainful look at Stefani. She, out of habit, makes that comment whenever they go anywhere. The fact of the matter is both Blane and Jared are very well-behaved boys. Many times David and Stefani have been approached by adults who comment, almost in an envious manner, on how well behaved the boys are. As most parents would prefer, they act out at home but in public are very respectful and nearly perfect kids.

Stefani smiles and turns forward. She glances over at David, who is driving. Clearly he has no interest in this dinner engagement and has less interest in driving her car. Stefani looks forward through the windshield and thinks, *Well, David we could have taken your car, but the only passengers allowed to ride in your chariot are your golf clubs.*

David slows, turns into a long driveway, and parks. Everyone exits the car and makes their way up the walk. As they hit the front steps, they are met by Jason Morgan.

"Hey there, Tanner crew, come on in."

The boys dart in and head for the family room like they've done so many times before. Jason laughs. "Guys, I think Mitch and Seth are in the family room playing Call of Duty." He looks at Stefani and David and adds, "As if they didn't already know."

The three laugh as they make their way through the foyer into the kitchen, where Mallory Morgan is preparing dinner. "Hey, guys."

Stefani walks up behind Mallory and gives her a soft hug. "Mallory, whatever you're making, it smells wonderful."

Jason walks over to the refrigerator. "David, how about a beer?"

"Yesssss."

Jason reaches into the refrigerator and pulls out two Coors Light bottles. He pops the top off each and hands one to David. David nods, takes a huge gulp. "Oh yeah."

Mallory walks over to the sink to rinse off a bowl of cauliflower. "Jason, why don't you and David go out on the deck? Stef and I will be out shortly with the food."

The two men bolt out as if they were just paroled from prison. Stefani walks over to the center island and fumbles with the cooking utensils lying on the countertop. "Mallory, what can I help you with?"

"There's nothing else to do but carry the stuff out. If you'd grab the salad bowl, I'll grab the dressing and bread. Jason has the steaks on the grill, and the table is already set."

As they head for the back door, Mallory yells out to the boys in the family room, "Guys, let's go. It's time to eat."

Moments later everyone is sitting down at the table nestled on a large, beautiful deck. The boys quickly devour their dinner so they can return to their Call of Duty session, but before they can leave, Jason stops the boys. "Hey, guys, instead of burning up the rest of the evening playing Call of Duty, why don't you walk over to the garage and shoot some ball at that high-dollar basketball hoop we had to buy because you were going to take up the game?"

The four boys look at Jason, their faces expressing dislike of the idea, but accept his suggestion and saunter over to the driveway. The court Jason built in the backyard butts up against the detached two-car garage located at the head of the driveway. As the boys toss the ball around, Stefani reaches over, grabs David's arm, and blurts out, "Jason, the garage door has so many windows."

Jason and Mallory have matching Chevrolet Tahoes parked in the garage. Both vehicles sit so high each can be seen clearly through the windows. Stefani continues, "Aren't you afraid the ball is going to go through a window and hit one of the cars?"

Jason looks forward and stares at Stefani with a cynical expression. "Stefani, I'd love to see it happen. At least that way I know my two sons aren't addicted to these stinking video games and actually do have some coordination. I'll bet you that hoop hasn't had fifty balls go through it since I put it up six months ago."

Mallory looks over at Jason and laughs. "Yeah, Jason … that's what we need, something else broken around here. How long has the lock on the outside basement door been broken? You've been fixing that for three months. Boy, if anyone wanted to break in to our house all they'd have to do is walk right into the basement. They could do it and no one would ever know they were in the house."

Jeff glances at Mallory briefly. "That's why I want to get a dog."

"Uh … as we have discussed so many times before, there will be no dogs in my house."

All four watch the boys shoot around. Jason, in a tone of disgust, utters out a final statement about the subject. "I'm not so sure things are better for kids these days. Sure, they have all the technology, but most can't even throw a baseball straight or ride a bicycle without falling off. It's nothing short of sad."

Jason and David lean back in their chairs and continue to add to the number of empty beer bottles on the table. Mallory sits back and sighs. She appears to have no immediate plans of cleaning up; if anything she looks like she intends on staying put for an extended period of time. Stefani sits preoccupied in thought as conversation drags. Out of the blue Mallory leans forward and puts her arms on the table. "Stef, what's up? You've been extremely quiet this evening."

Stefani quickly sits up, somewhat embarrassed. "Oh … I'm sorry. It's nothing … I'm fine."

David reaches over and rests his hand on Stefani's back. "She's a bit concerned about work."

Mallory cocks her head back as she squints. "What's going on?"

Stefani clasps her hands and rests them in her lap. "Well … no one is supposed to know officially until tomorrow, but we are being purchased by Aeron International. We had a meeting today with all the executives and were told many of us would either be transferred or dismissed."

Mallory falls back into her chair and covers her mouth with her hand. "Oh my God."

Stefani forces a half-hearted smile. "Yeah … not exactly what a person wants to hear. Richard Manchester of Aeron did say they have evaluated each executive's importance to the company and won't eliminate any of the valuable personnel, but who knows at this point?"

Jason sits up and shakes his head as he places another empty beer bottle on the table. "Stef, you're not going anywhere. You've been with that company for over fifteen years. You are far too valuable and a key reason why AMERI-GEN has been so successful."

Stefani looks down at her hands. "Thanks … but you never know."

Mallory looks over at David and then back at Stefani. "Stef … Jason is right. These guys aren't dumb and certainly recognize the value they have with you on their team. You'll be fine."

David lets out a soft beer burp and sits up. "Exactly."

Jason does his best to break up the tension and says in a sarcastic and very loud voice, "Now you want to talk about valuable … look at me. I'm getting on a plane tomorrow headed for Sheboygan, Wisconsin, to discuss cellophane issues with a cheese-wrapping process. Now there's something to feel secure about. I get to spend eight days watching American cheese slices get individually wrapped and pray every slice passes inspection or the plant gets shut down."

The group laughs as Jason flops back in his chair and stretches his arms out as if he has completed a terrific speech and is waiting for applause.

Stefani loosens up as the conversation continues. "I guess I just feel overwhelmed at the moment. This situation at work, the kids going to day care for the entire day now that school has ended for the summer. They both hate it so badly ... I guess I just need to relax."

Jason snickers. "No ... what you need is a large glass of wine and about four more after that one."

The group laughs again and then slowly settles down. Stefani looks over at Jason, who is sitting there comfortably with his eyes closed. "Jason, does it ever get old?"

"Does what ever get old?"

"All the traveling you do ... being away from your family for a week at a time or longer?"

Jason nods. "Sure it does, but you do what you have to do. Besides, I have Mallory here to hold the fort down while I'm gone."

Mallory cocks her head and looks over at Stefani. "Uh-huh, and someone needs to chip in a bit more around the fort when his noble ass is home."

David lets out a laugh. "Damn! It's like that over here, too?"

Jason bites down on his tongue and squints. "Oh, she's ruthless."

Mallory looks over at Jason and slowly nods. "Just remember this ruthless woman packed your bags for tomorrow's trip."

Jason leans over, wraps his arm around her, and gives her a tight squeeze. "I know you did, sugar."

David plops his empty beer bottle on the table and takes a deep breath. "That's why I love my job. I rarely, if ever, have to travel. I have the flexibility to come and go when I want, and the perks are great."

Jason wobbles his head back and forth and sticks his tongue out at David. "Oh, eat shit, Golden Boy."

David laughs. "That's right, big-boy, and don't you forget it."

The four stand and carry the dishes into the kitchen. Stefani looks down at her watch. "David, it's getting late, and the boys have to be at day care at eight tomorrow."

Mallory quickly adds, "And my lovely sons will be spending the next two weeks with their grandparents."

Stefani grins at Mallory. "Jason is gone for a week and the boys for two? What are you going to do?"

Mallory snaps her head back and forth and answers is a raspy voice, "Lots of cleaning and lots of alcohol consumption."

The women breakout into uncontrollable laughter. Stefani puts a glass in the sink, and then says, "Well, you enjoy your cleaning and alcohol. I'm going home to prepare for another day of the bump and grind."

Stefani glances at David and smiles. "David, let's go before I get the urge to stop and buy some wine and cleaning supplies."

David nods and sticks his head out the back door, yelling to Blane and Jared. Mallory walks over and puts her arm around Stefani. "Stef, don't you worry about your job … you'll be fine."

"Thanks … I hope so."

Stefani and Mallory hug briefly, and then Stefani turns and walks toward the foyer. "Jason, Mallory, thank you for a great evening."

Jason and Mallory follow Stefani to the front door, where she meets David, Blane, and Jared. David reaches out and shakes Jason's hand. Jason reaches down and gives Stefani a quick hug. "Stef, everything will be fine I know it."

Stefani nods and smiles. "Jason, have a safe trip."

"I will."

While the Tanners back out of the driveway, Jason and Mallory wave. Stefani waves back and watches until the front door closes. David lets out a huge sigh as they travel toward the freeway.

"Now seriously, David, was tonight that bad?"

"No, Stef, it wasn't that bad."

David starts working the steering wheel back and forth quickly as he drives. "This thing drives funny. Did you hit something?"

Stefani fires back, "No, David. Could it possibly be the car is old enough to be in high school and is nearly worn out? I wouldn't consider driving this car on a long trip. It makes all kinds of noises and runs rough, but every time I tell you it needs to go to a garage you tell me it's okay. I guess it will have to stop cold before we do anything, right?"

David stops working the steering wheel and continues to drive, not responding to Stefani's question. Stefani looks out the passenger window and gazes at the beautiful red sky as the sun is about to set. She turns and looks forward through the windshield. "David, you should be more careful what you say to Jason about work."

Clearly offended, David swiftly looks over at Stefani. "What do you mean?"

"The comment about how great your job is and how fantastic you have it with all the freedom and perks and how you come and go without answering to anyone."

"I wasn't being a jerk—I was stating fact. That's exactly how it is."

"I know that, but to a guy who has to travel so much and probably hates it … I'm sure he doesn't like having it rubbed in his face."

David shakes his head and sneers. "You're blowing this way out of proportion. If Jason doesn't like his job, then maybe it's time he looks for a new one."

"I just think you need to be careful what you say when it comes to how good you have it."

David is visibly becoming irritated. "If you think I'm going to feel guilty because of my job, you have truly lost your mind. I've worked hard to be where I am, and if people have a problem with that, then tough shit."

Stefani cuts her eyes at David and then stares forward through the windshield. "Nice, David, really nice. I'm sure the boys really enjoyed your little speech as well."

David looks over and then softly laughs. "Whatever."

Chapter 3

Stefani pulls into a parking spot at the Tender Heart Day Care Center just shy of 8:00 a.m. There is total silence in the car, and Stefani, trying to resist looking in the rearview mirror, knows the boys are totally infuriated about having to spend every weekday of their summer vacation at the prison for preteens. With the exception of a two-week Talented and Gifted Children's Camp at the UNC campus, the boys figure their summer vacation is shot before it has even started.

Stefani takes a deep breath. "Okay, guys, let's go."

Blane undoes his seat belt and says, "Mom, this totally bogus."

Stefani turns and looks at him. "Bogus?"

Blane, clearly annoyed, says, "Yeah, Mom. Bogus. I can't believe I have to spend my entire summer here with a bunch of babies."

Stefani undoes her seat belt and opens the car door. "Honey, I know you don't like this, but we don't have a choice. We've discussed this so many times. You and Jared are too young to be alone at home."

When Stefani opens Jared's door, he already has his seat belt undone and his backpack in hand. They walk up to the front door and enter. Stefani approaches the front desk and signs the boys in. Quickly they are met by their day-care mother, Mrs. Ellis.

"Hello, Tanner men. Are we looking handsome today."

Blane looks back at Stefani and rolls his eyes. Stefani smiles. "Good morning, Mrs. Ellis."

The woman grins. "Yes, it is, and we have a full day planned ahead of us." She puts one hand on Blane's shoulder and the other on top of Jared's head. "Let's head down to our room, men, and we'll get settled in."

Stefani watches the boys walk with Mrs. Ellis down the long hallway. Slowly Jared turns his head back and looks at her. "Bogus, Mom."

Stefani sighs and turns for the door. She feels terrible guilt that quickly shifts to total fear as she begins the brief drive to work. She looks at her face in the rearview mirror. *Well, girl, let's see what the day brings.*

She arrives at 8:25, makes her way to her office, and starts to go through her emails. "So far so good."

Tonya bursts into her office. "Stef, I haven't slept in thirty-six hours. This shit is killing me!"

Stefani pauses for a moment, knowing many of the lower staff will be victims of the acquisition cuts. "Tonya, relax.

You're getting yourself all worked up. Now what's on the agenda for today?"

Tonya stands in front of the desk, twisting back and forth at the hips as she chews on her thumbnail. "You have a meeting at ten with the IT department to review the new email protocol."

Stefani nods. "Anything else?"

Tonya drops her hands to her side and flips her head back. "God, I don't remember."

Stefani chuckles, stands, and walks around to face Tonya. "Why don't we try this again. Tonya, why don't you go and get us some coffee."

Tonya bows her head as she, too, laughs. "Good idea."

She turns and bolts out the door. Stefani watches Tonya speed-walk toward the corporate kitchen. *Lord, I hope no one steps in front of her.*

Stefani returns to her desk and moves the mouse. When her screensaver disappears she is greeted by a new email. She looks at the name of the author. "C. Roberts."

Suddenly she breaks out into a cold sweat and whispers, "Oh my God."

She tries to move the cursor to open the email, but her hand seems to be fighting her. Finally she manages the energy to click the email, and it opens.

> *Stefani, I would like to see you in my office at nine. We will be having a meeting with Wendell Sanders, Richard Manchester and Carl Adair.*

Stefani flops back in her chair. She looks up at the clock on the wall; it's 8:35. She places her elbows on the desk and leans forward, softly massaging her forehead with her fingertips. Her heart rate picks up, and she begins to feel somewhat lightheaded. She gets up and manages to walk to the bathroom. She looks into the mirror. Her makeup is perfect, but her expression clearly reveals her intense fear. She mumbles to herself, "I don't think I can do this."

She stands up and takes in a deep breath. She speaks loudly and boldly as she throws a paper towel in the trash can. "No, I'm not going to let this get to me. I'm fine, and I'm going to be fine."

Confidently she turns and walks back to her office. When she enters she is met by Tonya, who is anxiously waiting for her return. "Girl, what's up?"

Stefani grabs her bag. "I have a meeting with the bigwigs at nine."

Tonya's jaw drops. "No shit?"

Stefani turns and faces her. "No shit. I'll see you when I get back."

She exits and heads for Robert's office. Roberts has always been one about authority and image. Even though he splits time between locations, his office area covers one fourth of the executive floor. She approaches the secretarial desk that is just to the right of the closed, massive wooden doors isolating Robert's personal office from the rest of the sector.

Stefani looks down and sees April Winchester sitting at the desk. "Good morning, April."

April forces a smile. "Good morning, Mrs. Tanner. Mr. Roberts and the other gentlemen will be with you shortly. Just have a seat, please."

Stefani is about to jump out of her skin. She turns and finds a seat on one of the large leather couches. She looks at a huge iron clock mounted on the wall; it's now 8:55. She looks down at her watch and then turns and looks out the large window overlooking downtown Charlotte. She tries to maintain her composure, but her mind keeps repeating, *I'm about to lose it.*

The silence is deafening as Stefani patiently waits. Suddenly April jerks her head up and places her hand against the earpiece in her left ear. "Yes, sir."

April glances over at Stefani. "Mr. Roberts will see you now."

Stefani rises and musters a half-hearted smile. She gathers her belongings and takes a deep breath as she walks toward the large door. She hesitates before turning the doorknob. *Come on, Stef ... it's only your life.*

She opens the door and enters what could only be called the palace of corporate offices. Roberts stands while the other three remain seated at a small conference table with totally lifeless expressions on their faces. "Stefani, come in and take a seat."

Stefani nods and sits down across from the group of four. She sets her belongings on the floor beside her, interlaces her fingers, and rests her hands on the table.

Roberts leans back in his chair and says, "Stefani, the group and I have discussed in detail the magnitude of your importance to this company. Your years of dedicated service have proven instrumental in the continued success of AMERI-GEN.

Stefani sits up and smiles. "Thank you."

Roberts leans forward and rests his forearms on the table. "With that being said, it makes it very difficult to make certain changes in the corporate circle."

Stefani squints and slowly shakes her head. "Mr. Roberts, I'm not quite sure I follow you."

Suddenly Manchester loudly and without emotion intervenes. "Mr. Roberts is trying to say the organization no longer requires or has the need for your services."

There is a brief moment of silence as Stefani sits in total shock. Although she feared there was a possibility this could happen, the actuality never seemed realistic. She slowly looks at each individual. Wendell Sanders is staring at a blank legal pad positioned in front of him. Roberts briefly looks at Stefani and then lowers his head. Manchester and Adair stare back at Stefani with cold, empty faces. Stefani gathers her strength to reply. "So this is it? I'm out?"

Adair quickly responds, "Yes. We are transferring one of our top executives from Seattle. He will assume your responsibilities effective Monday."

Stefani, on the edge of breaking down, manages to continue the conversation. "Is there an opportunity for me to take a position within the organization in another capacity?"

Again Adair quickly responds, "No. We believe such maneuvering is counterproductive and leads to negative influences regarding company morale."

Stefani looks again toward Sanders and Roberts for support, but neither offers any eye contact. She looks at Adair and Manchester. "I just find it hard to believe my experience and hard work have no place with this organization."

Manchester stands, as does Adair. "Mrs. Tanner, you will be escorted by one of our staff to your office. The individual will watch you gather your personal effects and then accompany you to the front door. Once outside the building you are forbidden to reenter at any time. Should you do so you will be cited for trespassing and will be taken into custody by the authorities. You will receive the standard severance compensation, two weeks' salary and medical insurance for a period of thirty days. The severance check will be waiting for you on your desk."

Stefani sits totally shocked. "Excuse me, but have I done something wrong or illegal? Why am I being not only dismissed but literally thrown out of the building?"

Manchester removes his glasses and softly sets them on the table. "Mrs. Tanner, this meeting is over."

Stefani is barely able to stand. She reaches down and grabs her things. She walks toward the door, doing everything possible to hold back tears, but turns to ask one more question. "I have things on my ... there are things on the computer I used that are personal. May I download them?"

Adair quickly addresses her question. "During this meeting one of our IT department team members has examined your hard drive and has downloaded these personal items for you on a thumb drive. The staff member assigned to you will give you the drive. You are not to touch the computer in the office. Your login and passwords have been deleted from the system. As was explained earlier, you will collect your personal belongings and exit the facility. You will be out by twelve noon. Good day, Mrs. Tanner."

Stefani turns and weakly heads for the door. When she exits, a tall man is waiting for her on the other side of the door. "Mrs. Tanner, I will be accompanying you through this process."

Stefani looks at him, manages a weak smile, and nods. "I understand."

The two reach Stefani's office, where a stainless steel cart with boxes on it sits outside the door. Tonya watches from her desk in obvious disbelief as Stefani walks in and begins to collect her things. Finally, she grabs her jacket and scans the office one last time.

"Mrs. Tanner, I will push the cart to your car. We need to leave now."

Stefani nods and walks out of the office. Everyone in their cubicles is standing watching in total bewilderment. Many are crying as Stefani walks toward the elevators. The two reach the first floor and make their way to Stefani's car. She pops open the rear hatch, and the escort loads the boxes in her car. Once done, he turns and hands her an envelope. "This is your termination material, including a severance check."

Without saying another word the escort turns and swiftly pushes the cart toward the office building. Stefani watches him walk away and then pulls out her keys. She opens the door and climbs in. She puts her bag and other items she was carrying in the passenger seat and then reaches over and grabs her seat belt. After she latches the belt she slowly slides the key into the ignition. As she turns the engine over, she looks through the windshield. Seeing that the sign that displayed her name, designating this as her parking spot, has been removed snaps her last fiber of strength. Her head falls forward against the steering wheel, and she begins to cry uncontrollably. The professional world as she knows it has come crashing down, and for the first time in her professional life she has no idea what to do.

Chapter 4

Stefani backs her car out of the parking spot and exits the lot. As she merges onto the highway, she reaches down and picks up her cell phone. Just as she is about to call David, however, she stops. She doesn't know if it's embarrassment, shame, or the fear of how he will react, but she sets the phone on the console and continues to drive. She puts on her sunglasses in an attempt to hide the tears that continue streaming down her cheeks. Thoughts race through her mind as she drives on autopilot. *How could this have happened? What could I have possibly done to make me nonessential? What more could I have done to make me less expendable? What was the need to rush me out of the building?*

Stefani looks at herself in the rearview mirror and wipes her tears. "What the hell am I going to do? David is going to flip. What if they blackball me and I can't find another job in the area? David is established here, and I know he would never consider relocating ... Jesus ... I'm going crazy."

Suddenly she rockets off the interstate onto an exit ramp. When she reaches the end of the ramp she stops at a red light and sits motionless. As the light turns green, a thought enters her head, and she says, "Molly, I hope you're home."

Molly seems the obvious one to lean on at the moment. Jason is gone on his eight-day business trip, and the boys have left for their grandparents. It is a perfect opportunity to vent, cry, and more importantly drink.

Within twenty minutes Stefani pulls into the long driveway at Molly's house. Disoriented from the day's events, she drives up to the garage and stops. She places the car in park, turns off the engine, removes her sunglasses, and stares at herself in the rearview mirror. Her makeup is a mess. "God, I look like shit."

She stares out the windshield, not focusing on anything, but continues to run the entire morning through her head. She abruptly shakes her head as she clears her thoughts and opens the door to get out. Suddenly she stops and focuses on the image of the garage she has been staring at for the last few minutes. On the right, in the garage, she can clearly see Mallory's Tahoe through the windows, but the image on the left isn't of another Tahoe but of a car with a much lower profile.

Jason left this morning to go to Wisconsin. Whose car is that?

Stefani slowly climbs out of the car, turns, and scans the back yard. She gently pushes her car door closed to avoid making any noise and then walks over and peeks through the window. Sitting in the closed garage is a BMW 550i … David's BMW 550i. Stefani stands paralyzed and then covers her mouth with her hand. She turns and stares at the windows on the second floor of the house. Her body begins to shiver as she walks toward the deck. She stops and grabs the railing. She feels totally off balance and does her best to gather herself. She reaches down and slips her heels off to avoid making any noise as well as to improve her balance. She shakes her head, trying to make sense of everything. *What the hell is David's car doing here?*

Her question to herself is one she already suspects she has the answer for, though she is desperately reaching for a glimmer of hope that there is a legitimate reason for this. Her mind is racing with thoughts, but her body seems to be frozen. She breaks out into a cold sweat and her throat feels as if it is closing shut. Suddenly the deck feels as if it's swaying back and forth.

What am I going to do?

Initially she turns to get back in her car and drive home, figuring she'll confront David about this later when he gets home. Quickly, however, her thinking changes, and she knows she needs to find out right now what's going on. Her confidence in David telling her the truth is nonexistent.

How do I get in the house?

As she stands there and catches her breath, she remembers, *Jason hasn't fixed the basement lock.*

Stefani quietly works her way around to the side of the house and finds the stairs leading down to the basement door. She silently walks down the concrete steps and reaches the door. She closes her eyes, reaches out, and slowly turns the doorknob. The door opens and makes a soft creaking sound as it swings inward. Stefani walks in and gently closes the door behind her. She looks around and sees a set of steps leading upward. She approaches the stairs and then stops. *Do I really want to do this?*

She inhales deeply and then softly takes one step at a time, trying not to make a sound. She reaches the top of the steps and opens the door leading into the kitchen. Her heart is pounding violently, and she can feel sweat running down her neck. She stops to see if she can hear anything, but the house is silent. She continues into the living room and then moves toward the steps leading to the second floor. She stops again to see if she can hear anything … again nothing. She again quietly takes one step at a time, making her way to the top of the stairs. There she can hear the sound of a shower running. It sounds like it's coming from the master bedroom. She comes within reaching distance of the bedroom door and then carefully opens it. Moaning can be heard above the sound of the shower.

Stefani looks at the floor beside the bed. There lie a pair of men's dress shoes and a pair of dress pants. A dress shirt is tossed on a chair in the corner of the room. She quickly turns her head, pinches her lips together, and squeezes her eyes closed with every ounce of energy in order not to burst into tears. She easily recognizes the shoes and pants—the shirt she ironed for David two days earlier.

She hesitates and then heads toward the bathroom. She stops just short of the door and can hear a woman's voice crying out as she hyperventilates. Stefani closes her eyes and takes a deep breath. She enters the bathroom, where she can see two bare bodies through the glass shower door. The moaning is much louder, and the rhythmic sound of two wet bodies slapping together echoes throughout the tile bathroom. Stefani stands motionless as she grasps what she is seeing. Her breathing quickens, as her body shakes violently. Then, without warning, she lets out a bloodcurdling scream. She covers her face with both hands as David and Mallory grab for towels hanging in the shower.

Mallory collapses to the shower floor in tears as David throws the door open and says, "Stef, wait … don't leave."

Stefani, completely overwhelmed with emotion, grabs a vase off the vanity and throws it at David. The vase misses him and shatters when it hits the wall behind him. She steps backward and shakes her head. "Fuck you, David! Fuck you and your whore!"

Stefani turns and races down the steps. She bolts through the kitchen and out to her car. She jumps in, starts the engine, and tears out of the driveway. She flies down the road, crying hysterically. Her emotions have total control over her as she weaves in and out of traffic.

Stefani arrives home and manages to get inside. She then stops in the kitchen, leans against the cabinets, and slides down to the floor. As she breaks down, she cries uncontrollably. *What am I going to do? What have I done to deserve this? Where am I going to go?*

After moments of sitting in a trance, she slowly stands and walks to the bedroom. She opens the door to the walk-in closet and pulls out a large suitcase. She throws it on the bed and fills it with her clothes. Afterward she grabs another suitcase and enters the boys' room. She fills the suitcase with Blane's and Jared's clothes. She carries the two suitcases to the kitchen and then heads back to her bedroom to change into a pair of jeans, a T-shirt, and running shoes. When she returns to the kitchen, David is sitting at the table.

"Stef, we need to talk."

Stefani slides by him and grabs her handbag sitting on the counter. "No, David, we really don't."

David stands and blocks her from getting to the suitcases. "Where are you going?"

Stefani tries to push past him, but he grabs her wrists. Stefani snatches her hands away. "Don't you touch me! Don't you ever lay a finger on me again, you son-of-a-bitch!"

David opens his hands and holds them in the air. "Fine. Where do you think you're going?"

Stefani looks at the floor and then at David. She is surprised at her own emotions, surprised that she is filled with rage instead of pain. "I don't know, but I am going to pick up the boys, and I'll figure something out. Just get the hell away from me."

David crosses his arms and leans against the counter. "Okay, you take the boys and go clear your head. We'll talk about this in a few days."

Stefani slams her bag on the counter and squares off with David. He appears taken back by her sudden aggression.

Stefani nods and quickly crosses her arms. "Well, let me tell you how my day has gone so far, you piece of shit. At roughly twelve o'clock today I lost my job. Then about an hour later I find out my husband is fucking my best friend ... my best friend, David ... really?"

She chuckles sarcastically. "You have to think the day has got to get better."

David drops his head. "Stef, I'm sorry."

Stefani turns and grabs her bag. "David, there isn't anything to say. You're just a piece of shit."

David's attitude changes as he shifts to the defensive. "You go ahead and take the boys for a while, but don't think you're walking out of here with them forever and taking my stuff with you."

Stefani stops and stares off into the distance. She turns and stares into David's eyes. "You go ahead and worry about your stuff. I don't want your stuff, and I certainly don't want you."

As she turns, David whirls around and throws his keys through the window above the kitchen sink. "Yeah, you take your time, but you will not take my sons from me. That's one road you don't want to travel."

Stefani looks at the broken window and then heads for the door. "You're such an ass."

As she loads the suitcases in the Touareg and climbs into the driver's seat, her emotions again get the best of her, and she sobs heavily.

Chapter 5

Stefani heads for the Tender Heart Day Care Center. After parking she fixes her makeup and hair. She walks up to the front door and approaches the desk. Mrs. Ellis looks up. "Mrs. Tanner, what a pleasant surprise."

Stefani forces a grin.

"Mrs. Tanner, is everything alright?"

Stefani quickly nods. "Everything is fine. I'm here to pick up the boys."

Mrs. Ellis studies her face, and Stefani suspects she can sense something is painfully wrong, but the woman just smiles. "Let me call down to their room."

"Thank you."

In a matter of moments a door down the hall pops open. Blane and Jared burst out of the room and speed-walk to Stefani. Blane looks up at her and says, "Hey, Mom, you're early … what's up?"

Stefani feels a sense of relief and bends over and hugs both boys. "Nothing, guys. I just thought it would be nice to spend the afternoon together."

The three climb into the car, and Stefani pulls out of the parking lot. As she drives, she gets caught up in her thoughts. The day's events play repeatedly in her head. *How could so much happen in one day?*

Stefani's thoughts are interrupted by Blane yelling, "Mom!"

Stefani quickly looks up in the rearview mirror and snaps, "You don't have to yell."

Blane's jaw drops as he responds, "Mom, I've been calling your name for like a minute. What's wrong?"

Stefani remains silent. She does everything she can to fight back her emotions. As she drives, she tries to come up with a good reason for the three of them not to go home without upsetting them.

"Hey, guys … why don't we do something fun tonight?"

Blane perks up. "Like what?"

"What do you say we spend the night at a nice hotel and have room service bring us food, and then we can swim in the pool all day tomorrow?"

Out of nowhere Jared pipes up, "Yeah!"

Blane remains quiet as he looks at his mother's reflection in the rearview mirror. Stefani glances over and sees him staring at her. She winks, but his expression stays serious. "You and Dad had a fight, didn't you?"

Stefani's lower lip trembles as she looks at Blane. A tear rolls down her face as she tries to find the right words. "Guys, don't you worry about that. Let's try to have some fun."

Fifteen minutes later Stefani pulls into the Marriott parking lot. She drives up to the main entrance and undoes her seat belt.

"Okay, you two, I'm going in to get us a great room. You two stay in the car and don't unlock the doors for anyone, got it?"

The boys reply in unison, "Got it, Mom."

Stefani climbs out of the car. She locks the door with the remote and walks into the main lobby. She approaches the front desk and is greeted by a clerk. "Good afternoon, ma'am. How may I help you?"

Stefani rests her bag on the counter and pulls out her wallet. "I'd like to get a room for my two sons and me."

The clerk begins typing on the computer keyboard. "How many nights?"

Stefani hesitates. *How long will it take for me to figure things out? Hell, this could take weeks!* Finally, she says, "Just one."

The clerk types and smiles. "We're in luck. I do have a room. It has two queen-sized beds and a whirlpool tub."

Perfect, just what we all need, Blane and Jared in a whirlpool. What a mess this will be. Still, it's better than going home. "That will work fine."

"Great," the clerk says. "I'll need your driver's license and a credit card."

Stefani opens her wallet and pulls out her license and Visa. She hands the clerk the cards and watches him swipe the Visa through the credit card device. Suddenly his smile disappears. "Let me try again."

He swipes it again, and then he says, "Ma'am, I'm sorry, but this card has been declined."

Stefani is caught between shock and total embarrassment. "I'm sorry, try my MasterCard."

She hands him the card, and he quickly swipes it. Seconds later he looks at her and shakes his head. "This one was declined as well."

Stefani stands in utter disbelief. "I don't understand."

The clerk hands her back the credit card, clearly aggravated. "Ma'am, maybe you should contact the bank and see what the problem is." He quickly turns and walks away.

Stefani takes the card and walks toward the front door. She can see the boys sitting patiently in the car. *This is crazy.*

She pulls out her cell phone and dials the number embossed on the back of her card. Within seconds an automated attendant answers. After working through a series of options she finally gets a customer service representative. "Hello, this is Marie. How may I help you?"

Stefani looks around to see if anyone is close enough to hear her speak. "Yes, my name is Stefani Tanner, and I just tried to use my card and it was declined. Can you tell me why?"

"Yes, I'm sure I can. Please read me the account number and the last four digits of your social security number."

Stefani relays the information and waits.

The representative apologizes for the wait. "I'm sorry this took so long, but I do have an answer for you."

Stefani quickly paces in the lobby. "Okay, what's the problem?"

"Mrs. Tanner, this card was cancelled."

"Cancelled? How?"

"Mrs. Tanner, this account was terminated by a Mr. David Tanner. The card was not reported stolen—it was simply cancelled."

Stefani stands in devastation. "Can I reactivate the account?"

"Unfortunately, no. Is there anything else I can help you with?"

Stefani begins to weep. "No." She hangs up and covers her face with her hand. She can still see the boys in the car. *That son of a bitch has cancelled all the cards.*

Stefani looks at her watch. "I still have time to get to the bank."

Stefani jogs out to the car and hops in. She starts the car and pulls out of the parking lot. Blane looks at her, clearly confused. "Mom … I thought we were staying at the hotel."

"We are, honey. I just need to run to the bank first."

The three arrive at the bank. Again Stefani instructs the boys to sit tight while she runs inside. She enters the vestibule and approaches the ATM. She inserts her debit card, types in her personal identification number and requests a withdrawal of three hundred dollars. The screen turns bright green and displays the words "INSUFFICIENT FUNDS."

She leans forward and rests her head against the ATM. She takes a deep breath, walks into the lobby, and approaches a teller. "Can you tell me what the status of this account is?"

"Gladly. Just give me one minute."

The teller types on the keyboard and then tilts her head with a perplexed look on her face. "According to the system a large withdrawal was made earlier today. At the moment only the required minimum of one hundred dollars remains in the account."

Stefani stands motionless for a few seconds. The teller, appearing somewhat confused, softly asks, "Is there anything else I can help you with?"

Stefani remembers the envelope containing her severance check the escort gave her. She pulls the envelope out of her bag and opens it. Fortunately, she and David do their banking with the same organization Aeron International does. She looks down at the check and frowns. *Wow, I'll bet this hurt them, a check for $3,619.83.*

Stefani lays the check on the counter and asks, "Can I get this cashed?"

The teller looks it over. "Absolutely. Just sign the back. I already have your license, so this will only take a second."

The teller hands Stefani the money and her license. "Will there be anything else?"

Stefani tucks the cash neatly into her wallet and slips it into her bag. "No, thank you. That will be all."

She turns, exits the bank, and climbs into the car. She quickly notices the boys are getting restless.

Blane, clearly unable to hold his words any longer, leans forward. "Mom, what are we doing?"

Stefani turns and smiles at the two. "Let's go to the hotel and relax!"

Both boys grin, and Jared yells out, "It's about time!"

The three return to the Marriott, and Stefani works out the financial details with the front desk clerk. They finally get to their room, and the boys begin jumping from one bed to another. Blane races to the bathroom, and his voice echoes through the entire hotel room. "Check this tub out! Mom, it's bigger than the one we have at home!"

Stefani, for the first time all day, laughs as the boys' excitement influences her own feelings. She flops down on one of the beds, and the two boys crash beside her. She wraps her arms around both of them, and for a brief moment she feels a weak sense of peacefulness.

"Okay, guys, what do you say we put room service to work?"

Blane pops up. "Yeah! Let's get pizza!"

Stefani snorts. "Pizza? Are you serious?"

Jared squeezes her around the waist. "Yeah, Mom, let's get pizza, please."

She looks at both boys as if she is going to shoot their request down, all the time knowing they will get anything they want to eat. After a moment she takes a deep breath. "Okay, if that's all we have to choose from."

The boys jump up on the bed and celebrate. Stefani calls room service and orders a large pepperoni pizza and a two-liter bottle of Dr. Pepper. Roughly thirty minutes later the pizza and soda arrives, and the boys begin to eat while watching a movie on TV. Stefani sits in a daze. She knows the small amount of cash she has won't last long, and the last person she wants to talk to is David. Whenever she has something she can't tell David or if they have an argument, she confides in Molly. She gets up from the bed and walks over to the large window overlooking a beautiful patch of woods. The view quickly reminds her of many places in St. Michaels. As much as she hates to admit it, going back to the eastern shore of Maryland is her only option. She doesn't want to involve her parents and upset them, but right now she needs the support, she knows, only her mother and father can provide. No matter what challenges have confronted her in the past, these are the two people who could always make her feel safe and calm. Plus the privacy would allow her time to think. Stefani takes her laptop out of a bag and places it on the desk. She sits down and looks for flights to Baltimore. She finds a flight from Charlotte to Baltimore leaving in the morning at 6:35. She also finds a shuttle service that will run them from the Baltimore airport to Easton, Maryland. From there her parents can pick them up and take them home to St. Michaels, a short, ten-minute ride away.

While the boys watch TV Stefani slips onto the balcony and slowly closes the sliding glass door without the boys noticing. Fortunately she is able to reserve tickets on a flight and shuttle service, that she can pay cash for at the airport, over her cell phone. The total cost for this will put a huge dent in the money from her severance pay, but she needs to get away from Charlotte and David. The thought of being home with her parents brings comfort and a feeling of security. She walks back into the room and clears her throat to get the boy's attention.

"Hey, guys, I have an idea. What do you say we go visit Nana and Pop?"

Blane whips around from the TV. "Really? When?"

Jared turns and has pizza sauce all over his face. Stefani walks over and laughs as she wipes his face with a napkin. "How about tomorrow?"

Jared replies, "That would be awesome, Mom! Do you think Pop would take us fishing?"

Stefani hugs both boys. "I'm sure he would. I just need to call and let them know we're coming. You guys stay in here and watch the movie. I'm going out on the balcony to call Nana."

Twenty minutes later Stefani returns from her call, her eyes quite red. Blane looks at her and says, "Mom, what's wrong?"

Stefani sits down on the edge of the bed. "Nothing at all … I'm just excited about seeing Nana and Pop. It's been a long time since we've been to their house."

Stefani walks over and opens a suitcase. "Now, tomorrow morning we have to leave early, so let's not stay up too late."

The boys agree and clean up their pizza box. Blane walks over to his suitcase. "Mom, can Jared and I take a bath?"

Stefani knows where this is headed. "Sure … just don't make a mess, okay?"

"Okay," the boys declare in unison.

Stefani grins, knowing that's nothing but wishful thinking. She sits on the bed, pondering how to tell David she's going to her parents with the boys. She expands her chest and then hits his preprogrammed number on her phone. He answers almost immediately. "Hello."

"David, I'm going to keep this short. I'm on my way to my parents with the boys."

"Stef, how can you take the boys from me?"

"Are you serious? You want to ask how *I* can do something to *you*? I just caught you with my best friend, and you want to make *me* out to be the bad person here?"

"Do you think your car is safe enough to make the trip?"

Stefani laughs. "Really, David? Now you're concerned about my car? I think it'll make it."

"How long are you staying?"

"Well, let's see … the boys are off school until September, and I don't have a job. I'd say the best answer to that question is … I have no idea."

"Stef, you can't do this. The boys have Little League ball, not to mention the two-week-long Talented and Gifted camp."

"I think I can. Oh … and if by that you mean because I have no money, I'd like to thank you for canceling the credit cards and wiping out the checking account, you prick."

"I just didn't want you to make any drastic decisions while you weren't thinking lucidly."

"Thanks for the concern, asshole." Stefani throws a pillow across the room in anger. "Anyway, you know where the boys will be, and they'll be safe. If you try to report the boys kidnapped I've already notified the Charlotte police about our dilemma and told them where the boys and I will be and gave them the phone number. Oh … I'd not try to contact

Mom and Dad's house or make a surprise visit. Dad's a little enraged right now, and as you so eloquently put it so many times, he's a 'blue-collared redneck.' You never know what he might do in a situation like this ... I'll be in touch."

Stefani ends the call and collapses onto the bed. She buries her face into a pillow and begins to cry. She can hear the boys in the whirlpool laughing, so she knows she is safe from an interrogation from them. She turns her head on the pillow and looks out over the trees through the window.

Well, at least he thinks we're driving, so we won't run into him at the airport. I just can't believe this is happening. How can everything come crashing down so hard and at one time?

CHAPTER 6

When the shuttle rolls into Easton, Stefani's parents, Jack and Peggy Foster are waiting in the lobby of the terminal. Peggy hugs her and kisses her on the cheek while the boys all but attack her dad. Stefani lets go of her mother and walks over to her father. She looks him in the eyes and tears up as she quickly embraces him. "Hi, Dad."

"Hi, sweetheart … it's good to have you home."

The two hold each other tightly. "Thanks, Dad."

When Stefani was a child she would always go to her father when something was bothering her, and somehow he always made her feel everything was going to be all right. Certainly now she is looking for that same sense of assurance. He reaches down and grabs the suitcases. "Let's go home, boys. I think I heard the fish talking this morning."

Blane and Jared run for the door in excitement. Stefani looks at her dad and smiles. "You always did know the right thing to say."

Stefani's mother takes her by the hand. "Come on, honey. Let's go home so you can rest. You look so tired."

"Thanks, Mom."

Within minutes they reach the house and get settled in. Stefani walks into the kitchen, where her mother is preparing lunch. "Mom, one thing I never will forget, no matter where I go, is the smell of this kitchen."

"Honey, no matter where you go this is always your home. We wish it was under different circumstances, but it is so nice having you and the boys here. I know Dad is upset with everything that has happened to you, but he was so excited hearing you and the boys were coming home. He went out to the barn and put new fishing line on all the reels and bought enough bait to last for a year."

Stefani looks out the back window and can see the boys playing with their grandfather. Suddenly she breaks down and sobs. Joanna races over and holds her. "Mom, I'm so sorry."

"Honey, what are you sorry about?"

"Everything."

Stefani pulls a tissue out of her pocket and wipes her eyes. Her mother guides her over to the table, and both sit down. "Honey, what do you mean everything?"

Stefani looks at her with bloodshot eyes and an expression of total bewilderment. "What has happened between David and me. The embarrassment I'm putting you through. What it's doing to the boys, putting my career and my life so far out in front that I put you and Dad on the back burner."

Joanna smiles as she puts some distance between them so she can look Stefani in the eyes. She puts her hands on Stefani's upper arms. "Sweetheart, one of the toughest things a parent has to do is let their children grow up. Part of that process is letting them go be their own person. Sure it hurts, but it doesn't compare to the delight of seeing your child succeed and start a family of their own. You may have moved away from here, but love knows no distance, and Dad and I both know you never forgot about us or loved us less. You need to realize you didn't do anything to deserve what you're going through. We know you are a great wife and mother. Sadly, bad things do happen to good people. But you will get through this. Right now you need to focus on the good things in your life. You look out that window and see those two beautiful boys playing in the yard with your dad. Those boys are a gift from God. Nothing, no matter how bad, can best what those boys bring to your life."

Stefani wipes her eyes.

Joanna looks at her and grins. "And never forget, no matter what, this is your home, and we are always here for you."

Stefani reaches out and hugs her. "Mom, I love you so much."

"I know you do, honey."

Stefani leans back. "Thank you."

Joanna winks at her and then stands. "I've got to get this lunch finished, or I'll have three men looking at me with empty bellies!"

Stefani gets up and walks over to the back window. She sees her father showing the boys how to cast a fishing rod. She shakes her head. "Mom, you know, I never did get that right."

Her mom laughs and points at her with a large fork. "No … but your dad still talks about the way you used to hit a softball."

Stefani raises her eyebrows. "Yeah?"

"Honey, you and your sisters were always able to step on your father's toes and are the most precious things in his life. But … you were also the son he never had. He always said Stef was two people in one body, his athlete and his baby girl."

Stefani leans her head against the glass as she watches her boys laugh with her dad. *Why did I ever leave here?*

She turns and sighs. "Mom, do you think it would be alright if I used your car to drive into town?"

"Sure … I'll get you the keys."

Joanna heads for the living room and then walks back into the kitchen and hands her the keys. "Do you need any money?"

"No, Mom, I'm fine."

Stefani turns to walk to the living room. "Hey, Mom, you wouldn't happen to know what Mindy Williams is doing these days, would you?"

"Yes, I saw her about two weeks ago. She works for the school board over in Easton." Joanna laughs. "The things you two use to get into."

Stefani grins and walks away with her hands up. "Mom, let's not go there."

As she drives through St. Michaels and onto Easton, she finds she can't hold back the smiles as old memories come racing back. She reaches the Board of Education building in Easton, walks in, and takes her sunglasses off. As she is looking around, a woman at the front desk speaks up. "May I help you?"

"Yes, can you tell me where I can find Mindy Williams?"

"Certainly. She's in room 226. Just take the elevator to the second floor. You can't miss it."

"Thank you."

Stefani makes her way to the elevator and steps out on the second floor. She walks down the corridor to office 226. She softly knocks.

"Come in."

Stefani opens the door and sees a woman standing at a filing cabinet with her back turned toward the door. Without turning, she says, "May I help you?"

"Probably … if you'd turn your scrawny butt around."

The woman's outrage is apparent in her stiff posture. She slowly turns, mouth open to reply, and then she looks at Stefani standing there. Immediately she dashes over and hugs Stefani. "Oh my God! What are you doing here?"

"I thought I'd see what my old best friend is up to."

Mindy steps back and looks Stefani over. "Girl, you haven't aged a bit."

"Me? What about you? You still look eighteen."

Mindy laughs. "Liar." She looks up at the clock. "Hey, let's do lunch!"

Stefani looks around. "You sure you have time?"

"I'm good—trust me."

"Okay."

When they reach the parking lot, Mindy turns to the left. "Come on, girl. This one's on me."

Stefani grins and nods. "Okay … if you say so."

Mindy pulls a remote out of her bag, and a chirp can be heard coming from a BMW 325. Stefani puckers her lips. "Wow. Very nice!"

"Eh, marriage to a state trooper does have a few perks."

The two climb in and head out onto the main strip. Mindy asks, "You like Panera?"

"Absolutely!"

They arrive at Panera, order their food, and find a booth in a corner away from most of the congestion. They pay very little attention to who is sitting in the adjacent booths. Mindy grabs her drink, takes a big swallow, and asks cheerfully, "So what brings you up here? Seeing your mom and dad?"

When Stefani just places her hands in her lap and looks down at her food, Mindy's tone softens. "Stef … what's up?"

Stefani leans back and takes a deep breath. She forces a smile. "Mindy, things aren't good."

"Are your mom and dad okay?"

"Oh yeah, thank God for that."

"Then what is it?"

Stefani looks at Mindy and then brushes away a tear. "Well, in one day I lost my job and that very afternoon discovered my husband is screwing my closest friend in Charlotte."

Mindy drops her roll on her plate and is frozen in total shock. "Stef, I don't know what to say."

Stefani shrugs her shoulders. "Really, there's nothing to say. In a matter of hours I lost my job and my marriage."

Mindy, clearly devastated, places a hand on Stefani's arm. "What happened with your job?"

"We were bought out, and I was replaced by an executive already working for the new owners. He's transferring from Seattle. They escorted me out of the building and told me if I enter the building again I'll be arrested for trespassing."

"Arrested? And you did nothing wrong?"

"Nope. The new owners believe in cutting things off totally—no strings. You know, I thought my time and efforts would have meant more to them. I guess I was wrong."

"Jesus! And I thought the school board was bad."

Stefani smiles and continues, "So I thought I'd confide in my friend about what happened at work and found her in the shower with my husband at her house."

"Stef, I'm so sorry."

"Yeah, me too. Then to top it off, he cancelled the credit cards and withdrew all the money out of our savings and checking accounts. The only way I got up here with my sons was with my severance check they gave me when they escorted me out the door."

"So you're here with your sons … no job and no money?"

"Yep … and no car."

"Let me give you some money."

"Mindy, no, I don't need any. I'm staying with Mom and Dad. I figure I'll stay here until I can get an idea what to do."

"Stefani, I hope this doesn't offend you, but I hope your husband's dick falls off and bursts into flames."

Stefani snickers. "I've had similar thoughts."

"I want you to promise me something."

"Sure."

"If you need anything, and I mean anything, you call me."

"I promise."

The two finish their lunch and return to the Board of Education building, where Mindy drops Stefani off at her parents' minivan. "Stefani, remember what I said."

"I will. I promise."

"I call you in a few days, and we'll get together again."

"Sounds good … I'd like that."

Stefani climbs into the minivan and drives home. Instead of going inside, she sits on the front porch swing. She opens her handbag and pulls out a book she's been trying to find the time to read … now seems as good a time as any. She gets so caught up in the book she loses track of time until she hears her mom call everyone in for dinner.

"Mom, this smells great."

"Thank, you dear. Men, sit down and eat."

Afterward Stefani walks back onto the porch and sits on the swing. Jack walks out and sits beside her. "How you doing, Tiger?"

Stefani smiles. "Dad, you haven't called me that in years."

Her father crosses his feet under the swing. "Still seems right somehow."

"I like to hear it."

He leans back and puts his arm around her. "Honey, I know a good bit about what you're going through. Sadly, I don't have all the answers for you. I just want you to know Mom and I are always here for you and the boys, and you stay as long as you want."

Stefani tears up as she leans into him. "Dad, you don't know how much I love you and am so lucky to have you and Mom."

He pats her on the thigh. "I'm going to bed. I need some rest if I'm going to keep up with those boys of yours."

Stefani sits up straight. "Dad, don't feel like you have to cater to them every minute."

"Sweetheart … today was the most fun I've had in years. The boys and I will be just fine."

Stefani grins and hugs him again. "Dad, I think tomorrow I'll start the day off with a run. It always makes me feel good."

"Tiger, you do what you want, but I think I'll skip the run." He gets up off the swing and walks in the house.

"Goodnight, Dad."

Chapter 7

Stefani wakes just as the sun is breaking over the trees. She slips on a pair of running shorts, a T-shirt, and running shoes. She heads out toward the old boat slip at the end of the lane, the same route she used to run when she was in high school—four miles, to be exact. During her run she thinks about her job, David, and the great day she had with her parents and sons. She thinks about calling Mindy to see what's been going on in St. Michaels while she's been gone. Once she reaches the old boat slip she stands and stares out across the water. The smell of the salt air brings back so many memories, as does the peacefulness of the water, the very water her father worked on for over fifty years. Somehow the familiar surroundings give her a sense of peace and calm. Until she left for college, this was all she knew. Suddenly she realizes it's not the size of the city or the job that makes one happy. It's the people and the security that creates the happiness and stability. She looks down at her feet. She gently kicks an oyster shell off the dock and watches it disappear into the depths of the dark water. She takes a deep breath and then heads home. As she makes the final turn toward the house, she slows her run to a walk. She can see her father outside in the driveway talking to a man in a suit. There is a large SUV in the driveway and another car parked on the road with a man sitting in the driver's seat. Stefani walks up. "Hey, Dad, what's going on?"

"Honey, this man needs to speak to you. I'll be right in the house if you need me."

Stefani stands firm and nods to her dad. She looks at the man in the suit and asks, "How may I help you?"

"Ma'am, my name is Fred Mitchell, and I am here to deliver your new Range Rover to you."

Stefani squints in confusion. "My new what?"

"Your new Range Rover. If you'd like, I'll go through the features with you."

Suddenly Stefani is filled with rage. "Sir, I'm assuming this was purchased by a David Tanner and sent here for me. Well, sir, you can take this high-dollar vehicle back to wherever it came from because I am not accepting it or anything else from him."

The man in the suit calmly responds, "Ma'am, I'm from Chesapeake Motors of Annapolis. I sold this vehicle yesterday under the following conditions: one, it was to be put in your name solely; two, it was to be delivered this morning to you; and three, I'm not to tell you who purchased it."

Stefani shakes her head. "Sir, evidently you didn't understand what I said. I am not taking anything from David Tanner. Do you grasp what I'm saying?"

Jack, who has clearly been listening through the screen door, steps out onto the porch and walks down to her. "Honey, just listen to the man."

"Dad, no! I'm not going to let David try to buy his way into forgiveness."

"Tiger, just hear me out. When these guys pulled up here this morning not long after you left to go run, I told them the same thing and ordered them to get the hell out of here. But when this gentleman told me what he did, I had to apologize, and if you continue you'll have to as well."

Stefani looks at her dad. "What do you mean?"

"Honey, David didn't buy this car."

"What?"

"No, honey … he didn't"

"Then how can it be mine?"

The man who has been sitting in the car gets out, walks over to Stefani, and shakes her hand. "Hello. My name is Paul Ford, and I'm an attorney. I can assure you this is totally legal and no one by the name of David Tanner was involved in this transaction."

Stefani looks down and puts her hand on top of her head. "I don't understand."

"I represent a very good client who instructed Mr. Mitchell to deliver this vehicle to you. It is paid for in full and insured through State Farm for one calendar year. All you have to do is sign the transfer papers."

Stefani looks at her dad, who shrugs his shoulders.

"Okay, so I sign these papers … how do I know this won't come back on me somehow?"

Mitchell opens a folder. "This is the title. Once you sign this, the vehicle is yours."

Stefani takes the pen from Mitchell, glances over at her father, and signs the documents. Mitchell neatly folds the documents and gives Stefani her copies. "Here you go, and if we can … I'd like to show you all the features this vehicle has. It's nicest vehicle we had in our inventory. We pulled it off the showroom floor this morning."

Stefani sits in the driver's seat as Mitchell goes through a long list of features. She shakes her head. "This is unbelievable. How much did this car cost?"

Mitchell chuckles. "Um, that was also a condition of the sale. I'm not allowed to divulge that either."

Stefani climbs out of the car and looks at Paul Ford. "And this is totally legal?"

"Absolutely."

"So how does Mr. Mitchell get back to Annapolis?"

"I will drive him."

Stefani turns and looks at her dad. He smiles and throws his hands up. She turns back to Ford. "So, we are done here?"

"Almost."

He pulls out a leather binder and opens it. "This is a prepaid Exxon gas card worth one thousand dollars. Your PIN is written on this card."

Stefani turns again and looks at her father in total disbelief. The attorney continues, "And ... this is a cashier's check in the amount of twenty thousand dollars. I have contacted the local bank here in St. Michaels. They have everything ready for you to sign to deposit this check."

Stefani stands motionless with her mouth hanging wide open. She quickly reaches out. "May I see the check?"

He hands it to her. "Absolutely—it's your check."

Stefani examines the check, turning it over and then back again. "Who is this from?"

"Once again, ma'am, we were instructed to not reveal that information." He puts his finger on the back of her hand. "I promise you, as God is my witness, David Tanner has no involvement in any of this." He then turns and nods to Mitchell. "Ready?"

Mitchell nods. "Yes."

Both men shake Stefani's and Jack's hands. "It's been a pleasure," Ford says.

As the two men climb into the car, Stefani glances at the new Maryland license plates on the Range Rover. "That's it?"

Paul leans out of the car window. "Everything is taken care of. Enjoy the car."

The two men pull off as Stefani stands in amazement. Joanna has obviously been keeping the boys in the house, for once the men are out of sight they tear out to admire the new car.

Blane is clearly beside himself. "Mom, is that ours?"

Stefani fumbles through the papers. "It would seem so."

Jared climbs into the car. "Awesome."

Jack walks over and puts his hand on her shoulder. "Honey, I don't know what angel sat on your shoulder this morning, but if I were you I'd get cleaned up and get that check in the bank as soon as possible."

Stefani lets her arms flop down by her side and then looks over at her dad. "Dad … what just happened here?"

Chapter 8

Early the next morning Stefani calls Mindy and asks her to lunch. Once again they meet at Panera. Stefani gets there early and sits patiently waiting for Mindy to arrive. Moments later Mindy pulls up and walks in. The two get their food and sit. "Stef, I'm so glad you called. I really needed to get away from that place." Mindy studies Stefani's face. "You certainly seem to be in a good mood today."

Stefani puckers her lips and nods her head. "Yes, I am."

"May I be so bold as to ask why?"

Stefani leans back and pats the table with her hands.

"Mindy, in the last twenty-four hours I've gone from being flat broke with no car to having a brand new Range Rover, a prepaid gas card, and a nice chunk of change."

Mindy flops her cup on the table and stares at Stefani. "And this happened how?"

Stefani puts her hands up in total confusion. "I returned to my parents' house yesterday morning from jogging, and there were two men in my parents' driveway. Within fifteen minutes I had a new car and cash. At first I was upset because I knew David was behind it all, but the attorney assured me David had nothing to do with this."

Mindy, sitting with a stunned expression on her face, says, "So who did it?"

Stefani shrugs her shoulders. "I honestly have no idea."

"Wait … you have a brand new Range Rover and a huge amount of cash and have no idea who or where it came from?

"Not a clue."

Mindy shakes her head and squints. "Well, somebody had to purchase the car before it was given to you."

Stefani sips her tea. "That's what I figure, but how do I find out?"

Mindy looks out the window and then turns to Stefani. "Let me talk to Mike. As a state trooper, he has to have an idea how we can figure this out."

Mindy looks at Stefani and shakes her head. Stefani grins and begins to blush. "What?"

"Girl, this is better than any movie mystery I've ever seen. Stef, we aren't talking chump change here. Between the car and the cash, we are talking huge money!"

Stefani takes a bite of her salad and nods. "I know."

"Stef, we've got to get to the bottom of this. The suspense is killing me!"

"You? I'm the one who has all this stuff and no clue where it came from."

Mindy and Stefani finish their lunch. As they exit, Mindy reaches into her handbag and pulls out her sunglasses. She puts them on and shoulder-bumps Stefani. "Trust me … with Mike's help we'll get to the bottom of this."

Stefani walks over to the Range Rover. Mindy stops and stares. "Damn! Whoever sent it to you went all out!"

"I know … it's a beautiful car." Stefani continues to walk toward the car and then stops.

Mindy sees her standing there. "Hey … you okay?"

"Yeah … I was just thinking … I should be feeling overwhelmed with grief considering what all has happened. But since yesterday … I kinda feel excited."

"Good! You deserve it. Just remember it's your dick-headed husband who should be in pain, not you. Enjoy it."

"Thanks, Min."

"Don't mention it. And trust me … I'll be in touch soon!"

"I'm looking forward to it.

Stefani drives back to her parents' house. Joanna is working in the kitchen, and Jack is out on the dock fishing with the boys.

"Mom, who do you think sent me the car?"

"Honey, I have no idea, but they certainly wanted to get your attention."

Stefani gets up and walks over to the back door. She can see the boys and her dad laughing about something.

"Mom … maybe this was a blessing in disguise."

Joanna wipes her hands on her apron. "What do you mean?"

Stefani turns and rests her shoulder against the door frame. "Maybe this is a wakeup call for me. I've been so caught up in my work and have forgotten about the important things in my life. Look how Dad and the boys are enjoying each other. The little talks we've had in the last few days. Mom, I'm ashamed to admit it, but I forgot how much these things mean to me."

Joanna walks over and lightly touches Stefani on the cheek. "Sweetheart, we don't forget … life just has a way of changing things. Our time gets eaten up with other things."

Stefani reaches up and cups her mom's hand. "I know, Mom, but these last few days have been great even though I know I have huge issues to deal with. It's been great being home."

Joanna smiles at her and turns back to the stove. "I know, honey. It's been a blessing having you here."

Their conversation is interrupted by the telephone ringing. Joanna reaches out and lifts the receiver off the wall. "Hello … oh yes, Mindy, she's right here." She covers up the mouthpiece with her hand and says, "Just like old times."

Stefani laughs as she takes the receiver. "Hey, Mindy"

"I told Mike about the car, and he had a great idea."

"What?"

"Mike said whenever a car is purchased or the title is transferred it has to be documented."

"Okay, but how does this help me?"

"Mike has a buddy at the Department of Motor Vehicles. Although he's not supposed to do this … he said he'll get us the information if we get him the VIN number off the car. Mike's friend will print the material off. Mike will drop it off to me. I'll scan it then email it to you."

Stefani nods. "Sounds like a plan. Tell Mike I really appreciate it."

"Let me give you my email address so you can send me the number."

Stefani jots the address on the notepad her mom keeps on the counter.

"Mike said give him about an hour, and you should have it from me not long after. And, Stef …"

"Yeah?"

"You better keep me in the loop!"

Stefani laughs. "I'll see what I can do."

Stefani hangs up the phone and then fights off a smile. She leans against the wall and presses her thumbnail against her lower teeth.

Joanna has been watching her and casually comments. "Is everything alright?"

The question takes a moment to register, but then she quickly responds. "Yes … everything is great."

Stefani runs upstairs and pulls the car title out of the binder. She boots up her laptop. Aware her parents have no Wi-Fi connection, she plugs her air card in and sends Mindy the vehicle identification number. She notices the battery in her laptop is extremely low and plugs in the AC adapter. After doing so she lies across the bed and begins to finger through some of her high school yearbooks, which have rested undisturbed on a shelf for years. The old black-and-white photos bring back memories of a simpler time. The Friday nights after football games, the countless suicide sprints on the basketball court, the many games on the softball field, the endless hours spent studying that felt like pure torture, the days in the classroom with friends she hasn't seen since graduation, and the many short paragraphs, written on the inside covers of the yearbooks, each containing a very special message.

The reminiscing evokes a bittersweet feeling ... how great those four years were ... yet another reminder of how she left such treasured parts of her life behind while working desperately and tirelessly, searching for something new, rewarding, and certainly lucrative ... something she was certain she'd never find in the small world of St. Michaels.

Carefully she places the yearbooks back on the shelf, and then she walks to the window and looks out over the water. She is mesmerized by the small waves rolling across the bay. Her reverie is interrupted by the chime of an incoming email. She glances at her laptop still resting on her bed. She sits and taps the touch pad, making her screensaver disappear and displaying her email inbox. She gently bites down on her index finger when she sees a new message from Mindy. "Here goes nothing."

She clicks on the message, and it opens. "Mindy, you certainly don't disappoint."

She scans the message. "Okay ... the car was shipped to Chesapeake Motors. Then ... just the other day the car was purchased by ... Perceptive Insight, LLC, then transferred to Stefani Tanner."

Softly she puts her hands together in front of her face and then presses her lips against her index fingers. "Perceptive Insight? I've never heard of it."

Immediately she begins doing searches on Perceptive Insight, LLC. Although a few sites provide basic information, none go into any detail regarding the company's profile or officers.

She scrolls to the bottom on the last site she opens and finds the address of the company, 2256 Waterview Place, Oxford, Maryland.

Stefani is now totally confused. She stands up from the bed and looks out the window. "Who do I know in Oxford?"

Oxford is roughly thirty minutes from St. Michaels; however, if the ferry is running the time is less than half that.

As Stefani continues to stare out the window, she recalls what she's been through in the last week. Losing a job she loved along with suffering the betrayal of her husband and best friend should have her nothing short of bordering on a nervous breakdown, but somehow there exists a feeling of happiness, serenity, and excitement. Certainly the comfort of being home, a place that has always made her feel safe and secure, and with her parents has softened the blow. Blane and Jared being with her and the old, familiar surroundings all contribute to her peculiar sense of calm, but there is something else. The curiosity that consumes her has produced a sense of exhilaration. Who is behind the mystery of the new car? No one, with the exception of her parents and Mindy, knows what she's been through recently. She has been assured by the car salesman and the attorney that David is not involved. This unknown company with a person or people who insist on anonymity has all but made her forget about David and AMERI-GEN … at least for now.

Chapter 9

The next day Stefani completes her run, showers, and puts on the outfit she was wearing the day she was dismissed from AMERI-GEN. She walks into the kitchen, where her parents and the boys are enjoying breakfast. Joanna looks at her and smiles. "You look very nice this morning. You have plans?"

Stefani, never being able to tell her mother even a small fib, turns and says, "Well, not exactly plans … I'd say more of an inquiry."

The boys look at their grandfather, who just shrugs his shoulders and continues to eat. Stefani walks over, kisses the boys on the head, and hugs her dad from behind. She rests her hand on her mother's shoulder. "Boys, I'm going to take a short ride, and when I get back, what do you say we all go into town and have lunch and buy you guys some new clothes?"

The boys both appear less than enthused about shopping suggestion but agree. Jack smiles and nods. Joanna looks at Stefani and winks. "Honey, I hope you find what you're looking for."

Stefani shakes her head and grins. She walks out of the house and climbs into the Range Rover. She starts the engine and looks at the huge screen mounted in the dash.

"Okay ... there's the navigation button ... enter the address ... and voila!"

A soft, British female voice begins issuing directions that Stefani follows as if she were disarming a bomb. As she nears the destination, she can feel her heart rate increase and her palms sweat. When she turns onto Waterview Place she is somewhat taken back. The road is a long lane with nothing but forest on both sides. As she drives through the woods, she wonders if the GPS system has taken her far from her intended target. Unexpectedly, however, the road leads to an opening, a beautiful clearing overlooking Boone Creek. In it is one large building, an older structure built of brick with expansive windows and surrounded by tall oak trees and landscaping fit for a palace. Stefani drives up to the front of the building, amazed by the fortress image the structure exudes and mesmerized by the sheer beauty of the site. As she approaches the small parking lot near the main entrance, she can't help but notice the six cars in it: two Mercedes, one Jaguar, a BMW, a Maserati, and a huge Lexus SUV. She slips the Range Rover into an available parking space and turns off the engine.

Stef, what have you gotten yourself into?

She looks at the huge wooden double doors in the center of the building. Mounted in the middle of the door on the right is a beautiful brass plate displaying the name "Perceptive Insight,

LLC." She sinks back into the seat, and her shoulders slump. After taking a deep breath she opens the door and sluggishly slides out. Approaching the doors, her legs suddenly feel weak. She reaches the doors and stops. *Oh my God, what am I doing? How do I walk in and ask, 'Hey, did you give me the car and money?' What if I go in here and make a total fool of myself? This is crazy!*

Stefani reaches out and softly runs her fingertips across the solid oak door, almost testing the door to see if it is safe the way a child would cautiously extend a hand toward a strange dog. She reaches down, grasps the huge brass lever, and gives it a turn. The door opens easily, and she steps into an amazingly large foyer. Obviously the building is very old, but the décor is incredible. Stefani stands in awe as she glances over the interior. Suddenly she is startled by a voice saying, "Good morning. May I help you?"

To her right sits an older woman at a desk. She is dressed very nicely, and her smile easily cuts Stefani's growing anxiety. Stefani focuses on the woman, takes a deep breath, and releases an uncontrolled and embarrassed expression. She approaches the desk and gently taps her fingers together. "Yes, I have a question, and I'm quite certain it's the oddest you'll ever hear."

The older woman leans forward. "What might that be?"

Stefani pulls the car keys from her pocket. "Who may I speak to about a new car that was recently given to me?"

The older woman takes off her glasses and gives her a friendly if puzzled look. "I'm sorry?"

Stefani can feel her face getting extremely warm. "I know this sounds crazy, but a new car was delivered to me under the condition that the person or company who purchased it would remain unnamed."

"If that's the case, then what makes you think someone here purchased the car?"

Stefani takes another deep breath and sighs. "Paperwork I have on the car lists this company as the purchaser."

The woman presses her index finger against her chin and then puts her glasses on. "May I have your name?

"Yes ... Stefani Tanner."

"Let me see if I can find someone to talk to you."

She picks up the telephone and punches two numbers. "Mr. Davidson, could you come to the front for a second?"

There is a brief pause, and then the woman hangs up the phone. "Mr. Davidson will be with your shortly. Please have a seat."

Stefani smiles. "Thank you."

Minutes later a tall, slender man dressed in a suit enters the lobby. He walks over and extends his hand. "Good morning. My name is Duncan Davidson."

Stefani stands and shakes his hand. "Hello, I'm Stefani Tanner."

As they stand facing each other, the silence is deafening. Duncan tilts his head, obviously puzzled. "Ms. Tanner, is there something I can help you with?"

"Yes ... but I don't know quite how to ask."

Duncan can easily sense Stefani's nervousness. "Why don't we sit down, and you can explain to me how I can be of help."

Stefani nods, and the two walk into a spacious sitting area. Like the foyer, it is breathtaking. The panoramic windows overlooking the water create a tranquil setting. Stefani can't help but think how this place looks like something out of a magazine.

They sit, and Stefani says, "Sir, I know you're a busy man, so I'll get right to the point. I received a new Range Rover that was purchased by this company. I'm quite sure of this because paperwork I have on the VIN number verify this. I don't want to sound unappreciative, but I need to know why. I have been in the area for only a few days, and very few people know I'm here. I have never heard of this company nor do I know what you do here. I confident I don't know anyone who works here. Can you explain this to me?"

Duncan leans forward, rests his elbows on his knees, and rubs his hands together. "May I call you Stefani?"

"Certainly."

"Stefani, you have me in a very uncomfortable position."

"I do? How?"

"This company was created by two people, one of whom you're talking to. The other is the heart and soul of this firm and one of my closest friends. Unfortunately, he is out of the office at the moment. I don't know all the details regarding the car, and for obvious reasons I'd prefer not to speculate."

"So the car was definitely purchased by this firm?"

Duncan grins and drops his head. He pauses for a moment and then looks up. "Stefani, my suggestion to you is to set up an appointment with my partner. I think this way you'll get the answers you're looking for."

Stefani smiles and stands. "Mr. Davidson, I appreciate your time and candor. Should I make the appointment with the lady at the front desk?"

Duncan extends his hand and shakes hers. "Yes. Jean will gladly set you up with an appointment."

"Thank you."

"My pleasure."

Stefani turns and walks toward the front desk. She pauses and turns back. "Mr. Davidson, may I ask what your partner's name is?"

Duncan stops, looks down at the floor, and rubs his chin. He then slips his hands into his pants pockets and says with a smile, "Gavin Thorne."

Stefani stands motionless for a moment. *Gavin Thorne? I haven't heard that name in over twenty years. Is it even the same Gavin Thorne?*

Stefani continues toward Jean's desk. "Hello again ... I'd like to make an appointment to see Gavin Thorne."

Jean looks up at Stefani with a very suspicious expression. "Is Mr. Thorne expecting you?"

Stefani tilts her head. "Well, I'm not sure if he's expecting me but we have a mutual interest involving a recent transaction we need to discuss."

Jean types something into her computer and studies the screen. "Mr. Thorne has an opening at eleven tomorrow morning."

"That would be great."

"May I have your name?"

"Yes ... Stefani Tanner."

Jean types the information into her computer. Stefani rubs her hands together. "I'll see him at eleven tomorrow."

Stefani drives home on autopilot as she thinks about what she's learned. *Why would Gavin Thorne buy me a new car and give me money? Secondly, how did he know I was in town? This is crazy!*

Stefani pulls the Range Rover into her parents' driveway, shifts the car into park, and turns off the engine. She sits staring out the side window, totally consumed in thought. *There's no way David and Gavin know each other. But why would someone you hardly ever knew and haven't seen in over twenty years hand over the keys to a brand new car and twenty thousand dollars and prefer to stay totally anonymous? I just don't get it.*

Stefani enters the house and finds her parents and the boys just finishing lunch in the kitchen. Joanna says, "Hi, honey. How did everything go?"

Stefani lifts her eyebrows. "Not at all what I expected."

Joanna looks at Jack and makes a subtle gesture. He stares back at her with a puzzled expression and then realizes what his wife is trying to convey. "Hey, boys, what do you say we ride down to the docks and get some fresh bait?"

Both boys jump up and race for the pickup truck. They know the first one there gets to ride in the center and shift the gears while he drives. Joanna gives Jack an affectionate look as he walks out of the kitchen. "Thank you, dear." She then says to Stefani, "Sweetheart, why don't you sit for a moment?"

Stefani places her handbag on the table and slides into a chair. Joanna smiles and winks. "So, not what you expected?"

Stefani sighs. "No, but, honestly, I don't know what I was expecting."

"Did you find out who purchased the car?"

"I'm pretty sure I did."

"And?"

Stefani shakes her head. "Mom, I don't understand."

"Well, why don't we try to figure it out?"

Smiling, she fiddles with a fork that has been left on the table. "Mom, do you remember the name Gavin Thorne?"

Joanna pokes out her lower lip and squints. Suddenly she raises her eyebrows. "Wasn't he one of your ball coaches when you were in high school?"

"Yes ... he helped coach the team I played for the summer of my junior year."

Joanna picks up two forks and sets them on one of the dirty plates. "Didn't he marry Belinda Patrick?"

"Yes, he did."

Joanna crosses her arms and leans forward. "Then why are we talking about Gavin Thorne?"

"I'm all but certain he bought me the car and gave me the money."

Her mother takes a deep breath and then sighs heavily. "Wow … are you sure?"

"Mom, you can't repeat what I'm about to tell, you but Mindy's husband has a friend who works for the Department of Motor Vehicles. He ran the VIN number of the car and printed out all the owner information. The car was purchased from the dealer by a company named Perceptive Insight."

"Honey … isn't that illegal?"

Stefani winces. "Maybe not illegal... put possiblt frowned upon."

"Oh Lord."

"Mom … I went there today."

Joanna's eyes become huge. "You went there?"

"Yes, I did, and I spoke to one of the owners. He's a nice guy and obviously very close to the other owner. He didn't come out and actually say it, but I could tell he knew the car was purchased by the company."

"Well, then why didn't he tell you the company bought it?"

"Because I don't think it was his decision. In so many words he basically told me he was the number two guy at the company."

"So that makes Gavin the number one guy?"

Stefani shrugs her shoulders. "That would be my guess."

Joanna pours Stefani a glass of lemonade. "Why would he buy you a car and give you money?" She squints as she scratches the top of her head. "Better yet, how did he know you were home?"

"I have no idea."

Joanna looks at Stefani and smirks. "I do remember you girls on the team thought he was a hot ticket."

Stefani laughs and nods. "He was put together nicely."

The two sit there quietly for a moment, and then Joanna rises and cleans off the table. Stefani stands and helps clean up as well. Stefani wipes her hands on a towel and then walks over to the door and leans against the frame. "Mom, something doesn't feel right."

"What do you mean?"

Stefani turns and shakes her head. "In the last week I've lost my job, I'm pretty certain my marriage is damaged beyond repair, but I don't seem to be overwhelmed like I think I should be."

"Honey, sometimes it takes things like this a little time to sink in."

"Maybe, but for the last few days I've been more relaxed than I can remember ever being. I know being here with Dad, you, and the boys has made things so much easier, and I'm not surrounded by things that constantly remind me of my life in Charlotte ... but I still feel like I should be more upset."

Joanna wipes off the table and then turns and winks. "Maybe the thrill of a mystery person giving you a new car and money has occupied your thoughts."

"Maybe ... it is kind of exciting."

Joanna gives Stefani a disciplinary look. "Stefani, don't you let this get out of hand."

Stefani is taken back by her mother's statement. "Out of hand? What do you mean?"

"Honey, you have always been very levelheaded and never impulsive, but lately you've been put through a tremendous amount of stress. Don't let your emotions over-influence your decisions."

Stefani winks at her mother. "I promise I won't."

Stefani goes upstairs to her room to change out of her business attire and slips on a pair of shorts, a T-shirt, and running shoes. She skips back down the steps and yells out, "Mom, I'm going for a run. I'll be back in about an hour."

"Okay, honey. Be careful."

Stefani walks to the road, reaches back, and pulls her toes up toward her back to stretch her well toned thigh muscles. After doing both legs she takes a deep breath and then springs into a pace that borders on a sprint. As she runs, she is virtually oblivious to her surroundings. Her mind is filled with the day's events. *Gavin Thorne. What is the connection with him? How does he know I'm home? Better yet, what would make him think about me? Could he know David?*

As the thought of David and Gavin Thorne knowing each other goes through her mind, her pace picks up. This thought, however, is short lived. *There's no way they know each other.*

Stefani's pace returns to normal. Her feet barely make a sound as the soles of her running shoes tap the road. *Gavin Thorne ... yep, he was pretty hot years ago.*

Stefani runs to the end of the road, which leads to a pier and continues to the end of the pier, where she stops just short of the railing. She walks in circles with her hands on top of her head. Breathing heavily, she continues thinking about Gavin Thorne. She leans her head over the rail and looks down at the water. The dark water seems to mirror her life at the moment: everything so unclear and vague yet mysterious at the same time. As she looks out over the water, she grasps the railing tightly and as if looking for an answer from the bay asks, "Gavin Thorne, what is on your mind?"

Chapter 10

Stefani turns the corner and heads toward the house. Her dad is sitting on the porch swing by himself. She remembers the summer evenings when the two of them would sit on the swing and just talk about anything. She hits the driveway, slows to a walk, and then strolls up onto the porch and sits next to him.

He reaches over and puts his arm around her. "Been a long time since we did this, Tiger."

"Too long, Dad."

Jack kicks his hat back and takes a deep breath. Stefani looks at him and smiles. "The boys aren't working you too hard, are they?'

Jack laughs. "They're full of energy, but I still manage to keep up." He pulls her closer. "Sweetheart, the last few days have been great. Those are good boys. You've made your mom and me very proud."

Stefani sinks into her dad's side, and they sit quietly for a moment. "Dad, I'm sorry about what happened between David and me."

Jack turns and leans away. "Honey, what are you sorry for?"

"I must have done something to push him away."

"Tiger, you can drive yourself crazy trying to figure out why other people think the way they do. Bottom line is no matter what you did, it doesn't justify him straying. He was obviously only thinking about himself. He never gave thought to the damage he would do to you and the boys." He pulls her close again. "And I know in my heart you didn't do anything to push him away. Whatever drove him to do what he did is a problem he has, not you. Neither you or the boys deserve what happened, and don't you forget that."

Stefani starts to tear up and quickly wipes her eyes with her hand. "Dad, I was telling Mom earlier today that I'm confused."

"What about?"

"I should be devastated over what has happened. My marriage has been damaged possibly beyond repair, I lost my job, and until recently I was penniless. But ... I don't feel overwhelmed. Is that a bad thing?"

Jack laughs. "No, that's not a bad thing. Honey, things like this sometimes take time to hit home. That doesn't mean you're doing something wrong. I would imagine getting away from the surroundings down there and the people has made it somewhat easier. Plus, you have the boys with you."

Stefani looks at her father. "And being here with you and Mom has made me feel like I did when I was young ... always safe."

Jack looks back at her. "Tiger, no matter where you go or what you do, this place will always be here for you if you need it. You know the door is always open, and your mom and I love having you here." He says softly, "You just grew up too darn fast."

Stefani wraps her arms around him and squeezes tightly. "I love you, Dad."

"I know you do, Tiger. I love you, too." Jack kicks his foot forward and starts to gently rock the swing back and forth. "Mom told me you think you figured out who sent you the car and money."

"Yes, I think so."

"I don't believe I ever met this guy."

"I don't think you ever met him formally, but you'd remember him if you saw a picture from my ball-playing days."

"So what's his story?"

Stefani crosses her arms and nibbles at her thumbnail. "I really don't know. I mean I knew him … but not very well. I never had a real conversation with him that I can remember, and I haven't seen him in over twenty years. As a matter of fact, the only interaction I had with him was the summer of my junior year in high school. After that I saw him in passing a few times, but that was it. He was older and dated Belinda Patrick, and they got married. I have run this through my head a thousand times, and I can't make the connection."

Jack pops his lips and gives her a very serious look. "Does David know him?"

"I honestly can't imagine how. David never expressed any interest in the St. Michaels area. I can say with total certainty David doesn't have immediate access to the kind of money it takes to purchase a Range Rover and have a check cut for thousands of dollars. If he did why, of all people, would he channel it through Gavin Thorne? David and Gavin working together doesn't make any sense."

Jack leans forward and rubs his thighs with his hands. "Well, you've always been persistent. I know you'll pursue this until you get all the answers. Just do me a favor."

Stefani leans forward and rests her chin on his shoulder. "What's that?"

"Just be careful."

Stefani kisses her dad on the cheek and stands up. "I promise you, Dad, I will."

The two stand up and walk into the house. The smell of food fills the entire home. Stefani runs up the stairs and takes a quick shower. When she gets out she stands at the sink and looks closely at her face in the mirror as if she's staring at an old friend. *What do I say to Gavin tomorrow during our meeting? Hey, thanks for the car and money. Now have a nice day ... or, Gavin Thorne, I don't mean to sound unappreciative, but do you frequently give cars and large amounts of cash to people you hardly know …? I know … Mr. Thorne, thanks for the gift … by the way, are you crazy?*

Stefani pulls her hair back with a clip and takes a final look in the mirror. "Tomorrow's meeting should go smooth as silk … yeah, right."

She slips on a pair of shorts, a T-shirt, and some flip-flops. She heads down the stairs and enters the kitchen. After eating and cleaning up, she walks over and places her hand on her mother's back. "Mom, I'm going to town for a while. Do you need anything?"

"No, honey, I'm good."

"Okay. I'll be back soon."

Stefani heads toward Easton. She knows this isn't a formal business meeting; at this point she's not sure what kind of meeting it will turn out to be. She drives past a few stores and then parks in the Nordstrom's lot. Much to her surprise, the perfect outfit, appropriate for her meeting tomorrow, is on display in the store. *Not too bold but not too passive. Perfect for a person who has no idea what they're doing.*

Stefani begins to snicker but stifles it when a sales associate approaches her and asks, "Miss, is there anything I may help you with?"

Stefani turns and says, "Yes … I'll take this in a size two, and I'll need a pair of matching shoes."

Chapter 11

The next morning Stefani wakes earlier than normal. She slides out of bed and slips on a pair of shorts, a T-shirt, and running shoes. After hesitating momentarily, she reaches into her bag and pulls out her iPod and ear buds. Glancing at the clock, she leaves her room at 4:50 a.m. and creeps down the stairs. The front door creaks as she eases it open. The warm, humid air cuts through the screen door and hits her in the face. She walks toward the road while putting the ear buds in. A bashful smile crosses her face as she passes the Range Rover and begins her morning jog. Oddly, her pace is much slower than usual. Reaching down, she hits the button on the iPod, and the *Richard Marx Greatest Hits* collection begins to play. People always joke about her music preferences, but to her there is something special about music from the '80s. The morning seems surprisingly peaceful, and unlike her normal runs this one seems to have no purpose. Instead of the usual route, Stefani heads for the marina. Her pace remains slow and smooth as her mind slips away from the running and focuses on Gavin Thorne. *God, he had a great body ... broad shoulders, muscular arms, and that tan. The dark brown hair and those legs—oh my God, those legs.*

Stefani reaches the marina and stops. Looking over the boats tied into each slip, as if each is sleeping, she quietly walks to the end of the pier and looks out over the water. As she scans the bay, she can't help but notice how relaxed she feels. The sense of peacefulness confuses her again. *Stef, you're going to have to step back into reality. Your life is totally upside down no matter how you feel at the moment.*

She takes a deep breath and exhales hard. She looks up at the sky. "Maybe ... but I'm going to enjoy this as long as I can."

Her return trip is at her normal pace, and she arrives in virtually no time. When she walks into the house, Joanna is in the kitchen cooking breakfast. Jack is sitting at the table reading the paper, and the boys are still in bed. Stefani walks into the kitchen and sits down.

Joanna is facing the stove scrambling eggs but turns her head to ask, "How was your run?"

"It was great. I went down to the marina and looked around."

Jack looks up at Stefani over his glasses. "The old place is starting to look run down ... like some of the people around here."

Joanna cuts an eye at her dad and laughs. Stefani gets up, walks over to the cupboard, and gets a glass. She fills it with tap water and then returns to her chair. "Oh, I don't know, Dad. The place looks like it did years ago. It's like most things around here ... even though it ages, it still stands the test of time."

Before turning back to the paper, Jack says, "Well, honey, I can assure you the test of time gets more difficult every year."

The kitchen becomes silent as Stefani fumbles with the glass in her hand, preoccupied in thought. Joanna looks at Jack and then back at Stefani. "Honey, you okay?"

Stefani continues to stare at the glass and is totally oblivious to her surroundings.

"Stefani."

Stefani jumps and sits up straight. "Yes?"

Joanna laughs, looks at Jack, and winks. "Got your mind elsewhere?"

Stefani glances at her dad, who is smiling, causing her to blush. "No, just sitting here."

Suddenly the loud rumble of feet coming down the steps can be heard. Jack folds up the paper and rubs his hands together. "Joanna, I think they smelled your food."

The boys burst into the kitchen and fly into seats at the table. Joanna turns and laughs as she pours each a glass of milk. Stefani grins as her father and the boys each tuck their napkin into their shirt collar.

"I see they have picked up a few of Pop's habits."

The five finish breakfast, and immediately the boys race upstairs to take a quick shower. The plan is to go into town with their grandfather to get a new propeller for the boat. Stefani laughs as Jack gets up and puts on his cap. "Dad, you don't have to take them everywhere you go."

Jack rinses his coffee mug in the sink. "Tiger, we're fine."

He winks and walks out the back door. Joanna strolls over and watches him make his way to the garage. She is smiling as she turns to wash the breakfast dishes. Stefani gets up and grabs a dishtowel to dry.

"Mom, are the boys running Dad too hard?"

"Sweetheart, I haven't seen your father this happy and energetic in years. These boys have made him twenty years younger."

"I just don't want him to think he has to cater to every beck and call."

"When Dad gets tired he'll let them know."

Joanna hands Stefani a wet plate. "That man has slept completely through the last three nights. That's the first time in years he hasn't gotten up and walked the floors two or three times. He wakes up refreshed and happy. There's no medicine his doctor could give him that would work the magic these boys have."

They continue to wash dishes without saying a word. Joanna finally cuts the silence. "So, are you ready to meet Mr. Thorne?"

Stefani takes a deep breath, sighs, and then laughs. "I don't know."

Joanna chuckles as she hands Stefani the last of the dishes. "Well, it's the only way you're going to get some closure with the car and money thing."

"I know."

Stefani hangs up the dishtowel and sits down at the table. "Mom, I have worked in a high-pressure, very intense business environment for years, but I don't think I've ever been as insecure about a meeting as I am right now."

Joanna sits down and rests her chin on her hand. "Maybe you're a little unsure about this meeting because you're not totally certain what all you want to know and what questions are out of bounds."

Stefani looks down at the table in embarrassment. "Mom, when I think about this meeting and Gavin Thorne, it's like I'm seventeen again and giddy as ever. I shouldn't be like this ... I'm married with two kids."

"Maybe this is why it's been a little easier for you to deal with everything."

"What do you mean?"

"Well, it's not every day a girl gets a new car and a boatload of money. Obviously he did this for a reason."

Stefani flops back in her chair. "But why?"

Joanna smiles at Stefani. "I don't know … why do you think?"

"Mom, I have no idea."

Joanna gets up and wipes the stove top. "I remember a teenage girl, years ago, who had a bit of a crush on one particular coach."

"I'm not sure it was a crush."

"Honey … who are you trying to kid? It was a crush."

Stefani grins as she nibbles on her thumbnail. "He was pretty hot."

Joanna glances over her shoulder. "Maybe a little of that teenage girl is still around."

Stefani looks up at her mom and turns away, trying not to smile. "I guess I'd better get ready and go see if I can get some answers to these crazy questions."

Stefani goes upstairs and pulls out the new outfit she bought yesterday. She showers and takes her time doing her makeup and hair. After putting on her suit and shoes, she walks downstairs and finds her mother vacuuming the carpet in the living room.

Joanna turns the vacuum cleaner off. "Honey, you look terrific."

"Thanks, Mom."

"What time do you think you'll be home?"

"I don't know."

Joanna winks at her. "I hope you get the answers you're looking for."

Before Stefani can respond Joanna turns the vacuum cleaner back on and proceeds to sweep. Stefani grins and heads for the door. As she makes her way down the porch steps, she can hear her dad and the boys in the garage working on the boat motor. Climbing into the Range Rover, a sense of satisfaction comes over her. For the first time since the Aeron International incident, she feels somewhat like her old self. Is it the suit, the car, or the two together? She can't tell, but it feels right. She fastens her seat belt and starts the engine. As she drives toward Perceptive Insight, however, she can feel her stomach tense up. Her mind begins to race. *What do I say to Gavin? What does he look like now? Will he blow me off? Will he be mad? Should I really be doing this?*

Stefani's confidence is quickly replaced by nervousness and uncertainty. Every meeting she has ever initiated, she has been prepared for. She'd always made sure no stone was left unturned, no question would be a surprise. Now, however, she has no idea what to expect. *Maybe I should call and cancel.*

That thought quickly leaves her mind; she knows quite well this may be the one and only shot at getting answers to her questions. She continues to drive with her mind racing. *I think I'm going to throw up.*

Chapter 12

Stefani again makes her way to the office at Waterview Place. As she slows, she recognizes a car that wasn't in the lot during her previous visit. Parked off by itself is a Bentley Continental GT.

Stef, I think you may be way out of your comfort zone.

She takes a deep breath and parks. She grabs her bag and exits her car, looking looks down at her suit to make sure everything is perfect. She walks toward the front door and once again reaches down and turns the handle. As she does, she can feel her heart rate accelerate. Quietly she enters and walks over to Jean, who looks up. "Good morning, Ms. Tanner."

Stefani forces a smile through her nervousness. "Good morning."

"Mr. Thorne is presently on the telephone ... he will be with you shortly. You're welcome to have a seat while you wait."

Stefani looks around and sees a small chair positioned against a wall. She chooses to sit there out of the way and hopefully unnoticed. As she waits, she looks at the décor again. *This place is phenomenal.*

The wait, although somewhat lengthy, could take longer as far as Stefani is concerned. *What am I doing here? I need to get out of here!*

Suddenly Jean gets up from her desk and walks toward her. "Ms. Tanner, Mr. Thorne will see you now."

Stefani begins to feel faint, but she nods and stands. "Okay."

"Please follow me."

The sound of their heels tapping the hardwood floors echoes throughout the wide corridors as the two reach a set of oak doors. Jean opens the right door and walks in with Stefani cautiously following. Her heart is racing as if she has just run a 10K race. The office is spacious and its décor similar to the rest of the building. Floor-to-ceiling windows overlook the water, and the furniture is made of beautiful wood.

"Mr. Thorne is in the conference room through those doors … he will be with you shortly. Why don't you have a seat in front of his desk?"

Stefani walks over and sits. "Thank you."

Jean turns and leaves, softly closing the door behind her. Stefani scans the office. Everything is neatly organized. She notices a number of pictures of two boys situated throughout the bookcase behind the desk. She squints to focus on the photos. Some look like school pictures; some are athletic photos. Both boys are very attractive and fit. As she continues to study the photos and the office, she is startled by the sound of the conference door opening. She waits only a second, but it seems like an eternity, and she feels paralyzed as she tries to rotate toward the door. Slowly she turns her head, and her breath swiftly leaves her. A man walks through the door dressed in a very expensive, custom-made black suit and a gold tie. His hair is short and combed to the side. There is a hint of gray on the sides, but the face and eyes are the same as they were so many years ago. It's the same Gavin Thorne. She quickly looks him over again and can tell he is still physically fit. As Gavin walks toward her, she stands and smiles.

Gavin extends his hand. "Ms. Tanner, it's great to see you."

Stefani blushes. "It's great to see you as well."

"It must be twenty years and then some since I saw you last."

Stefani nods, feeling a bit more at ease. "I believe so."

After their hands separate there is a brief, awkward pause. Gavin rubs his hands together. "Please have a seat."

Stefani sits. "Thank you."

As Gavin walks around his desk, Stefani notices his left ring finger is bare with no tan line. He sits down, and the two look at each other briefly; he seems almost as afraid to speak as she is. Finally he says, "Ms. Tanner—"

Stefani cuts him off. "Please call me Stefani."

Gavin nods. "Okay ... Stefani, I have to admit I was surprised when I saw your name on my schedule for today."

Stefani smiles. "Probably as surprised as I was when I made the appointment."

Both laugh, and some of the tension in the room eases.

"So ... Stefani, how can I help you?"

Stefani takes a deep breath and slowly exhales. "Mr. Thorne—"

"Gavin."

Stefani laughs again. "Gavin ... did you get a chance to speak with your partner?"

He gives her a slightly confused look. "Duncan? I have spoken with him, but I'm not quite sure if I know what you're referring to."

"Not long after I arrived in St. Michaels I received a brand new Range Rover and a large amount of cash. Two men delivered the car and money and told me under no circumstances could they disclose where each came from."

Gavin sits quietly and nods. "That's sounds pretty exciting."

Stefani fidgets with her bracelet. "Well, I couldn't imagine who would send me such nice gifts, so I did some research."

"Oh?"

Stefani smiles and sighs. "I have access to some DMV data, and I discovered the Range Rover was initially purchased by your company. Then the title was transferred to my name. I can only assume the money came from the same place."

Gavin leans back in his chair, puckers his lips, and sits quietly for a few seconds. Then he leans forward, stands up, and walks toward the windows overlooking the water. Stefani remains seated and follows him with her eyes. He reaches the windows and leans forward, resting his hands on the large sill. "I didn't see this coming."

Stefani tilts her head to the side. "See what coming?"

"You figuring this out."

Gavin turns and sits against the ledge. "It was to remain anonymous."

"I don't understand. Why would you send me a beautiful new car, money and not tell? I guess my first question is how did you even know I'm in town or remember who I was for that matter?"

Gavin slides his hands in his pants pockets. He looks down at the floor and then up at Stefani. "May I ask you a favor?"

"Yes."

"Would you have dinner with me tonight?"

"Dinner ... I'm not sure that would be a good idea."

He stands and walks toward her, stopping about five feet away. "Um … not as in a date, but I think I owe you an apology and an answer. I'd feel a whole lot more comfortable if I could explain myself away from here."

Stefani watches every move Gavin makes. Her insecurity must be apparent because he quickly says, "Trust me, we will be in a safe place, and you can tell anyone you want that you're with me. If at any time you feel the need to end the evening, I promise you I will drive you home with no questions asked."

Stefani is between guarded and curious. "Gavin, I don't know what to make of all this. This borders on the bizarre, and I don't know what to do. If you really think about it, we don't even know each other very well."

"I understand. If you'd prefer not to go, I totally appreciate your position. I would just like the opportunity to explain myself so you don't think I'm … some sort of nut."

She looks at Gavin and can tell he's embarrassed. "I tell you what. I'll have dinner with you tonight, but you have to make me one promise."

"Okay."

"You have to be totally honest with me and tell me the names of everyone who was involved in this."

"I don't understand."

"What I'm saying is if someone else was involved in you knowing I'm in town, buying the car, and giving me the cash, you have to tell me."

Gavin nods. "Absolutely."

Stefani sits frozen for a few seconds but then says firmly, "Deal."

Gavin grins and takes a step closer. "What time should I pick you up?"

Stefani stands and squints. "How's … six sound?"

"Perfect."

She eases out a small smile and then extends her hand. He takes it and shakes her hand softly. "I'll see you at six."

"Okay."

Stefani turns toward the door with Gavin following behind. Suddenly she stops and turns around. "Exactly where are we going, and how do I need to dress?"

Gavin looks down and rubs his chin. "You know, I wear suits all the time, and, if it's okay with you, I'd like to relax a bit. What do you say we go to Bodie's?"

"Bodie's?"

"Yes, it's a nice place … but casual. They have great seafood and steak. And, if you're a vegetarian, they have tremendous salads."

"Where is it?"

"On the water in St. Michaels. I guess they've been there about ten years or so. I go there frequently and have never been disappointed. They have a beautiful long beach there as well. It's just a very nice place."

"Okay, so when you say casual, you mean …?"

"I like to wear a golf shirt and shorts."

"So you mean really casual."

"We can go somewhere else if you'd like."

Stefani laughs. "No, no … that's fine. I'm just trying to take this all in."

"Okay … so six?"

"That's fine."

"At your parents' house?"

Stefani squints playfully. "As if you didn't know."

Gavin blushes and points his finger at her. "Right."

Stefani turns and reaches the door, but Gavin opens it for her. He escorts her to the front door and says, "I'll see you at six."

"Okay."

Gavin watches her climb into the Range Rover. He waves and then closes the door. Stefani sets her handbag on the passenger seat and starts the car. As she heads toward home, she can't help but smile. *Stefani, what are you doing? You've gone from detective to dinner date in a matter of an hour. This is absolutely crazy.*

She plugs her iPod into the stereo, and again Richard Marx begins to play. As she drives, her mind is totally consumed with Gavin. *What's his story? Where's Belinda? What do they do at Perceptive Insight? Geez, at this rate I'll need a notepad to keep track of these questions.*

Once again the confusion Stefani has been experiencing kicks in. She knows she should be feeling overwhelmed with what's happened with David and work, but right now both are the farthest things from her mind. She feels guilty, but yet she's feeling no sadness. Maybe it's because her termination from Aeron International was groundless and what David did was unforgivable. Either way she hadn't done anything wrong, and this is just a simple dinner date ... well, not even a date. It isn't hard to justify things when you know you have been treated unfairly and your trust has been shattered. Stefani sinks into the soft leather seat as she drives toward her parents' house. For the moment she feels the same peace she felt this morning when at the marina. She only has one concern at the moment ...

What will Mom and Dad think?

After the short drive Stefani pulls into her parents' driveway. As she exits the car, she sees her mother sweeping the front porch. She walks up and stops at the base of the steps. "Mom, you never stop, do you?"

Joanna laughs as she pushes a small pile of dirt off the porch. "You know they say a woman's work is never done." She looks at Stefani and says, "Judging by the distinct glow on your face, your meeting went well."

Stefani looks up and rolls her lips in between her teeth. She pauses for a moment and then looks down and grins. "Yes, it went well."

"So Gavin sent you the car and money?"

"I think so."

"You think so?" Joanna rests the broom against the wall and walks toward the porch swing. "Honey, maybe you should come sit with me for a moment."

The two sit down. Stefani looks at her mom and smiles. "Mom, I think the last time we did this I was going off to college, and you were warning me about aggressive guys."

Joanna wipes her hands on her apron. "So, tell me about your meeting."

"Well, honestly there isn't much to tell. I met with Gavin."

"Same guy?"

"Oh, yes … same guy. Little bit of gray hair, but, oh yeah … same guy."

Joanna tilts her head in disapproval. "Stefani."

Stefani laughs. "Okay, Mom, okay."

Stefani lets her hair down and slips off her shoes. "There really isn't much to tell. I must say his office—his entire building—is beautiful. It's a very professional setting, and the atmosphere is incredible."

"Okay, honey, Gavin is still a hot ticket, and his place of business is impressive, but what about the car and money?"

"I asked him, but he asked for a favor instead of giving me an answer."

"He asked you for a favor?"

"Yes."

"What's he want?"

Stefani takes a deep breath and squints as she looks at her mother. "He asked me to dinner."

"Stefani Marie, I know you refused his invitation."

"Well ... not exactly."

"Stefani, I know your marriage is going through a very difficult time, and what David did to you and the boys is heartless, but you are still a married woman with two sons."

Stefani reaches over and rubs Joanna's hand. "Yes, Mom, I know that. We both agreed this is not a date. He just didn't want to discuss this in his office. We are going to a place called Bodie's. He promised me he'd bring me home the moment I wanted to leave or felt uncomfortable. "It's no different than all the dinner meetings I attended for work."

"Well ... I still don't know if I'm onboard with this ... but ... it's your call."

"Mom, I'll be fine. Trust me."

Joanna stands and grabs the broom. "I will say this ... he's not trying to sweep you off your feet."

"Why do you say that?"

"Bodie's isn't exactly a romantic setting. I mean it's a very nice restaurant, but not where you would take a woman on your first date."

"Exactly, Mom ... it's not a date."

Stefani slips her shoes back on and follows Joanna into the house. Jack and the boys are sitting at the table with a part off the boat motor.

Joanna sees this and shakes her head. "What is this? You have a garage with a workbench, and you're working on the kitchen table?"

Jack glances up at the boys, grits his teeth, and bulges his eyes. "Joanna, the light is much better in here, and I can't see these little parts without good light."

Joanna shakes her head and then walks over to the sink. Jack looks up at Stefani, who is leaning against the doorframe shaking her head. He raises his index finger to his lips. "Shhh."

The boys see him and do the same. Stefani laughs out loud. "Somebody's gonna get it good."

Clearly trying to change the subject, her dad says to her, "So, Tiger, how'd your morning go?"

"Not bad."

Joanna turns and surveys the table. "Boys, run upstairs and get cleaned up. We are going to the grocery store, and I don't want you to see your grandpa get a whipping."

The boys look at each other and scamper upstairs. Jack looks at Stefani and then at Joanna. "Okay, I'll clean up."

He stands and puts the parts in a cardboard box. As he finishes, he glances at Stefani. "Tiger, what would you like for dinner?

Joanna strolls over and rests her hand on her husband's shoulder, "Stefani won't be eating with us tonight."

"Oh?"

Stefani gives her mother a scornful look. "Mom."

Jack looks back and forth at the two, clearly confused. "What?"

Joanna pats his shoulder. "Stefani is going out to dinner with Mr. Gavin Thorne."

Her father gives Stefani a disapproving look. She hasn't gotten one of those from him since she threw her glove after making an error in junior high softball.

"Dad, really it's nothing. It's no different than a business meeting. It's not a date."

He stands motionless for a second and then picks up the box. "Okay, but I don't think the boys should know about this."

Joanna takes off her apron and hangs it on a hook on the back of the door. "That's why we'll be in Easton when he picks her up."

Stefani winks at her mother and then looks at her dad.

His concern is clear in his expression and his tone as he says, "Stefani, don't get yourself into a pickle."

"I won't, Dad. I promise."

Chapter 13

Stefani is home alone. She has been reading a magazine but totally aware of the time.

Four-thirty ... I should get ready.

She showers and then stands wrapped in a towel in the bedroom trying to decide what to wear. *Gavin said casual. He's wearing a golf shirt and shorts ... hmmm, polo shirt and shorts.*

She puts on a nice-fitting pair of khaki shorts and a white blouse. She slips on some wedges and looks in the mirror. *God, I've dressed for corporate executives for years, but I can't decide on an outfit for a casual dinner at a local joint?*

Stefani knows it's not the atmosphere as much at is it is who she's dressing for. She carefully applies a bit of makeup and fixes her hair. She stands in front of a full-length mirror. *Well ... I hope this is okay.*

She walks downstairs and sits in the living room. She nervously picks up a magazine and fumbles through it as she glances up at the clock ... 5:55. She leans forward and peeks through the sheers on the window as they dance in the breeze. She flops back against the chair and shakes her head. *Stefani, you're crazy.*

Suddenly she hears a soft hum and the sound of gravel being compacted. "Oh, Lord."

She leans forward and can see the Bentley in the driveway. Her heart rate picks up, and she hears the car door close. Seconds later the front steps creak as Gavin walks up and taps on the door. Stefani sits frozen for a moment and then closes her eyes and takes a deep breath. She gets up, walks over, and opens the door. Standing on the other side of the screen door is Gavin, dressed in a casual, button-up shirt not tucked in, tan cargo shorts, and flip-flops.

Stefani smiles and opens the screen door. "Hello."

"Hello to you."

Gavin looks around. "Are your parents here?"

"No, they went into Easton to shop with my sons."

"Oh. I was hoping to say hello … I haven't seen them in years. Are they doing well?"

"Yes, very well. Dad is running himself to death trying to keep up with the boys, but they are healthy. I'm certainly thankful for that."

Stefani looks down at Gavin's attire. "You did say casual, didn't you."

Gavin looks down at his clothes and then up at Stefani. "Yes ... I can go change if you'd like."

Stefani breaks out into laughter. "No ... it's just so different from how you were dressed this morning."

Gavin snickers. "It's nice to get away from a suit sometimes."

Stefani looks down at his feet. As she does, she can't help but notice the bulging calf muscles she remembers from years ago. "Flip-flops, huh?"

"Yes." Gavin looks down at her feet and says, "Flip-flops ... um, I can go get a pair of shoes."

Stefani continues to laugh. "Actually, if it's okay, I'd prefer to wear flip-flops."

"By all means."

"Give me one second."

Stefani walks upstairs, slips off the wedges, and slides on her flip-flops. She returns to the living room, where Gavin is still standing. She makes her eyes big and smiles. "Now this is much better!"

The two walk out to the car. Gavin hurries ahead and opens the passenger-side door for her. After she is comfortably seated, he gently closes the door. She buckles her seat belt, quickly scans the dashboard, and slides her hands across the soft leather seat. Gavin climbs in, buckles his seat belt, and starts the car. He reaches up to the visor and pulls out a pair of Maui Jim sunglasses and puts them on. "I'm not trying to be cool—my eyes don't handle direct sunlight very well. But, if cool works for you, we'll say that."

Stefani laughs and shakes her head. "Cool it is." She continues to study the car. "This car is beautiful."

"Thank you. Someone suggested I test drive one, and once I did I was sold."

Stefani bites her lower lip and then goes out on a limb. "Bet it doesn't drive as nicely as a Range Rover."

Gavin continues to look straight ahead and grins. "They're close."

"Oh, are they?"

Gavin nods and glances over at her. "I've driven a Range Rover a few times."

"Oh, have you now?"

Gavin turns back, still smiling. "I have one at home. It does very well in the snow."

Stefani laughs as they continue toward Bodie's. Once they arrive Gavin pulls up to the main entrance. A teenage boy walks over to the driver's side door as another young man open's Stefani's door. "Good evening, ma'am."

Stefani stands and looks over at Gavin, who is already out of the car. He walks around to join her. She watches the teenager drive off in Gavin's car and then looks at Gavin with raised eyebrows. "Valet parking at Bodie's?"

Gavin smiles and nods toward the door. "I come here a lot."

As the two enter the restaurant, they are met by the host. "Good evening, Mr. Thorne. We have your favorite table ready for you."

"Thank you, Jim."

Gavin and Stefani are led to the table. The view overlooks the bay and a large, sandy beach. Stefani sits as the host slides her chair in for her. She looks out over the water. "This is absolutely beautiful."

"This is why I call this my favorite table."

The waitress appears. "Good evening, Mr. Thorne."

"Hello, Lindsey. This is Mrs. Tanner."

"Good evening, Mrs. Tanner."

"Good evening."

The waitress recites the day's specials. Gavin inclines his head toward Stefani to indicate she should order first. Stefani shakes her head. "So much to choose from. I think I'll have the stuffed flounder with a side salad."

The waitress looks at Gavin, who looks at Stefani and then back at the waitress. "That sounds great. I'll have the same."

The waitress walks away, leaving the two alone. Stefani, feeling much more relaxed, crosses her hands and rests them in her lap. "Okay, Mr. Thorne, interrogation time."

"Uh-oh."

Stefani laughs. "So a Range Rover and money … why?"

Gavin takes a deep breath and exhales hard. He rests his forearms on the table and raises his eyebrows. "Because you needed them."

"I needed them?"

"Yes."

Stefani leans forward and rests her forearms on the table as well. "And how did you know I needed them?"

Gavin puckers his lips for a second and then tilts his head. "Okay, here goes. Recently I was at work, and everything was in total disarray. I mean everything was going wrong, and the harder I tried the worse it got. Finally I had enough and decided I was going to get away from the office and eat alone to clear my thoughts. I decided to go to a restaurant that I hadn't been to in ages. While I was sitting in the booth, working on my tablet, I heard a voice in the next booth. It was a voice I hadn't heard in years, but as soon as I heard it I knew who it was."

Gavin nervously fumbles with his napkin.

"So—and please forgive me for eavesdropping—I listened to the conversation. I couldn't believe what I was hearing.

I thought I had a bad day. That angelic voice told a story that made me feel guilty for even thinking I had a bad day. She lost her job and discovered her husband was being unfaithful in the same day. I continued to listen as she told her friend she was staying with her parents but had no means of transportation and was virtually out of money because of her husband's manipulative actions.

Gavin takes a deep breath and sighs heavily.

So ... that afternoon I went back to my office, and I called the dealership where I buy my cars. I told the sales manager what I wanted. I then called my lawyer and told him to process everything but—no matter what—not to tell anyone who these things came from. Obviously, we both underestimated your investigative skills."

Stefani stares at Gavin and then looks down at her napkin. "Gavin ... I don't know what to say. Thank you hardly seems like enough. Honestly, I feel guilty for accepting everything."

"First of all you don't need to say anything. Secondly ... do not feel guilty."

The food arrives, and they continue with small talk. After completing their meals Stefani puts her hands in her lap. "That was absolutely delicious!"

"I'm glad you liked it. They never disappoint me here."

Stefani glances at Gavin and then bows her head with a grin. Gavin bows his head as well.

"Stefani, I know this isn't a date, but this is one of the nicest evenings I've had in a long time."

Stefani looks at Gavin with a totally dropped guard. "Me, too. I really appreciate everything."

Gavin looks at his watch and then says in a tone that sounds like he's trying hard to be casual, "Um, it's only seven thirty ... would you like to take a walk on the beach?"

Pleased that it appears he doesn't want the evening to end, Stefani looks out the window and smiles. "Sure. I think I can handle that."

As they stand, Gavin looks out at the flags on the deck, which are flapping strongly. "Looks like the wind has picked up a bit ... might be chilly."

"Oh ... I'll be okay."

Gavin waves to the waitress, who immediately walks over. "Yes, Mr. Thorne?"

"Lindsey, can you get Mrs. Tanner a Bodie's sweatshirt? Pink ... and I'd say ... a medium."

"Yes, sir."

Lindsey returns with a sweatshirt and hands it to Stefani.

"Thank you, Lindsey."

"My pleasure, Ms. Tanner. Mr. Thorne, may I get you anything else?"

Gavin looks at Stefani. She shakes her head no and laughs. "I'm perfect."

Gavin reaches out and takes the small binder from Lindsey and signs it. "Lindsey, we're good. Thank you for a great dinner."

"It's been my pleasure. You both have a great evening."

Gavin and Stefani walk out onto the back deck and then down on the sand. Stefani shivers. "Brr … it is a bit chilly." She puts the sweatshirt on and smiles. "Good guess on the size."

"I get lucky every now and then."

Gavin reaches down and slips off his flip-flops. Stefani does the same. Gavin holds out his hand for her flip-flops and carries them with his. They walk for a few yards, and then Stefani breaks the silence. "So what does Perceptive Insight do?"

Gavin shrugs his shoulders. "Well … we actually do a few things. About five years ago my partner Duncan and I worked together and were frustrated with our employer. So we finally got up the courage and ventured out into the insecure world. We wrote a screenplay that luckily was optioned. We then wrote another, and before we knew it we were not only writing but also producing. We then branched out into the restaurant world, and that has worked for us.

Actually, Bodie's was our first restaurant. Our most recent endeavor has been commercial development, so we'll see how that goes."

"So Bodie's is yours?"

"Yep."

"It's a great place."

"Thanks ... I think it will always be my favorite."

"Wow ... you've been busy and obviously successful."

"Yes, we've been very fortunate, and I'm lucky to have the best partner to work with."

They continue to walk without saying anything. Again Stefani risks another question. "I hope I'm not crossing any lines, but I noticed you don't wear a wedding band."

Gavin glances at her and obviously forces a smile, and she wishes she could recant the question. "I'm sorry. I should not have gone there."

Gavin laughs. "No ... that's fine. There's really nothing to tell. Belinda and I married and had two great boys. But honestly ... we couldn't have been more wrong for each other if we tried to be. It's not like things were brutal, but we were legally married roommates with very different ideas and wants. One day she came home and said she'd had enough and was tired of being miserable ... so she left. That was six years ago."

"Right before you ventured out in business?"

"Yep."

"Bet she regrets that."

"Oh, she's made some comments and attempts, but nothing ever came of them. Basically, we have two common interests and have agreed to remain amicable for them."

"That's good."

They reach a pier and walk out to the end. Gavin wipes a bench of with his hand. "Would you like to sit?"

"Okay."

They sit looking out over the water. The sun is setting, and the colors are stunning.

"Gavin, why?"

Gavin looks at Stefani. "I'm sorry. I don't understand."

"Why?"

"Why what?"

Stefani gets up, walks over to the rail, and turns to face Gavin, who is still seated.

"Gavin, there are hundreds of people around here who have lost their jobs. Many have marriages that didn't last. Did you buy them cars and give them money?"

He rests his elbows on his knees and rubs his hands together. "No."

"Then why me? Why would you give me all this stuff and not want me to know it was from you?"

Gavin joins her at the rail and rests his forearms on the top plank. Stefani waits for an answer almost to the point of aggravation. He shakes his head and sighs. "To protect myself."

"To protect yourself ... from what?"

Unlike the rest of the evening, Gavin seems to find it difficult to make eye contact with her. "I'm not so sure you want to hear this story."

"I don't?"

"No."

Stefani turns and walks away from him and then turns and storms back. "Yeah, I think I want to hear it. You give me a car and money with no real reason why. Yeah ... I'll take my chances."

He turns and faces her. "Because I didn't want to have to go through a second time what I went through the first time."

"What are you talking about?"

Gavin puts his hands on top of his head and closes his eyes. He takes a deep breath and then looks at Stefani. "You."

"Me? What did I do?"

"Nothing … you did nothing."

Stefani crosses her arms and paces back and forth. "Gavin, you're not making any sense. You tell me I'm a problem but I did nothing. Gavin I have enough going on in my life right now. I don't need games." She turns and looks out over the bay. "I think I'm ready to call it a night." Stefani shakes her head, turns, and starts walking back toward the restaurant.

Gavin takes a deep breath and blurts out, "I didn't want to have to wonder 'what if' again!"

Stefani stops and turns. "What if? What are you talking about?"

Gavin lets his arms flop down to his sides. "This is why I wanted to keep the car and money anonymous."

"Gavin, you're talking in circles."

Gavin turns and faces the bay again. He firmly grasps the top rail with his hands and says quietly, "Before you say anything, please let me finish."

"Okay."

Gavin inhales deeply and then closes his eyes as he exhales. "Over twenty ears ago I was working for a guy while I was in college and shortly after I graduated. One day he comes up to me and asks me if I'd be interested in helping him coach a girls' softball team. At the time I was playing ball three nights a week and traveling all over the place to play on weekends. I felt I didn't have time for this. He kept after me, and the only reason I agreed was because he was my boss. So about a week later he walks up to me and tells me we will be having our first team meeting at the sponsor's house. The meeting was scheduled for Thursday night, ironically the one night I didn't have a game ... so I go."

Gavin reaches up and scratches his head.

"I walk into the family room, and it's full of girls. I glanced around, and then suddenly, as if someone hit me in the face, I saw the most beautiful girl I'd ever seen. She had long, beautiful blonde hair, and these eyes—oh my God, those eyes, they were incredible. I can't tell you a thing that went on at that meeting. All I remember was this girl who had swept me off my feet. Funny thing ... I had no idea who she was. I had dated plenty of girls in high school and college. There were some I was more attracted to than others, but I had never had any girl, before or since, affect me like the one at that meeting did. I knew right then I had to meet her. Well, after doing some checking, I found out she was going to be a senior in high school that fall, and I had just graduated from college, so I knew that would never fly. Plus, I found out her parents had a high standard of ethics and integrity, and I didn't want to start off on a bad foot with them, so I decided I would wait until the following summer and ask her out when she was eighteen. I still felt the six-year difference was a lot, but I couldn't help it. She was the most amazing girl I had ever been around. As the season went, on I learned more about her ... her voice, her walk, her smile, her laugh, how committed she was to her academics, what a great athlete she was ... she was perfect. By the end of the summer she had stolen my heart completely. I started dating Belinda, figuring I'd just play the field until the following summer, and then I'd get up the nerve and ask her out. I patiently waited and then ... I learned late that winter she intended on going to the University of North Carolina."

Gavin glances down at his feet still feeling the pain from the devastating news.

"That was quite a blow, but I thought maybe we could still date and see how it went. I know most people think love at first sight is some kind of pseudo-poetic delusion that doesn't exist, but I'm telling you it's real. Trust me ... I speak from experience. Well ... when she left for college, she left St. Michaels behind. It was then I realized this area would never allow her to become everything she wanted to be. I knew I'd never get the chance to see where things may have gone between us. Funny thing is ... I wasn't even sure she would have agreed to go out with me in the first place. I was honestly heartbroken. I had never felt that way before and didn't know what to do ... so I cashed out. I don't want to say I gave up ... but something inside of me seemed to die. I married Belinda and just accepted life for what it was. I became totally reactive to the events in my life and was a person without any direction. As much as it hurt ... I accepted the reality I was going to live my life without knowing what possibly might have been, and with the certainty that the girl who I knew was my soul mate ... was gone forever."

Gavin sighs as he looks out over the bay. "Over the years the pain of the perfect girl being gone wore off, and I just moved on. I was fine right up until one particular day at Panera, and all these feelings came rushing back. I promised myself I'd not get openly involved, but ... I couldn't imagine what would make a man who has the most perfect gift in his life as his wife pursue another woman. So ... I guess you can call it selfishness, but I wanted to be there for her and take care of her like I always imagined I would have."

Gavin turns, looks at Stefani, and softly shrugs his shoulders. "I'm sorry. I know it all sounds ridiculous, and if anyone heard me tell this story they'd think I'd lost my mind, but ... it's the truth."

Stefani walks forward and rests her forehead softly against his chest. He hesitantly reaches up and gently rubs her upper arms. "I didn't mean to upset you."

She lifts her head. "You have nothing to be sorry about." She lightly touches his cheek with her hand. "That was the most beautiful thing anyone has ever said to me."

Gavin gives her a bittersweet smile. "Just wish I had said something to you before you went away to college." He looks deeply into her eyes and murmurs, "These are the same eyes that grabbed a hold of me so many years ago."

They continue to stare into each other's eyes for a brief moment. Then Gavin lowers his head and looks at his watch. "I better get you home. I don't want your parents to worry."

Stefani sighs and nods. "Okay."

The ride home seems to take so little time. After they pull into the driveway, Gavin turns off the car and sits looking forward through the windshield. "Thank you, Stefani."

"For what?"

"For listening to my story."

"Gavin, I should be thanking you and apologizing to you."

He turns and looks at her. "You already thanked me by being with me tonight. This was the best night I can remember."

Stefani smiles as she gazes into his eyes. "I better go."

"Can I walk you to the door?"

"Sure."

The two walk slowly up the steps and to the front door. She reaches out and grabs his hand. "Thank you for the most remarkable evening."

"Trust me … the pleasure is all mine."

Stefani looks down at the floor and then up again. "Gavin, do you think maybe we could do this again before I head back to Charlotte?"

"I'd really like that."

She reaches into her handbag and pulls out a pen and two pieces of paper. "Tell you what … you give me your cell phone number, and I'll ask you out. This way you can see how easy it would have been years ago."

Both laugh as Gavin writes down his number and hands it to her. She then writes her number on the second piece of paper and places it in his hand. "Here ... just in case you're interested."

Gavin grins as Stefani winks. He nods. "I'll see you soon?"

Stefani quickly leaps up and kisses him on the cheek. "You can count on it."

Chapter 14

The next morning Stefani sleeps in and doesn't go for her morning run. As she lies in bed, she stares at the ceiling thinking about the night before. She repeats Gavin's story over and over in her head, each time falling more and more in love with it. She reaches over and picks up the small piece of paper with his cell phone number written on it and smiles as she runs her finger over the number. She slowly sits up and glances out the window. Then she walks over and places the paper in her handbag, puts on a robe, and goes downstairs. Joanna is in the kitchen cleaning up the breakfast dishes.

Stefani looks up at the clock. It's eight-thirty! *When was the last time I slept this late?*

"Mom, where are Dad and the boys?"

"They ran into town to get gas for the lawnmower and Lord knows what else."

Stefani sits down and takes a deep breath. Joanna walks over and sits in front of her. "Did everything go okay last evening?"

Stefani looks at her mother and shakes her head back and forth. "Mom ... I can honestly say I about the most confused human being on the face of the earth."

"Why would you say that?"

"Gavin."

Joanna leans back and puckers her lips. "Oh boy."

"No, Mom ... he's ..."

Stefani pauses and grabs the top of her head with both hands. "Mom, how am I supposed to feel?"

"Honey, I'm not sure I understand. How are you supposed to feel about what?"

Stefani looks at her mother and then lets her head fall backward. "I felt like a seventeen-year-old again last night on my first date. Nervous but exhilarated. Mom, we just sat and talked. That's all. It's just the things he said that made me think about everything. He wasn't smooth-talking ... he was sincere and honest. It made me think about where my life is and where it should be."

Joanna covers Stefani's hand with her other hand. "Sweetheart, you're vulnerable right now. Anything said to you that is kind will make you think."

Stefani shakes her head back and forth. "No, Mom, he wasn't trying to take advantage of me or anything remotely close. We just talked, and it seemed so right. It was like the two of us had known each other for years and were so comfortable with each other."

Joanna interrupts her. "Stefani, you're in a weak position. It's natural for you to want to hear nice things."

"No, Mom, it wasn't like that at all."

Still looking a bit skeptical, Joanna says, "I'm glad."

Stefani pulls back and shakes her head. "So how did last night go? Did the boys behave?"

Joanna looks her in the eyes. "David called here last night. He said he tried you on your cell but you didn't answer." Stefani quickly tenses up. "What did he say?"

"Well, he wants to see the boys and wants to talk to you."

Stefani stands and walks over to the sink. "He is the last person I want to talk to. He didn't try to call me last night. I had my phone with me the whole time in case you or the boys needed me. He's just trying to play headgames with all of us. I'm sure he thinks, if we see him as bold enough to call here, we will be intimidated. The thought of talking to him makes me sick."

"Honey, I know, but what about the boys?"

"Mom, he destroyed all our lives. He not only betrayed me but the boys as well."

"I know he did, but it sounds like he's talked to a lawyer."

"Oh, I'm sure he has."

"Stefani, I don't know much about the law, but you're going to have to deal with this sooner or later."

Stefani walks over to the back door and leans her forehead against the screen. She can feel the soft breeze gently caress her face when she closes her eyes. "I know."

Joanna walks over to her and hugs her from behind. "Sooner may be better than later."

Stefani turns and nods. She returns upstairs to her bedroom and sits on the bed. She picks up her cell phone and pulls up David's number. She hesitates and then hits the send button. *Okay, asshole, let's see what you have to say.*

The phone rings twice, and then David answers, "Hey, Stef."

"I understand you called last night."

"Yes."

"What do you need?"

"Stef, I don't want to make this any harder than it already is."

"Really … that's mighty nice of you, David."

David's voice cools, his irritation clear as he says tersely, "Fine. I want to see the boys, and I want to see them soon."

"David, I don't think you're in any position to start dictating things."

"Quite the contrary, I have spoken to an attorney. You have three days to bring the boys back to Charlotte. Even though you haven't kidnapped them, we are still married, and I have the right to see them. Not to mention they both have camp starting soon."

"So I'm supposed to jump when you say jump? Well, let's see, David, since you've frozen any access to money I had … how do I hire an attorney?"

"Stefani … I'm sorry, but that's not my problem."

Stefani gets up and paces. "David, you are truly a piece of shit."

"Stef, I'll see you in a few days."

He hangs up, and she throws her phone down on the bed and slowly slides down the wall, crying as she reaches the floor. Quickly she gathers herself and begins running everything through her head. *How can this be happening?*

She sees her handbag sitting on the table next to her. She picks it up, pulls out the small piece of paper, and runs her finger over the phone number. She leans forward, grabs her cell phone off the bed, enters the number, and saves it as "Gavin."

She then creates a new text message to Gavin. "Good morning. Hope you have a great day."

She pauses for a moment, putting her thumb over the delete button. Slowly she slides her thumb over the send button, takes a deep breath, and presses down. She flops her hands down beside her, letting the phone tumble out of her hand. She pulls her knees up to her chest, crosses her arms on them, and buries her face in her forearms. She sits motionless while her conversation with David runs through her head. Suddenly her phone vibrates. She looks over, and the phone moves slightly toward her as it vibrates again. She picks it up. The display shows "One new message from Gavin."

Stefani hesitates and then takes a deep breath. She opens the text, which reads, "It started off great, but I received a text message, and now I don't see how my day can get any better. I hope you have a great day as well."

Stefani smiles and puts the phone on the floor. *Stefani, what are you doing?*

Moments later she hears the boys and her dad walking through the house. Stefani quickly gets up and jumps into the shower. As the warm water flows through her hair and down her back, she finds her thoughts flitting back and forth between David and Gavin. The more she thinks, the more she wants to see Gavin again—and soon. She turns off the shower and dries herself. After wrapping her hair in a towel, she stands and stares at the mirror. *Okay, how do you contact Gavin and tell him you want to see him?*

She dresses and goes downstairs. The boys are sitting at the table with their grandfather, each with a bowl of ice cream. Stefani leans against the door frame and laughs. "Hmmm… eating healthy, are we?"

Jack looks up and grins. "This is a mid-morning power booster."

The boys look up at Stefani, and Blane quickly adds, "Yeah, Mom, it's for power."

"Oh, well, I'm glad to see you'll have all the power you need."

Joanna walks over and rubs Stefani's back. "Honey, would you like to have something to eat?"

"No, I think I'm going to run into town for a moment." She looks down at the boys eating their ice cream. "Hey, guys, what do you say we go see a movie tonight?"

Both boys perk up. "Yeah!"

Stefani laughs. "Dad, is it okay if I leave these guys with you for a few hours?"

Her father looks up with a drip of ice cream on his chin. He tilts his head back and mumbles, "Honey, we're fine."

"Okay, I'll be back in a few."

Stefani heads into downtown St. Michaels and parks along the curb. She gets out and window shops, heading in no particular direction and with no sense of urgency. As she walks, she sees an older couple walking hand-in-hand in front of her. Suddenly she feels an emptiness inside her. With the exception of Blane and Jared, she can't remember the last time anyone has held her hand, and of course that is something totally different. She turns and enters a small art gallery. Looking around, she notices a picture of the bay taken from the pier located at the end of her parents' lane. As she stares at it, an older lady who works at the gallery walks over. "Hello. May I help you?"

Startled, Stefani turns quickly. "Hello ... I was just admiring this picture. Do you know when it was taken?"

"I'm not exactly sure. My guess would be in the late eighties."

The clerk walks over and stands next to her to look at the picture. The clerk sighs and says, "It's funny, isn't it?"

Stefani turns her head toward the clerk. "What's that?"

"How one can live here and never realize how beautiful and rare things around here are. Sometimes the most precious things are right in front of you, and somehow it just gets missed."

Stefani nods and replies in a very soft voice, "I know exactly what you mean."

The clerk touches Stefani's arm softly. "Honey, you look around as much as you like."

Stefani stops her. "How much is this piece?"

"Two hundred dollars."

Without a second thought Stefani blurts out, "I'll take it."

The clerk smiles and wraps it up for her. Stefani walks out and gently lays the picture in the back of the car. She climbs into the driver's seat and pulls out her cell phone. *I'm losing it!*

Stefani laughs as she creates a new text to Gavin. "Hi. Hope I'm not bothering you, but I have a question."

She sits impatiently waiting. Within seconds her phone vibrates.

"Hi. Never a bother. I have an answer."

She laughs. "What's your schedule look like around 5?"

"Nothing pending. What do you have in mind?"

"Meet me at the high school at 5."

"The high school?"

"Yes, around back."

"Okay. Is everything alright?"

"Yes, everything is fine."

"Okay I'll see you at 5."

Stefani smiles and nods her head quickly. She races home, totes the picture upstairs, and leans it against the wall. Then she takes a deep breath and walks over to an old hope chest located against the far wall of her room. She removes the pillows on top and opens it. Neatly organized, the chest is full of things from her childhood. She briefly looks some things over and sets them aside. She reaches down and pulls out a ball glove. "Ah! There you are."

She slips the glove onto her hand. The leather has dried, but it stills feels perfect on her hand. She puts the other items back neatly and closes the chest. She takes the glove and slips it into a large shoulder bag hanging on the closet door handle. She changes into a pair of shorts, T-shirt, and running shoes and then throws the bag over her shoulder. She walks downstairs and into the laundry room. On a shelf is another glove and an old softball. She grabs both and drops them in her bag. As she leaves the laundry room, she sees her mother out at the clothesline. Her father and the boys are out on the boat. She writes a note and leaves it on the table.

I'll be home around six. Boys, be ready to go to the movies.

Stefani drives to the school and parks next to the softball field. She walks out, shuffles around third base, and then makes her way through the gate and sits on the bleachers. Moments later Gavin's Bentley meanders through the lot and parks next to Stefani's car. He gets out, wearing a suit, looks around, and waves when he sees her sitting on the bleachers. He takes off his jacket, places it in the backseat, and then walks over. "Good afternoon, Mrs. Tanner."

"Hello, Mr. Thorne."

Gavin looks around at the infield and then grins at Stefani. "Doing a bit of reminiscing?"

Stefani returns the smile. "Mayyyyybe. Want to help?"

"Help?"

Stefani reaches into the bag, pulls out a glove, and hands it to Gavin. "You still know how to work one of these?"

He laughs. "I think I can hold my own."

"Good!"

Stefani grabs the ball and heads for the field. "Come on."

The two walk out onto the field. Gavin stops after a few steps. "Wait."

Stefani turns. "For?"

Gavin removes his tie, folds it up, and then stuffs it into his back pocket. "Just loosening up."

Stefani walks toward third as Gavin makes his way toward the plate. Stefani grins. "Ready?"

"I hope so."

Stefani whirls and zips a throw at Gavin. He gracefully catches it chest high. He pauses, holding the glove in the same spot for a moment. "Wow, that felt good."

He pulls the ball from the glove and throws it back. Stefani smoothly picks it out of the air, looks at him, and smiles. "See, all you had to do was use the basics back then."

"The basics?"

"Yes. Had you asked me to play catch about twenty years ago, there's no way I could have refused."

Gavin laughs. "That easy, huh?"

"Mayyyyybe."

They continue to throw for a few minutes, saying only a few words. Finally Gavin catches one and instead of tossing the ball back looks down at the ground.

Stefani drops her hands to her side. "What's wrong?"

Gavin looks up with a half-hearted smile. "I wish I would have done this years ago."

Stefani pulls her glove off of her hand. She walks toward the bleachers again and sits.

Gavin follows and sits beside her. "Funny how quickly times flies."

She nods. "Yes, it is."

Gavin hands Stefani the glove and rests his forearms on his knees. He bows his head and shakes it back and forth.

Stefani sees a hint of sadness on his face. "Is everything okay?"

Gavin lifts his head and stares through the fence at third base. "I remember watching you play third. You moved so smoothly and quickly. Everything you did was with such intensity. Everything about you was perfect. You were the most amazing and beautiful girl on the field, and I would just stand there in amazement."

Stefani glances out of the corner of her eye and can see Gavin is too embarrassed to look at her. She reaches down, puts her glove in the bag, and then tries to relieve Gavin's feeling of awkwardness. "So you're saying I've lost my flair?"

Gavin looks over at her and then quickly down again. "No ... you've gotten even better."

He looks her in the eyes, and they stare at each other for a few seconds.

Stefani scans his eyes and can feel herself leaning toward him. Suddenly she stops and widens her eyes, and then she immediately looks down and away. The two sit quietly again, but Stefani feels she's crossed a line and is now very uneasy.

As though attuned to her thoughts, he takes a deep breath and rubs his hands together, and asks in a casual tone, "Soooo ... besides playing catch ... what else does Stefani Tanner enjoy doing?"

Stefani shrugs her shoulder and smiles. "I don't know ... lots of things."

"Aw, come on ... there has to be one thing you really enjoy."

Stefani puts her hands on the bleacher and rocks back, grinning as she taps her toes on the board below her. "Well, there is one thing, but it really sounds dumb."

"What is it?"

Stefani scrunches her face and admits, "I like to shop in old antique and trinket stores."

"Why would you think that's dumb?"

"I don't know ... shuffling through junk isn't the most popular thing in the world."

Gavin shrugs his shoulders. "Sounds kinda fun, if you ask me."

Stefani grins and then bows her head. "Actually, there's a reason why I like to explore these shops."

"And why is that?"

Continuing to look down, she shakes her head and snickers. "I'm too embarrassed to tell you."

"Why?"

"Because it's crazy, and basically it's a pipe dream."

Gavin leans over and bumps Stefani's shoulder with his. "I'd like to hear it."

Stefani looks at him. "Okay ... but if you laugh at me, I'm going to be very mad at you."

"I promise."

"I do it for my mom and grandmother."

"Why is that crazy?"

"Because what I'm hoping to find will never be found in an antique store or flea market."

"What are you trying to find?"

She leans forward and wraps her arms around her legs. "I can't believe I'm telling you this."

"Come on, now ... you can't leave me hanging."

"Okay, let me tell you the whole story. Then maybe it won't sound so ridiculous."

"Deal."

"My grandfather fought overseas in World War I. One day he and a Russian soldier got caught in a bad situation, and the Russian soldier got shot. My grandfather pulled him into a ditch and bandaged him up. Then when it got dark my grandfather carried him, on his shoulder, all night long until they got to a place where the Russian soldier could get medical treatment. Basically, my grandfather saved his life. Sometime later, after the soldier recovered, he went looking for my grandfather. When he found my grandfather he gave him a box. As it turns out, the soldier was related to a guy named Peter Carl Fabergé."

Gavin's eyes widen. "Peter Carl Fabergé, as in …"

"Yep, that one … my grandfather opened the box, and in it was a brooch. The brooch was called 'Eternity.' Apparently my grandfather had told the Russian soldier about how he and my and grandmother were going to get married when he returned home, and he wanted my grandfather to give it to her as a wedding present. He also wanted my grandfather to know that he was eternally grateful to him for saving his life."

"Wow! That's quite a story."

"There's more."

"Oh … I'm sorry."

Stefani laughs and swats Gavin on the knee. "Anyway, my grandfather gave my grandmother the brooch, and it quickly became her most prized possession. I only saw it once when I was very young. It had a large, aquamarine gemstone in the middle surrounded by diamonds. There were four arrows that surrounded the center setting, representing eternity … it was beautiful."

"So your mom has it now?"

Stefani shakes her head and puckers her lips. "No … one day while my grandparents were grocery shopping someone broke into their house and took it … They never saw it again."

Gavin's chin drops, and he exclaims, "That's terrible!"

Stefani nods. "I don't remember, but my mom claims my grandmother cried for months. It tore my mother to pieces having to watch my grandmother hurt so much. I think what hurt my grandmother the most was the fact that my grandfather got it while in the war and what it stood for … Mom said she never totally got over the guilt."

"It wasn't her fault someone broke into the house."

"I know … but their whole world was each other … it meant everything to her. It was the fact that it was a gift from my grandfather. It doesn't seem significant now, but my grandfather was considerably older than my grandmother. Even though everyone told him that didn't matter, it was so important to him that she get a little older before he proposed to her. She meant everything to him, and he was her only true love. He wanted everything perfect when it came to her, and she loved him with all her heart."

Gavin shakes his head as he rests his elbows on his knees. "What about their homeowner's policy?"

"I don't think they got a dime … regardless, I don't think the money would have made my grandmother feel any better."

"That's a sad story. Did you ever look into what it would cost to replace it?"

Stefani laughs. "Yes, I did. There were a number of them made, and occasionally they come up for auction. But … you can buy a very nice Italian sports car for what they sell for."

"Ouch!" Gavin scratches his head. "There is certainly something to be said about the name Fabergé and jewelry ... CHA-CHING!"

"Exactly ... so that's why I like to roam through the antique shops. There's a little part of me that hopes one day I'll stumble across an Eternity brooch and get it for a song."

"Would you keep it or give it to your mom?"

"Oh, I'd give it to Mom ... then somewhere down the road I'd have it again. I know it wouldn't be the original, but somehow I think it would help fill the void."

Gavin looks at her. Stefani grins and bumps him with her shoulder. "See? I told you it was a crazy story."

"Stefani, I'd say it is one of the most wonderful stories I've ever heard. It certainly shows how much you cared for your grandmother and love your mom. If more people felt like you do ... well, let's just say it's pretty special."

"You want to know something?"

"What?"

"You're the only person I've ever told that to."

He looks at her and softly smiles. "Thank you for trusting me with that."

Stefani smiles back at him, and he quickly clears his throat and changes the subject. "So ... how are you making out?"

Stefani shrugs. "Pretty good." She takes a deep breath and then sighs. "Well, actually, … I guess I'll find out in the next few days."

"What do you mean?"

"I have to return to Charlotte in a few days to see my husband and discuss our present situation. I also have to take my sons so they can see him and go to camp. The thought of them not being with me tears me apart."

"Wow, that sounds pretty nerve-racking."

Stefani turns, grateful for his understanding. "It sure is."

"How are you getting down there?"

She leans over and bumps his shoulder with hers. "I thought about taking a nice new Range Rover."

Gavin laughs and softly shoulder-bumps her back. "I think we can do better."

"We?"

"Well … I meant we can arrange a better way to get you to Charlotte."

Stefani looks at him with a curious squint. "Oh, really?"

He looks down and laughs. "I think so. When are you leaving?"

"The day after tomorrow."

Gavin pauses and then looks at her. "Do you plan on coming back?"

Stefani can sense concern in his voice. "Yes … in a few days."

Gavin smiles in obvious relief. "That's good."

Both sit quietly for a moment. She turns and bumps her shoulder against Gavin's again. "I better go. I promised my sons a night at the movies."

He looks over and nods. "That sounds like a good idea."

The two walk to the parking lot. Stefani opens the door on her car while Gavin leans over the driver's side of his car and rests his forearms on the roof. "Stefani, you remember how to get to the Easton Airport, right?"

"Yes."

"Okay … be at hanger 'F' at eight in the morning the day after tomorrow."

"Hanger 'F'? Why?"

"Trust me."

Stefani squints at Gavin as he slips into his car. She stands motionless as he starts the car.

He rolls down the passenger side window. "Remember, eight."

She presses her tongue against her upper lip and nods. "Okay, eight."

Gavin winks and drives off. Stefani climbs into her car and sits, and then she shakes her head and laughs. *Gavin, now what?*

Chapter 15

Stefani returns to her parents' house and walks into the kitchen. Joanna is sitting at the table working the crossword puzzle in the local newspaper. Stefani quietly slips in the chair next to her and begins to run her index finger around the pattern on the tablecloth.

Joanna neatly folds the paper and takes her glasses off. "Okay ... what's up?"

Stefani shakes her head and sighs. "Is it that obvious?"

Joanna laughs. "Honey, I watched you deal with a number of issues while growing up. I think I know when something is on your mind."

Stefani shrugs her shoulders and then looks at her mother. "Why does everything have to be so hard?"

"Sweetheart, life has a way of throwing things at you, and many will never make sense no matter how long you analyze them."

"I know ... but I have to take the boys back to Charlotte the day after tomorrow. They have camp, and David wants to see them. Mom … you, Dad, and the boys have been what's held me together lately. I don't know if I can handle not having Blane and Jared around."

"Are you going to stay in Charlotte after you drop the boys off with David?"

Stefani flops back into the chair and exhales hard. "I don't think so." She crosses her arms and slowly shakes her head. "I thought about it, and I'm going to ask Tonya if I can stay with her for a few days, but I'd like to come back here. I can think things through more clearly here … where I want to head with my career, what I really want to do with the situation with David, and most importantly how my decisions will affect the boys."

Joanna nods in agreement. "I think that's a good idea. You know David will take care of the boys, and in no time they'll be in camp for two weeks. They'll be safe, so that will allow you to focus on what Stefani needs to do."

Stefani sighs heavily. "Hopefully Stefani makes the right decisions."

"I'm sure she will."

Stefani stands and turns for the front porch. "I'm going to give Tonya a call. Hopefully she won't mind a roommate for a few days."

"I'm sure she'll be excited to have you."

Stefani saunters onto the porch and sits on the swing. She pulls out her cell phone and dials Tonya's number.

Tonya answers immediately. "Stefani! Where the hell have you been?"

"I'm at my parents' house. The boys and I came up."

"That's good to hear. How are your mom and dad?"

"They're great."

Stefani pulls her legs up to her chest and tilts toward the arm of the swing. "Tonya ... I need to ask you a favor."

"Okay."

"Would it be alright if I stayed with you for a few days?"

"Sure, but—"

"Tonya, I have a lot to tell you. Getting fired wasn't the only thing that went wrong the last time you saw me. Things aren't good between David and me right now. That's why I need a place to stay while I get the boys settled in and ready for camp."

"Stef, if you come back here and stay anywhere but with me, I'll kick your tiny ass."

"It will only be for a couple days."

"I don't care if it's for a few months. I have the room. The one thing I got from my divorce was the house. It's not the Taj Mahal, but one thing this old house has is plenty of space."

"You're sure?"

"Jesus, Stef, do I need to draw you a picture? Yes ... I have plenty of room and would love to have you here. When will you be here?"

"The day after tomorrow."

"Good! Then I'll see you the day after tomorrow."

Stefani lays her head back and laughs. "Tonya, it's great to hear your voice ... I really appreciate this."

"I can't wait."

"Thanks for letting me stay."

"Stef, just get down here."

"Okay ... I'll talk to you in a few."

Stefani ends the call and then stares out across the open field on the other side of the road. Somehow the emptiness and mystery of the field seems to make sense to her. She gets up and walks into the house, climbs the stairs, and enters the boys' room. She places their suitcase on their bed and folds their clothes. With each garment she neatly tucks into the case she finds it harder to hold back her tears. *God, what am I going to do? What have I done to deserve this? Please help me.*

She finishes the packing and leaves a few outfits out for the next two mornings. Since being back in St. Michaels, the boys have found it very pleasing to sleep in their underwear, a habit David practiced and one the boys believe is something all grown-up men do. Stefani always preferred they sleep in pajamas—maybe to hold onto her "little boys" as long as possible—but she knows those days are quickly slipping away.

After finishing, she heads back downstairs and discusses what the next few days hold in store for everyone. Although the boys aren't excited about leaving St. Michaels, the anticipation of going to camp has been building for weeks. Stefani promises they will return to St. Michaels after camp is over, which seems to satisfy the boys. This plan, however, does little to comfort her.

The next day flies by as everyone prepares for the journey back to Charlotte. Long after the sun sets, Stefani tucks the boys in and then heads for her bed. As she lies still, staring into the darkness, she reaches over and picks up her cell phone. She slowly types a text message. "Gavin, I'm looking forward to seeing you tomorrow morning but I'm not sure I'll be the best conversationalist."

She rests her phone on the end table and turns to face the wall. Suddenly her phone vibrates.

"Stefani, I won't be there in the morning. You just have a safe trip and let me know when you get there."

Stefani sits up in bed and quickly returns a message. "The boys and I have a long drive ahead of us in the morning. If you're not going to be there, is it necessary for us to show up?"

"Stefani, just be there. Promise me."

Stefani shakes her head and sighs. "Okay, but please tell me you haven't bought us tickets on a charter flight. You've already done more than enough."

"Stefani, I haven't purchased any tickets for you. Just be there."

"Okay, we'll be there."

The next morning everyone is up and out the door early. Joanna and Jack hug Stefani and then each boy. The three climb into the car and buckle up, and Stefani starts the car and drops it into reverse. Jack puts his arm around Joanna as they back away from the car.

Joanna smiles and says, "Call us when you get there."

Stefani, fighting back tears, says, "I will. I promise."

Jack leans down and winks at the boys. "You guys be good, and we'll see you in a few weeks."

Blane and Jared wave as Stefani backs out of the driveway and puts the car in drive. Everyone exchanges one last wave as she pulls away. Stefani slips on a pair of sunglasses and quickly wipes away a hint of a tear. Once again she feels a sense of emptiness as she heads back to the place that has turned her life upside down. Only the thought of a stop at the Easton Airport keeps her from losing control and being consumed by her emotions.

When she turns onto the road heading toward Easton Airport, Blane asks, "Mom, where are we going?"

"We need to find Hanger "F."

The two boys look around, and then Jared yells out, "There it is!"

He points to a large metal building located away from the others. Stefani stops the car and looks. "Yep, that's it."

She drives the car toward the building and parks in one of the five spaces available in front of what looks like an office attached to a large warehouse. She turns the car off, and the three climb out. They walk through the door and enter the office, where they are greeted by a tall man dressed in a formal uniform.

"Mrs. Tanner?"

"Yes."

"I'm Roger Wells. I'll be with you throughout the day." He looks down at the boys. "And you guys must be the Tanner men."

The two boys smile and nod.

"Mrs. Tanner, we'll be ready in a few."

He turns and takes a few steps toward a small, separate office. "Danny, can you get the Tanners' bags and load them?"

"Yes, sir."

Danny walks over to Stefani. "Ma'am, may I have your keys to your car?"

Bemused, Stefani hands her keys over and then stops Roger. "Um ... what exactly is going on?"

Roger pauses and then smiles. "We'll be departing for Charlotte in a few minutes."

Stefani raises her eyebrows. "In what?"

"Mr. Thorne's plane."

"His plane?"

"Yes ... if you'd like, you can board now and get comfortable."

Stefani stands with her mouth open and then looks down at the boys. "Ooookay."

They follow Roger through a large door leading into the hanger area. Sitting in the center of the hanger is a beautiful Gulfstream G550. Stefani's mouth drops again. "This is his plane?"

Roger quickly responds. "Yes, one of the finest jets ever made."

Stefani turns to Roger. "And you're his pilot?"

"Yes. You won't find a better man to fly for."

A young woman sticks her head out the door of the jet. "Captain Wells, we're all set up here."

"Great, Megan. We're good down here."

Roger turns and faces the Tanners. "Shall we board?"

Stefani takes each boy by the hand, and they carefully climb the steps into the plane. As they enter, Megan greets them. "Welcome aboard, Mrs. Tanner. I'm Megan Bostick, and I will be taking care of you during the flight. If you have any questions or need anything, just ask."

Stefani stands in amazement looking over the interior of the stunning corporate jet. "Thank you."

Megan turns to the boys. "Guys, once we get you seated and belted in, we have Xbox 360 and PlayStation 4 hooked up to the monitors."

Blane blurts out, "Alright!"

Megan turns to Stefani. "Ma'am, if you'll pick a seat, we'll get you secured and be on our way."

"I can sit anywhere?"

"Yes."

Stefani looks around and sees a huge captain's chair next to a window. "I think I'll take that one."

Stefani sits down, and Megan helps her buckle up. Stefani softly rubs the leather arms of the chair and asks, "Does Mr. Thorne fly often?"

"Oh … about once a month. He and a few of his colleagues fly to the west coast for meetings."

The plane is pulled from the hanger. Once outside, the sound of the engines can be heard as Roger prepares for departure. They taxi out, and then the jet streaks down the runway and becomes airborne. Stefani is amazed how quiet the plane is. She has flown many times on commercial planes, but none compare to this.

Roger's voice comes through the intercom. "Mrs. Tanner, we have an estimated arrival time at Charlotte of nine thirty. The skies are clear, and this should be a pleasant flight. Just sit back and relax, and we'll be on the ground in no time. If you need anything just let Megan know."

Stefani allows herself to sink into the comfortable seat. She glances out the window as the ground quickly increases in distance. Even though she knows she's headed for an unpredictable meeting with David, she can't get her mind off Gavin. She looks over and sees the boys playing video games. She turns her head back, looks out the window at the beautiful clear blue sky then closes her eyes again, and releases a relaxed smile. *Gavin Thorne, what are you doing to me?*

Chapter 16

After landing, Roger walks from the cockpit. "Did you enjoy the flight?"

Stefani stands and sighs. "Yes, very much. It was the smoothest flight I've ever taken."

"Great! Honestly, this plane could fly itself ... it's a pleasure to pilot."

After everyone exits the plane, Roger escorts Stefani and the boys through a private door into the terminal. As they walk through the door, Stefani sees a man, dressed in a black suit, holding a sign that displays her name. Stefani walks over and says, "I'm Stefani Tanner."

The man smiles. "Hello, ma'am. If you will tell me where you need to go, I will drive you."

"Drive me?"

"Yes. I have been instructed to take you and your sons anywhere you need to go in our corporate limousine."

Gavin.

"Okay … can you take us to my friend's house? She lives at 1305 Red Oak Circle."

"It will be my pleasure."

In minutes their luggage is loaded and they are headed to Tonya's house. Stefani pulls out her cell phone and creates a text message. "Gavin, this is so nice of you, but you have to stop. I'll never be able to repay you."

She hits send and then lays her head back and closes her eyes. She can feel the fatigue setting in, but strangely she feels relaxed. Suddenly her phone vibrates.

"Stefani, first of all you have nothing to repay, and you owe me nothing. Just you and the boys be safe, and I look forward to seeing you soon."

Stefani drops her phone into her bag and runs her fingers through her hair. *Gavin, Gavin, Gavin.*

Within thirty minutes the limousine pulls up in front of Tonya's house. Tonya races out to meet Stefani and the boys at the curb. She gives Stefani an enthusiastic hug and says, "God, girl, it's so good to see you."

"I missed you, Tonya." Stefani pulls back, squints, and tilts her head. "Hey, did you take off work to be here to meet us?"

Tonya begins laughing hysterically but gathers herself and looks at the boys. "Hey, guys, why don't you grab your bags and carry them into the house."

The boys dart inside, leaving Stefani, Tonya, and the driver at the curb. Stefani reaches into her wallet and pulls out a twenty. She offers it to the driver, but he quickly refuses. "Ma'am, everything is taken care of. The last thing I was instructed to do was hand you this envelope. You have a good day."

As the driver climbs back into the limousine and drives off, Tonya turns and looks at Stefani. "A friggin' limo? Are you serious?"

Stefani laughs. "It's a long story."

The two walk toward the house. "Tonya ... how are you able to get away from work?"

When Tonya again laughs, Stefani shakes her head. "What am I missing here?"

"Shit, girl ... about twenty minutes after they asked you to leave, they cleaned house, and I was one of the bodies they threw out on the street."

"Tonya, I'm so sorry."

"Oh, to hell with those pricks. I wouldn't want to work for those assholes anyway. Now tell me how the hell you managed to get a limousine to bring you to my house."

"Trust me, Tonya ... tonight after the boys are asleep we'll open a bottle of wine, and I'll tell you everything."

The two walk into Tonya's house. Stefani strolls over, sits down on the large sofa, and opens the envelope. Inside is a note and a business card from Lloyd, Hughes, and Webster, LLP. The note is handwritten.

Ms. Tanner,

> *Please contact me upon your arrival in Charlotte. We look forward to assisting you with your legal needs.*
>
> *Sincerely,*
> *Carlton Lloyd*

Stefani takes a deep breath and then gets up and approaches the boys. "Guys, I need to make an important phone call, so I need you to be quite for a little while."

Tonya walks toward her. "Stef, is everything okay?"

Stefani shakes her head. "Not really ... I need to make—"

"I heard. Go in my bedroom and close the door."

"Thanks."

She walks into the bedroom, closes the door, and dials the number on the card.

"Lloyd, Hughes and Webster, how may I assist you?"

"Hello. My name is Stefani Tanner, and I have a letter from Carlton Lloyd instructing me to call him."

The receptionist politely puts her on hold, and seconds later Carlton Lloyd is on the line. "Ms. Tanner, I'm Carlton Lloyd."

"Hello. How are you?"

"I'm well, thank you. Ms. Tanner, we need to meet as soon as possible to review your present situation and decide how you want to handle things."

"Okay, let me make sure my friend can watch my sons, but I should be there in an hour or so."

"That works perfectly. I'll send our driver over to pick you up."

"I'm at 1305—"

"Our driver knows where you are. He picked you up from the airport."

"Oh … okay. I'll be ready in an hour."

Stefani hangs up the phone and walks out into the living room. "Tonya, I hate to ask you for more, but is there any way you can keep an eye on the boys for a while?"

"Stef, you know that's no problem."

"Tonya, I owe you so much."

"Oh … later tonight, when you tell me what the hell is going on, is payback time."

"Deal."

Stefani calls the boys into the living room. "Guys, Miss Tonya is going to watch you for a few hours until I get back. Until then you guys better behave. Got it?"

Jared smiles. "Yes, Mom."

Stefani looks down at Blane, who has a look of concern on his face. "Honey, I'll be right back, okay?"

Blane nods. Stefani bends down and hugs them both. When she rises she looks at Tonya.

"Stef, we'll be fine." She reaches out and squeezes Stefani's hand. The weak smile Tonya gives conveys she has a pretty good idea what's going on.

Stefani nods. "Thanks."

In no time the limousine pulls up to Tonya's house. Stefani walks out, and the driver opens the door for her. "Hello again, ma'am."

"Hi."

The driver closes the door for Stefani and then climbs back into the driver's seat. Stefani scans the familiar sights as they travel closer to downtown Charlotte. The chauffer glances back through the rearview mirror and comments, "Ma'am, I know it's none of my business, but I'd hate to be battling you legally."

Stefani squints as she looks at his reflection in the rearview mirror. "Oh? Why is that?"

"Ma'am ... Lloyd, Hughes, and Webster is the most powerful law firm in Charlotte."

"Really?"

"Oh yeah."

Moments later the limo pulls up to a high-rise office building in downtown Charlotte. The driver gets out and opens Stefani's door. She climbs out and walks through the revolving door into an impressive lobby, where she is greeted by a receptionist. Stefani gives the young woman her name and says she has an appointment with Carlton Lloyd.

After making a brief phone call, the receptionist smiles and says, "Ms. Tanner, Mr. Lloyd will see you now. He is located on the fifth floor. The elevator is to your left."

"Thank you."

When Stefani arrives on the fifth floor, she is greeted by an older man dressed in a very nice suit. He extends his hand. "Mrs. Tanner?"

Stefani shakes his hand. "Yes."

"It's a pleasure to meet you. I'm Carlton Lloyd. If you will follow me to our conference room, we can get started."

"Okay."

Stefani follows him down a short hallway and into a conference room where two other well-dressed men are sitting at a large table. As Carlton escorts Stefani to a seat, the other men stand and approach her. They introduce themselves as Charles Hughes and Steven Webster.

Carlton pushes Stefani's chair in behind her as she sits. The three men sit down around the table and open up leather binders with notepads inside. Carlton slides on a pair of glasses. "Ms. Tanner, we have been briefed on your situation but need more detailed information."

Stefani looks at the three. "Are you referring to my dismissal from AMERI-GEN or my domestic situation?"

"Well, we can certainly look into your dismissal as well, but right now let's focus on your domestic dilemma."

Stefani sits up and takes a deep breath, clasps her hands, and rests them in her lap. "There's really not much to tell. After my dismissal I drove to my friend's house to talk to her about what happened that morning. When I got there, I noticed my husband's car parked in their garage. I entered the house and found my husband with my friend in the shower."

Charles Hughes speaks up. "So you entered the home without being invited?"

"Yes ... I have done that for years."

Steven Webster remarks, "That won't be a problem."

Carlton pulls off his glasses and clasps his hands together. "Ms. Tanner, as difficult as it is, we need to know what you saw ... exactly."

Stefani looks at the three men and then down at the table. Hughes stands up, picks up a box of tissues, and walks it over to Stefani. He rests his hand on her shoulder. She looks up at him and smiles. Taking a tissue, she sighs. "I saw my husband and my friend Mallory in the shower together."

"So it's safe to assume they were engaged in sexual intercourse."

Stefani begins to tear up and wipes her eyes with the tissue. "Yes … I could hear the slapping noise of their bodies hitting one another, and Mallory was moaning very loudly. I walked into the bathroom, and there they were."

Stefani flops back in her chair. "Then I tried to get a room at a local hotel that evening, but my husband had all the credit cards cancelled and withdrew all the money out of our accounts. I literally had no access to any money. Fortunately, when I was released from AMERI-GEN, I received a severance check. Otherwise I had nothing."

The three sit quietly writing notes. Carlton puts his pen down and leans back in his chair. "Ms. Tanner, we must decide how you want things to go."

"I don't understand."

"We can try to handle this as amicably as possible, or we can find every speck of dirt on your husband and drive him into the ground. It's entirely up to you. Obviously your husband tried to make things difficult for you, so my question is … how badly do you want to damage him?"

Stefani sits back and takes a deep breath. "I really never gave this much thought. I'm not totally sure my marriage is over."

Hughes taps his pen on the table. "Ms. Tanner, now is the time to act. All we need is for you to tell us what you want. You have the best team available, and we can be as passive or as aggressive as we need to be. We will only strike in the manner you instruct us to. If you want to try to work things out, we understand."

Stefani looks at the three men who are patiently waiting for an answer. "I can't create a situation with my sons that may in the future backfire on me. Even though he did what he did, I'd like things to go as agreeably as possible. But if David and his attorneys get nasty, then I want to tear into them and burn him."

Carlton looks at the other two men. "Gentlemen, I think we know all we need to know at this time. Ms. Tanner, I'll have our driver take you back to your friend's house."

"Thank you."

Carlton escorts Stefani down the hallway and to the elevator. Stefani takes a deep breath and looks up at the ceiling. Carlton appears to sense her nervousness. "Ms. Tanner, are you okay?"

Stefani looks at him. "Yes … well … no." She wipes her eye with a tissue. "This is all new to me, and everything is coming at me so quickly. I'm just afraid I'm going to make a wrong decision or do something that will come back to haunt me later. I'm just confused."

Once they are in the elevator, Carlton turns to her. "Trust me, you are not the first person to feel the way you do. We are fully aware of the fear and anxiety tied to a situation like this. You must have faith in me and my team. We will make sure you and your sons are protected and will only proceed with that solitary focus in mind. As things develop, I will be contacting you on a regular basis. I'm confident you will find things will go more smoothly than you expect."

The two reach the main entrance, and Stefani stops, smiles at Carlton, and extends her hand. "Thank you for you kindness, Mr. Lloyd." She exits and heads for the car, but then she turns back. "Mr. Lloyd, may I ask a question?"

"Certainly."

"How did you know I needed an attorney?"

He walks out to her and places his hand on her elbow. "Ms. Tanner, you are obviously very important to someone, someone who wants to make sure you and your sons are protected and not taken advantage of." Carlton winks and grins. "Trust me ... you are in good hands."

Stefani looks down. "Would this someone be from St. Michaels, Maryland?"

Carlton smiles. "He made it very clear to me and my colleagues you would call all the shots but to make sure you were represented and protected to the best of our ability. I can assure you, just as I did him, you and your sons will be represented, and you will be exactly where you want to be when this concludes.

Stefani looks up and nods. "Thank you."

"Ms. Tanner, we'll be in touch soon."

Stefani climbs into the limo, and the car pulls away.

Chapter 17

Stefani returns to Tonya's and makes her way through the front door. When she walks in Tonya is sitting on the couch watching TV. Stefani looks around. "Where are the boys?"

"About an hour after you left, I went in to check on them in the bedroom. They had the TV on and both were sound asleep on the bed."

Stefani walks into the room and sees the two curled up on the bed. She pulls the covers up over them and kisses each on top of the head. She quietly closes the door and returns to the living room.

Stefani smiles at Tonya. "How about a little wine?"

"Works for me."

Tonya pulls the wine from the refrigerator and grabs two glasses. She sets the glasses and wine on the coffee table. Stefani kicks off her shoes while Tonya pours each glass half full. Stefani reaches forward for a glass, leans back against the couch, and takes a sip. "Wow, that's good."

Tonya grasps the remote and turns off the TV. "Okay, girl, what's going on?"

"You don't waste any time, do you?"

Tonya laughs. "You know me."

Stefani cradles the wine glass with two hands and sighs. "Tonya … the day I was let go, I thought I'd hit rock bottom. I was afraid, mad, upset, and had no idea what to do. I didn't want to call David, so I drove to Mallory's house. I knew she'd be home, and Jason had left for a week-long business trip. I thought I could spill my guts to her and try to make some sense of everything before I went home. Well, when I got there I noticed David's car hidden in their garage. I went inside and found David and Mallory in the shower together going at it."

"Oh my God!"

"Yeah, not exactly what I expected."

"So what did you do?"

"Well, I managed to get to my parents' house in St. Michaels, and then things really got out of the ordinary."

"What do you mean?"

"One morning two guys show up at my parents' house. Once they left I was the owner of a brand new Range Rover and a huge amount of cash."

"How's that work?"

Stefani smiles and looks at Tonya. "Someone from my past, someone I hardly knew, overheard a conversation I was having with an old friend and sent me the car and money but did his best to remain anonymous."

"Wait … someone sends you a brand new car and gives you cash and doesn't want you to know who he is?"

"Nope."

"Stef, what the hell's wrong with this guy?"

Stefani looks at Tonya and grins. "Not a thing, Tonya … he's perfect."

Tonya takes a huge swallow of wine. "Wait. I'm missing something here. This is a guy from your past, someone you hardly know … he sends you stuff, wants to remain anonymous, and you want me to believe he's perfect?"

"Yep."

"How do you know he's perfect?"

"Well … the friend I was speaking to when our conversation was overheard is married to a state trooper. He has a friend who works at the Department of Motor Vehicles. He bent the rules a bit and printed off a list showing the entire history of the car. When I saw who purchased the car … I confronted him about the car and money."

Tonya is sitting with her mouth hanging wide open, totally consumed with Stefani's story. "Okay … what did he do? What did you do? Girl … I'd have been a bundle of nerves."

"We went to dinner … just as friends. I cornered him and insisted he explain himself. Once he did … it was perfect."

"Ohhhh no … you've got to give me more that simple-assed answer."

Stefani runs her finger around the rim of the wineglass. "Okay … he used to coach my softball team when I was seventeen. He was a hunk, but he was dating another girl, and I never really got to know him. As it turns out, he wanted to ask me out but knew the age difference wouldn't be well accepted by most, particularly by Mom and Dad."

"Well, so far he sounds like he has some moral fiber."

"It gets better." Stefani takes another sip of wine. "After dinner we walked on the beach, and he told me how the first time he saw me he was swept off his feet. How hard it was to not ask me out. He had a plan to approach me after my high school graduation the next year but found out I was going to UNC, and he knew once I left I wouldn't come back. So … he gave up."

"That's sad. Did he ever marry?"

"Yes, he did. I got the feeling he wasn't happy but stayed married for their kids. Judging by the number of pictures of his sons in his office I'd say they mean everything to him."

"I'm beginning to like this guy."

"We walked and talked. Then one day I tricked him into meeting me at my old high school, and we played catch. I couldn't help it, but I wanted to see him again."

"Catch? Girl, this guy bought you a car, gave you cash, and you counter with a game of catch?"

Stefani breaks out in laughter. "Yeah … we both played ball at one time."

"Uh-huh."

Stefani is laughing harder. "Sad, huh?"

Tonya takes another large gulp of wine. "Whatever works … although, had it been me, I may have rethought the playing catch thing."

Stefani looks around the room and then back at Tonya. "He flew the boys and me down here on his private jet and set me up with the most powerful law firm in Charlotte."

Tonya's eyes grow huge. "So this guy is really loaded!"

"I don't know how wealthy he is. I know he owns a business and has some other interests, but that's all I know about his professional life."

"Stef, wake up! You don't own a jet and send people new cars and cash unless you're rolling in dough."

"I guess … but he's never acted like he's wealthy. He's just a laid-back, caring guy."

"And a guy who's stealing your heart."

"Doing what?"

"Come on, Stef. Quit being naïve. When you talk about him, your face glows. You perk up and get starry-eyed."

"Get out of here."

"Seriously."

Stefani sets her glass on the table and leans back. "Wish I knew then what I know now."

"What do you mean?"

"To be totally honest, I had a crush on him back then. I never imagined he was interested in me. Now that I know this, I can't help but wonder how things might have turned out."

"So what do you plan to do?"

"I don't know. I have to work my issues out with David. I've got the boys to consider. I need to find a job."

"And you have the prince up in Maryland."

"The prince, huh?"

"Damn right. Stef, you know every woman has a dream about the fairy tale."

"The fairy tale?"

"You know … meeting the one guy who loves you unconditionally, makes you happy, makes you feel safe, and gives everything he possibly can. His entire existence is to be there for you. Not because he has to … because he wants to. His whole world is you. That's what every woman wants."

Stefani closes her eyes. "Sounds amazing."

"Yes, it does … and, Stef … I don't mean to upset you, but the man you are married to doesn't come close to any of that.

Stefani turns and fights back tears, squinting her eyes and pinching her lips tightly together. Tonya reaches over and gently brushes the hair away from Stefani's face with her finger. "You're one of the best people I know. You deserve the fairy tale."

Stefani lays her head back and closes her eyes. "Tonya … what am I supposed to do?"

Tonya sets her glass on the coffee table and throws her head back against the couch. "Stef, if I had the answers, I'd tell you. The only thing I know is you'll know more after you and David get to working on your issues. When you see what his position is and how he acts during the meetings, you'll know if you want to try to make your marriage work."

"I guess."

Tonya looks at Stefani. "And I'd certainly not walk away from Prince Charming just yet."

"How did my life get so screwed up?"

Tonya tilts her head forward and puckers her lips but says nothing, just sitting quietly for a moment.

Stefani turns and looks at her. "What's wrong?"

"Stef ... maybe this was meant to happen."

Stefani quickly sits up. "Are you serious?"

"Yes ... a bump in the road to make you think about where you are and where you should be. Every now and then we need to be jerked up to make us realize what's important and what's not as important as we think. All I'm saying is you're a smart woman ... just make sure you think everything completely through before you make a decision."

"Something tells me that's easier said than done. Tomorrow I have to drop the boys off with David. Then I'm flying back to St. Michaels the following day." Stefani drinks the last of her wine and then sets her glass on the coffee table. "Maybe the time to myself will help me sort out everything."

"Stef, I've known you too long. You'll get through this ... trust me."

Stefani leans forward and hugs Tonya. "Tonya, you're the best. Thank you for everything and for being here for me."

"I wouldn't have it any other way."

Tonya gets up, collects the wine bottle and glasses, and heads for the kitchen. She stops at the door and then turns. "Hey, what's his name?"

Stefani smiles. "Gavin."

Tonya makes a funny face. "Gavin … geez … the guy even has a sexy name."

Chapter 18

The next morning Stefani wakes the boys up early and gets them dressed. It is all she can do to hold back her emotions, knowing David will have them before they go away to camp. The thought of David filling their heads with ideas that she may be the cause of the problems at home nearly rips her heart out.

"Boys, you'll be staying with your dad and then going to camp, okay?"

Blane sits down on the bed. "Aren't you coming home, too, Mom?"

Stefani sits next to him and pulls Jared to her. "No, guys … I'm going back to stay with Nana and Pop for a while. But I'll call you, okay?"

Jared looks up at Stefani. "Why, Mom?"

"I just want to make sure they're okay and want to spend some time with them."

The boys both hug her as she does her best not to lose control of her tears.

"I love you guys."

"We love you, too, Mom."

Tonya walks into the bedroom and clearly senses the emotional strain, for she says brightly, "Hey, Stef, why don't you take the boys in my car? I know they've never ridden in a classic like that."

Blane turns around. "Classic? Dad always said it was a piece—"

Stefani snaps, "Blane!"

Tonya laughs. "Boys, there's not another like it on the road." She flips the keys to Stefani and winks. "Try to keep it under one twenty."

Blane's eyes widen. "One twenty?"

Tonya sways her shoulders back and forth as she walks out of the room. "That's before you really stomp the gas."

Stefani and the boys climb into Tonya's car and head for the house. To shield the boys from her tears, she slips on her sunglasses and turns on the radio. It's the shortest ride home Stefani has ever driven. As she turns onto Ardent Drive and then slowly pulls into the driveway, her heart begins to race. She slips the transmission into park and sits for a moment. The front door opens, and David steps out.

The boys explode out of the car and race up the walk. "Dad!"

David drops on one knee and hugs the boys. Stefani climbs out of the car, adjusts her sunglasses, and stays in the driveway. David stands and looks at her. "Hey, guys, why don't you go inside and look things over while I get your bags."

The boys run into the house as David meanders toward the car. Stefani crosses her arms and looks down. David approaches her and then stops at a safe distance. She finds it impossible to give him any eye contact. David takes a deep breath and then slips his hands into the back pockets of his shorts. "So ... how have you been?"

Stefani turns away, looks up, and nods. "I've been getting by."

"I'm sorry to hear what happened at work."

Stefani chuckles. "Yeah ... made for one hell of a good day. Then find out your husband is fucking your good friend and to top things off have every access to your money blocked. Yep ... I'd say it was a splendid day."

"Stef, I blocked the money so you didn't make any impulsive decisions that you might have regretted later."

She turns and looks him in the eye for the first time. "Gee, thanks. I feel so special knowing you had my best interests in mind."

"Stef ... it was a one-time thing with Mallory. It meant nothing to me."

"Oh, bullshit. Do you really think I'm going to believe the one day I'm not at work I catch you fucking Mallory for the first time? Really? Something tells me my luck doesn't work that way."

David shakes his head. "Well ... where do we go from here?"

"I don't know. All I know is my children are in my house, and it kills me to know I can't be with them, but I have no desire to be in that house with you."

"So you have no plans or intentions?"

"What, David ... you screw me over and then expect me to cater to your inquisitive mind?"

"No ... I just want to know what you want."

"David ... I'll let you know when I decide."

David steps back and scuffs his shoe on the walk. He turns and looks out over the yard. "My attorney called me."

"David, don't even try to intimidate me."

"Really ... maybe that's a statement I should throw at you."

Stefani stands motionless, staring at his face. David turns and looks back at her. "Yeah ... he told me you're being represented by Lloyd, Hughes, and Webster. How the hell did you pull that one off?"

Stefani suddenly feels a sense of strength. She takes a step closer to David and slides her hands into the front pockets of her shorts. "Well, David, that's none of your business."

"Really ... so what do you plan to do, Stef?"

Stefani pushes her tongue inside her lower lip. "I'm not sure yet, but I do know one thing."

"Yeah ... what's that?"

"You mess with either one of those boys or try to hurt me, and I'll have your nuts cut off and shoved down your fucking throat."

David stands motionless as Stefani takes a step back toward the car. Just then the boys come out of the house, each with a Popsicle in his hand. They walk up to Stefani. She drops to her knees, kisses both boys, and hugs them tightly. "Guys, I will see you in a few weeks. You behave and be careful!"

"Yes, Mom."

"If you need anything you have my cell phone number. Even if you just want to talk, you call me, okay?"

Both boys look at her with expressions of concern. Blane forces a smile. "Okay, Mom."

The three stand for a moment, and Jared starts to sob. Stefani hugs them both again as she fights back her own tears. "Guys, everything is going to be okay. I promise."

Jared wipes his eyes and nods. In the distance a loud click can be heard as David opens the front door. Stefani smiles and hugs the boys once more. "Now you guys go inside with your dad."

The boys turn and walk up the sidewalk. As they reach the front door, both turn and wave. Stefani waves back and smiles. She holds her hand to her ear making a telephone sign with her finger and thumb as she whispers, "Call me."

Both boys nod and walk into the house. David gives Stefani a blank look and then follows the boys, closing the front door behind him.

Stefani turns and climbs back into Tonya's car. She to weeps uncontrollably as she backs out of the driveway. "God, I hate that son-of-a-bitch!"

She returns to Tonya's, where the two have a heart-to-heart talk for the remainder of the day and into the early hours of the morning. The next day is filled with the same: emotional talks, wine, and tears. The following morning Stefani gathers her bags and heads for the front door. She turns and grabs Tonya's hand. "I don't know what I would do without you."

"Stef, I'm always here when you need me."

"I know you are."

The sound of the limousine pulling up out front can be heard. "Guess it's time for me to go."

The two embrace. Tonya takes a deep breath and blurts out, "Call me when you land."

"I will."

Stefani turns and opens the front door. The driver grabs her bags and loads them in the trunk as she climbs into the car. She smiles and waves one last time. Tonya gives her a thumbs-up. The driver closes her door and takes her to the airport, where the Gulfstream is idling and waiting for her return to St. Michaels. Before she knows it she is back on the ground in Easton, her bags are loaded in the Range Rover, and she's headed for her parents' home. After pulling into the driveway, she grasps her bags and walks into the house.

Joanna calls out to her, "Honey, let me help you with those."

"It's okay, Mom. I'm fine."

"Your dad went to the store for me. Would you like a cup of tea?"

Stefani smiles at Joanna and hugs her. The "cup of tea" offer was always her mother's way of asking if she wanted to get anything off her chest. The two sit, neither saying a word. Stefani is lifeless as she cradles her teacup.

Joanna takes a sip of her tea and clears her throat. "So how did things go?"

"Well, I can't say my meeting with David was pleasant."

"So what do you plan to do?"

Stefani looks up. "I don't know. I guess I need to start looking for a job."

"Do you plan on looking in Charlotte or around here?"

Stefani's lower lip quivers as she turns away and looks out the window. "I don't know … it's so complicated. If I try to find work up here, then I have to pull the boys out of their school and enroll them in a school here. If I decide to do that, then my marriage is over. Then the complications really begin. David will demand visitation rights, which will be almost impossible between here and Charlotte. If I go back to Charlotte, the boys can stay in their school, and if I land a job that's great, but I'm not sure I want to be with David."

Joanna reaches across the table and covers Stefani's hand with hers. "Sweetheart, I know you're going through a very difficult time, and you know we're here for you."

Stefani wipes a tear from her eye. "I know, Mom, and that's one of the reasons I want to stay here."

Joanna grins and then tilts her head. "What's the other reason?"

Stefani looks at her mom and then shrugs her shoulders. "You think there's another reason?"

"Honey, I'd venture to say there's definitely another reason."

Stefani shakes her head. "Mom, I wish I had your perceptive ability."

Joanna laughs. "Stefani, you don't need to be clairvoyant to see the obvious."

"Is it that noticeable?"

"Well … let's just say you seem to be very happy when certain people come to mind."

Stefani smiles as Joanna gets up and walks over to the refrigerator, saying, "I think we'll have fish tonight."

Stefani sits and plays with a napkin. "Mom, would it be okay if I skip dinner tonight?"

"Sure … is there anything I can do?"

"No … I just want to take some time and do some thinking."

"Honey, you do whatever it is you need to do."

"Thanks."

Stefani goes upstairs and lies across her bed. She pulls the pillow closely as if hugging it for support. She runs the events of the meeting with David and leaving the boys with him through her head over and over again. As she lies there, she notices the pink Bodie's sweatshirt hanging on the back of the desk chair. She rolls over, pulls her cell phone from her bag, and enters a new text message. "Gavin, the trip on your plane was incredible. Hope to see you soon."

She lets her hand flop down on the bed but keeps the phone tightly clenched in her hand. Moments later the phone vibrates.

"Glad you're back safely and hope everything went as you wanted. It would be great to see you soon."

Stefani lies there rereading the text. Finally she responds, "Any chance maybe we can go for a drive later?"

"Sure. Have any place in mind?"

"No, just a drive to clear the head."

"Sounds great. Any particular time you want me to pick you up?"

"How about 7?"

"7 it is. I'll see you then."

Stefani lays the phone down on the bed and curls up around the pillow. She begins to smile as she closes her eyes. Before she knows it, she drifts off into a much-needed sleep.

Chapter 19

Stefani sits by the front door and watches the clock. Minutes before seven she hears tires rolling through the gravel driveway. "Mom, Dad, I'll be home later."

"Okay, dear."

She exits the front door and skips down the steps. Gavin smiles as he climbs out of the car. "Hey there."

"Hey to you, Mr. Thorne."

Gavin smiles as the two get into the car. He latches his seat belt and then looks over at Stefani. "Where to?"

"Anywhere you want."

"Want to ride out to the island?"

"Sounds perfect."

As Gavin drives, he scans the scenery. "You know, I haven't been through here in years. So much to see, and yet it seems like so little time to appreciate it."

Stefani looks down at her lap and then turns to Gavin. "Tell me about Gavin Thorne."

He glances over at her and grins. "Tell you about me? What do you want to know?"

"Well, I know you're a successful businessman, a very giving person, and very good looking."

Gavin gives her another look and laughs. "If I didn't know better, I'd say you were trying to close a business deal with all those compliments."

"No, I want to know the guy I never got to know when I was younger."

Gavin takes a deep breath and looks out the side window. "Stefani, I don't want to disappoint you, but there's really not much to tell."

She reaches over and softly rests her hand on his. "I want to know about Gavin the man."

He looks down at Stefani's hand resting on his. "The other night when I told you the story about you sweeping me off my feet and how badly I wanted to ask you out … that was the first time I ever told that story to anyone. Later I thought it over and wasn't sure it was the best thing I could have done."

"Why?"

"Because it was in the past and can't be changed, and I didn't want to add more stress to your life."

"Gavin, I loved that story."

He looks at her and smiles. "You really don't want to hear this,"

"Ah, yes I do."

Gavin shakes his head and sighs. "I married Belinda to try to erase the memory of you. I still remember the day of my wedding when Belinda and her father turned the corner at the far end of the aisle and walked toward the altar. I wanted to run away as fast as I could. I knew I didn't love her. The entire time, all I could see was you in that wedding gown and how happy I would have been … but it wasn't you. The entire time I was engaged, all I did was think about you and how I wanted to break off my engagement, but I knew too many people would be affected, and everything about the wedding was set. I couldn't risk embarrassing my family, so I went through with it. The way I justified getting married was by telling myself you were gone and never coming back. Looking back, it wasn't the possibility you may never have loved me … the pain was the fact that I never knew for sure if maybe you might have."

Gavin looks out his window and sighs again. "I never got the chance to find out." He looks at Stefani. She is staring at him with a huge tear in her eye. She lifts his hand from the center console and places it into her lap and interweaves the fingers of both her hands into his large hand. "Gavin, I would have fallen in love with you."

Gavin pulls the car into the parking lot of the marina, and they climb out. Head down, he slowly walks toward the pier, and Stefani follows closely behind. At the end, he leans over and stares at the water below.

"Gavin, are you okay? Did I say something wrong?"

Gavin turns away for a moment, puts his hands on top of his head, and walks in a circle. "No, you didn't say anything wrong, but part of me was afraid to hear what you said."

"Why? What did I say?"

He turns toward her and shoves his hands in his pockets.

"I dreamed for so many years about you. What it would have been like to have a life with you. To share things with you, good times, bad times … everything. But the one thing that kept me from going crazy was that I'd convinced myself it would have never happened because you wouldn't have gone out with me. That was the one thing that helped me deal with the mistake of never approaching you and seeing if we ever had a chance. Not a day goes by that I don't regret trying to be part of your life."

Gavin turns back toward the rail and stares at the water. Stefani walks up behind him, reaches out, and pulls his arm to turn him toward her. She can see the pain and sadness in his eyes as she presses up against him and wraps her arms around him. She closes her eyes and lays her head against his chest.

After a moment, Gavin wraps his arms around her and softly embraces her. He gently rests his cheek on top of her head and sighs. "I dreamed about this moment forever." Continues to hold her, he murmurs, "And it's better than I ever imagined."

Stefani lifts her head and smiles. "I think so, too."

They stand there motionless, staring into each other's eyes. For the moment nothing else exists. Then Gavin smiles and says, "The setting sun makes your eyes sparkle. It's amazing how your eyes can affect me just like they did so many years ago. I could look into them forever."

Stefani smiles and squeezes him tighter. She can feel the solid core of his body.

Gavin slides his hands down her arms. "Hey, if it's okay, I'd like to show you something."

Stefani looks at him with curiosity. "What?"

"Something that is special to me and I'd really like you to see it."

"Okay."

When they're back in the car, Stefani leans over, grasps Gavin's hand again, and leans her head on his shoulder. She rubs his hand and looks up at him.

He glances at her and smiles. "What?"

Stefani lays her head back on his shoulder. "Nothing … I was just thinking."

"About what?"

"You told me I swept you off your feet."

"Yes, you did."

"I think you've returned the favor."

They drive down a wooded back road, and then Gavin turns onto a paved lane. About a quarter mile down the lane, he stops at a closed iron gate. Stefani looks at the gate and then at Gavin. "Does this mean I can't see your surprise?"

"Don't give up on me yet." He pushes a button on the steering wheel, and the gate opens.

Stefani's eyes widen. "Wow." As they continue traveling on the winding lane, Stefani looks at their surroundings in puzzlement.

"What is this?"

"Just give me about twenty more seconds."

The lane turns to the right, and suddenly she can see a huge stone mansion. Stefani sits up and stares in amazement. "Wow! Is this a castle?"

"Not exactly ... this is home."

Stefani turns with her mouth hanging open. "This is your home?"

"Yes."

Gavin drives up to the front of the mansion. The lane turns to cobblestones, and he stops the car under a large stone carport with a path to a set of tall wooden doors. The entire house is breathtaking.

Gavin looks at Stefani as she studies the building. "Would you like to see the place?"

Stefani turns, still slightly shocked. "Yes, I would."

"Good! Sit tight for a second."

Gavin gets out and then walks around to Stefani's side of the car. He opens her door and extends his hand to help her out. "Ms. Tanner, welcome to the Thorne house."

"House?" Stefani looks at the magnificent structure and shakes her head. "Gavin, this is amazing."

"Come inside."

Gavin walks her to the entrance and pushes one of the doors open. He motions to her to enter. "Please."

Stefani steps in and looks at the beautiful entrance hall. "Gavin, this is incredible."

"Thank you ... now do me a favor."

"What's that?"

"Go anywhere you want, and make yourself at home."

"I'll get lost."

Gavin laughs. "No, you won't … I'll be right behind you."

Stefani stops. "Let me take my shoes off."

"That's not necessary, trust me."

Stefani smiles, turns, and walks into the main living room. She studies the décor and softly runs her fingertips across the furniture. She turns and makes her way through the kitchen, where she stops in astonishment at the sight of the two stainless steel refrigerators and matching commercial ovens and stove. "Gavin, you live here alone?"

"Just me and my sons when they come home. Hopefully you'll get to meet them soon. I like to entertain my associates and their families here. It makes it much easier to have everyone here rather than making other arrangements. Plus if other members of my family come to town they have a place to stay."

Stefani turns to Gavin. "How about you give me the tour?"

"Okay."

Gavin takes her through the house, showing her the family room, theatre, gym, den, his office, and the dining room that seats twelve.

"How many bedrooms are there?"

"There are nine."

"Nine bedrooms?"

"Yes."

"Wow ... how many bathrooms?"

"Eleven."

"Gavin, this isn't a house it's a hotel."

He laughs. "I don't know about that."

Gavin watches Stefani as she looks things over, and it's clear he's enjoying her being in his home.

"Want to see where I go to unwind?"

"Okay."

Gavin leads her through the family room and stops at the door. "Close your eyes."

She smiles and takes a deep breath. "Okay."

He opens the door and guides her outside by the hand. She can feel the floor texture change. "Can I open my eyes now?"

"Not yet ... give me one second."

He lets go of her hand, and she hears a click. Suddenly, soft music plays in the foreground, with the sound of water running as a backdrop. Then he returns and takes hold of her hand. "Okay ... open your eyes."

Stefani looks and is awestruck by what she sees. In front of her is a huge stone mass standing at least twenty feet tall, and the waterfall cascading down it feeds a lagoon-style swimming pool. The entire area is accented with palm trees and beautiful decorative lighting. Teak lounge chairs and tables are strategically placed around the pool, and to the side is a tropical hut that houses a wet bar and a large grill.

"Gavin, this looks like a resort."

"Like it?"

"Like it? I love it!"

"I come out here to get away from things. My sons go down the waterslides hidden in the rock and swim in the pool. I just like it because it makes me feel like I'm away from the day-to-day hassles around here. I just feel relaxed when I sit and listen to the waterfall."

"Gavin, this house is the most beautiful thing I've ever seen."

"I'm glad you like it."

Stefani walks over to the water and slips off a shoe. She dips her toes in and slowly twirls her foot around. She closes her eyes, runs her hands through her hair, and then opens her eyes and smiles. She slips her shoe back on and then walks back to Gavin. "You didn't show me one room."

"I didn't?"

"No."

"Which one?"

"Your bedroom."

Gavin blushes and looks down. "I didn't want you to think I was trying to imply anything by asking you here."

"I'd like to see it, if you don't mind."

"Okay."

He turns to enter the house as Stefani squeezes his hand tighter. They make their way through the house, neither speaking until he pushes a wooden door open. "Here it is."

Stefani walks in and looks around. The room is huge. It is decorated beautifully, with a king-size bed in the center of the room.

Gavin points to the right. "The master bathroom is through there."

Stefani pulls Gavin back by the hand and turns him to face her. "Gavin, you are the most amazing man I've ever met. You are so successful yet so grounded. You are giving and caring, and there's not an ounce of arrogance or egotism in you. Gavin … you're perfect."

He bows his head and blushes. "I don't know about that."

Stefani pulls him closer, reaches up, and softly places her hands on his cheeks. She stares into his eyes. "You have only one flaw."

"What is that?"

"You never asked me out."

She stands on her toes, closes her eyes, and gently presses her lips against his. She slowly pulls away and opens her eyes. Gavin is standing motionless with his eyes still closed. He gradually opens his eyes and smiles. Stefani closes her eyes again and leans forward. Gavin meets her this time, wraps his arms around her, and pulls her tight. She can feel his arms shivering as they continue to touch. She slowly pulls back while softly sucking on his bottom lip, looks him in the eyes.

He looks back at her. "Stefani, I've waited so long, and I never thought I'd ever get a chance to be this close to you."

"Gavin, I've realized you're not the only one who has waited so long."

They lean into each other and kiss again passionately. Stefani runs her tongue against his, and she can feel her body weaken as his powerful arms hold her.

As he pulls away, he looks at her and murmurs, "I don't ever want to let you go."

"Then don't."

Again their lips meet. Stefani wraps her arms around his shoulders as he begins to kiss her neck. He slowly pulls back and looks into her eyes. She stares back and then sighs. "Gavin, I want so badly to show you how much I care for you … but right now I can't."

He softly kisses her and looks at her eyes again. "Stefani … I want you to know you never have to explain yourself or doing anything you don't feel comfortable doing. All I want is for you to be happy."

As he continues to stare at her, Stefani smiles and tilts her head. "What?"

"I love you so much…you've touched a part of me no one else ever has."

Stefani smiles as tears build in her eyes. "I can't remember the last time someone told me that." Gavin runs a finger across her forehead, moving her hair away from her face. "Even though those are the words I've been wanting to say … they don't seem to express how much I care about you. I never thought I'd ever get the chance to tell you that."

Stefani wraps her arms around him and pulls him close. "Gavin, you're more than perfect."

"No, Stefani … you're the one who makes everything special. You're the gift everyone prays for. You're everything I've ever wanted and so much more."

"I thought all those years were an eternity," he says, smiling down at her. "Truth is … I'd wait a lifetime for you."

Chapter 20

Gavin drives Stefani to her parents' house. He climbs out of the car, walks over, and opens her door. When she gets out, the two embrace. Gavin kisses her forehead. "I wish this night never had to end."

She looks up and then softly kisses him. "Me, too."

Gavin holds her hand as he leads her to the front to door, where they stand quietly looking into each other's eyes.

Stefani grins. "You do know we could have done this about twenty years ago … but someone …"

Gavin snickers. "I know, I know."

Gavin leans forward, and the two kiss passionately for a moment. Then he pulls away. "You better get inside before your dad is out here with a shotgun."

Stefani laughs and hugs him one more time. "I'll talk to you soon?"

Gavin winks. "I'll be counting the minutes."

Stefani turns and opens the door. Once inside, she turns back. "Gavin …"

"Yes?"

She just smiles and shakes her head. "You already know."

Gavin grins and turns for the car. Stefani peeks through the sheers to watch him drive away. She takes a deep breath and turns to find Joanna standing in the kitchen doorway looking at her,

"Stefani … I think we need a cup of tea."

Stefani sighs and puckers her lips. "Oh boy."

She follows her mother into the kitchen, sits down at the table, and asks, "Where's Dad?"

"He's lying in bed watching TV."

"Is he okay?"

"Yes. He's tired, but I think he misses his fishing buddies."

Joanna walks over and sets a cup of tea in front of Stefani.

"Thanks."

Joanna sits down and takes a sip. Hoping to avoid the lecture she expected was coming, Stefani brightly stresses. "Mom, the time the boys and I have spent here has been great."

Her mom nods. "Yes, it has, but I'm a little concerned."

Stefani sits still just like she did when she was young and about to be scolded for something she had done wrong. "Oh?"

"Honey, I know I keep repeating this, but you have been through so much recently. I just don't want to see you get hurt more or get yourself in a situation that puts more stress on you."

Stefani looks at her mother and tries to force a smile. "Mom …"

"Yes?"

Stefani shakes her head as the tears flow freely. "Why does everything have to be so hard?"

"Sweetheart, that's life … everyone gets rained on now and—"

Stefani cuts her off. "Mom, it's time we had a real woman-to-woman talk."

Joanna takes a deep breath. "Ooookay."

Stefani reaches over and holds Joanna's hand. "Mom, before you comment or say anything let me finish."

"I promise."

Stefani leans her head back, looks at her mom, and smiles. "Recently I have learned so much and realized so many things. Some things I should have known or paid attention to, and some I just realized about myself that I never knew before."

"That sounds like a good thing."

"Mom, so good that I'm feeling things I never felt before." Stefani takes a sip of tea. "So here goes … I thought losing my job and discovering David cheating on me was the end of my world. I'm embarrassed to admit I came home because I had nowhere else to go, but that's what happened. I really thought I'd hit rock bottom. I get here and feel guilty because I have to tell Dad and you what's happened and ashamed because I haven't shown you the attention you deserve but come crawling home when I'm lost."

"Stefani," Joanna protests, "we've been through this before … that's what we're here for."

"No, Mom, that's not true! You're not only here for me to fall back on … you're here for me to show how much I love you and Dad and express how much I appreciate everything you and Dad have ever done for me."

"Honey, we know you do."

"But, Mom, there's so much more. I never realized it until I saw Dad spend time with the boys, the same way he did with me when I was younger. Mom, I loved to play catch with him, then come in the house, and you'd always have a great dinner waiting for us. When I saw that happening with the boys and the fun and excitement in their eyes, it made me realize David never spends time like that with them. I see the way you and Dad are toward each other, the unconditional love … I never had that with David. I was too caught up in my job, trying to be the perfect businessperson, and David was doing his thing. For some stupid reason I always thought I had to leave home and St. Michaels to be successful. The truth is I couldn't have been more wrong if I tried."

Joanna smiles and squeezes her hand. "Sometimes you have to leave to find what you want. Sometimes leaving home and moving far away is part of that."

"But, Mom … can I sit here, look you in the eye, and tell you that worked for me? No. But I get here, and everything feels right. I feel safe and secure. I know the boys are safe and secure. Then out of nowhere, someone reenters my life, and he makes me think and feel like I know I should."

Joanna leans back and tilts her head. "Stefani—"

"Mom, please let me finish."

Joanna rolls her lips in and nods.

"Mom, I know what you're going to say, and I know I should see it that way, but he's different."

"Different?"

"He's so genuine. He's compassionate, giving, and wholesome. Mom, he has never—not once—tried to take advantage of me. Remember when he gave me the car and money and didn't want me to know who it was from? He overheard Mindy and me talking about what I was going through at the restaurant and sent these things to me to help me. He never once expected anything in return and had every intention of remaining totally anonymous. I was the one who sought him out. I went to his place of business and asked why. Then, when I have to go back to Charlotte, he flies me and the boys down on his jet, puts me in contact with the most powerful law firm in the state, pays for everything, then flies me home."

"Stefani, I hear everything you're saying, and I'm more than sure he's a tremendous person, but why would he do all these things for someone he hasn't seen in over twent years or never really knew?"

Stefani looks down at the table and then up into Joanna's eyes. She shrugs her shoulders and smiles as a tear streams down her cheek. "He loves me."

Joanna quickly sits up straight. "Stefani!"

"Mom, stop, please. Before you say another word, let me tell you the story he told me. Then you tell me what you think."

Joanna shakes her head but reluctantly agrees. "Go ahead."

"When I confronted him about the car and money, he asked if we could talk in private outside of his office. I agreed and had dinner with him. We took a walk, and he told me how when he first saw me so many years ago at our first softball team meeting he wanted to ask me out. When he found out I was only going to be a senior in high school, he knew he couldn't. Beside the fact he felt it was wrong, he knew you and Dad would frown upon it and forbid it. So he planned to wait until I graduated and was going to ask me out."

"But didn't he date Belinda then?"

"Yes … they were fixed up by mutual friends, but he didn't expect it to last."

"Well, evidently it did—he married her."

"Just let me finish. He had no plans of staying with her, but when he found out I was going away to UNC, he told himself I was leaving and never coming back. Mom, he wanted to date me then but felt there was no chance. He told me he settled for Belinda because I left. He had children with her but never was truly in love with her … something was missing. He stayed because of the devotion to his kids. Once they were older, he and Belinda parted their ways. Mom, he sacrificed so much happiness for years for his kids. That's exactly the opposite of David's mentality. David sacrificed his children's home because of his own selfishness. Then, more than twenty years later, oddly, Gavin's sitting in a restaurant … the same one I enter. He overhears my story, and all his feelings for me come racing back. But because he was unsure of my position or if I would have even agreed to go out with him back then he doesn't make a formal approach. He doesn't even make an approach at all. He just helps me out when I needed it most. What kind of guy does that?"

"Well … I have to say he sounds like a great person."

"Mom, he is. And the more we talked, the more I learned about him and realized the guy I had a crush on so long ago is perfect. He stayed in the area, became very successful, but it never went to his head. He has his priorities in order and knows what's important. He's helped me realize what's important. He's helped bring me closer to you and Dad. Mom … I love him."

Joanna slowly stands and walks over to the sink. She pours her tea out and turns toward Stefani. "Honey, you're a grown woman and have always been levelheaded, but how can you be sure you're in love with him? You hardly know him."

"I' ll admit I've spent very little time with him, but he makes me feel ways I've never felt with David or anyone. Mom, he has all these qualities—he's smart, good looking, successful, confident yet humble, and very compassionate. I could go on and on, but I think you understand."

"Stefani, I understand, but you've got to look at the whole picture. You have a life in Charlotte. You have a home, and the boys are enrolled in school there. I know David did something to you and the boys that was horrendous, but are you sure you're ready to walk away from your marriage?"

Stefani sits quietly fumbling with a napkin as Joanna returns to the table. "Sweetheart, I know you've had so much thrown at you in such a short period of time, and I'm sure Gavin is a great guy, but you have to keep things in perspective. He happens to be at the right place at the right time, and he helps you keep your mind off things, but the reality is you're going to have to deal with everything sooner or later. I'm not sure Gavin fits in your life right now. Maybe down the road when you have things sorted out something could grow, but right now it might be best to focus on other things."

"What am I supposed to do, Mom? Turn my back on him?" Stefani stands up, walks over to the window, and looks out. "I can see it now ... Gavin, thanks for the car and money, and I certainly appreciate your generosity and company, but I think it's best if we part our ways."

"Stefani, I didn't mean that you should be nasty but just slow things down."

"Mom ... things aren't moving fast."

"Really?"

"Yes, Mom ... really."

Joanna looks at her. "But you love him."

Stefani bows her head and slowly nods. "Yes ... I do."

Chapter 21

The next morning Stefani gets up before daybreak and goes for a run. Her talk with her mother made total sense, and deep down she knows her mom is right, but that does little to ease her pain. She slows her run to a walk as she approaches the pier. She walks around in circles with her hands on her hips, catching her breath. The thoughts of David and Gavin continue to race through her head. Finally the frustration becomes too much, and she kicks the bottom bar of the pier rail. "Damn it!"

She flops down on a bench, burying her face in her hands as she rests her elbows on her knees. Moments later she throws her head back and takes a deep breath, wiping tears from her face. She stands and begins a quick run back to her parents' house. She turns the corner into the driveway and then stops at the Range Rover. Extending her arm, she softly runs her fingertips down the side of the car and peers through the driver's side window. Resting her head against the glass, she looks over the beautiful interior of the vehicle. As she backs away from the window, she sees her reflection in the glass. After a brief standoff with her image, she smirks. "Yeah, Stef, what are you going to do?"

She enters the house and hears Joanna in the kitchen. "Mom, I'm going to take a shower."

The warm water cascades down her body as she stands motionless, totally caught up in thought. She exits the shower, wraps up in a towel, and lies across the bed, recalling her time with Gavin in his bedroom. As she does, she rolls onto her side, pulls her legs up to her chest, and smiles. She closes her eyes and can feel him touching her, causing a chill to shoot through her body. When she opens her eyes, she sees the Bodie's sweatshirt hanging on the chair. She reaches over, grabs her cell phone, and types a new text message to Gavin. "Hey, really need to see you."

"Okay. Is everything alright?"

"Yes. Just want to see you."

"Is this evening too late?"

"No, that's perfect."

"Dinner?"

"How about if we just take a walk and talk?"

"Sounds great to me. What time should I pick you up?"

"I'll be in Easton, so why don't I meet you at the ferry in Oxford? We can walk the shore there."

"Are you sure everything is okay?"

"Yes. I just want to see you."

"What time?"

"6?"

"I'll see you at 6."

"See you then."

Stefani spends her day walking the shops in St. Michaels. At five-thirty she heads for the ferry and parks in the lot. She looks in the rearview mirror and checks her hair, and then she sinks into the seat as she looks out over the water. The peacefulness mesmerizes her, and she doesn't notice Gavin pull up beside her. She jumps when she hears him close his car door, and she climbs out of the car as he walks toward her. He wraps his arms around her and kisses her forehead as she rests her cheek against his chest. She interlaces her fingers of her left hand into his right hand and leads him toward the beach. While holding his hand, she grabs his arm with her right hand and presses her face against his shoulder as they walk.

When they reach the sand, Gavin stops and Stefani continues until their hands separate. He watches Stefani, who stops just a few steps ahead of him, and stands still as she continues to face forward. "Stefani, are you okay?"

She doesn't turn to face him but nods in acknowledgement. Gavin walks up behind her, wraps his arms around her waist, and presses his lips against the back of her head. Suddenly Stefani bows her head and begins to weep. She quickly covers her mouth with her hand. Gavin gently turns her to face him, and she hides her face in his chest.

Gavin embraces her as she continues to cry. "Stefani, please tell me what's wrong."

She sobs heavily while attempting to answer. Gavin softly massages her upper arms and gently creates distance between them so he can see her face. She looks up at him with tear-filled eyes. She squints, causing more tears to race down her face. Again she buries her face into his chest and continues to cry.

"Stefani, please talk to me."

Stefani manages to mumble from his chest, "I can't."

Gavin stands there and continues to hold her until she is able to gather herself. Finally she reaches into her pocket, pulls out a tissue, and wipes her eyes. She looks up at Gavin and gives him a shaky smile. "I'm sorry."

"Why?"

"Why? Look at me."

He tilts his head and then gently wipes a tear from her cheek. He smiles. "I am, and I love what I see."

She lets out a weak laugh and then softly punches him in the chest. "Yeah, right."

"May I ask what's wrong?"

Stefani turns, crosses her arms, and walks away from him. "Gavin, why does everything have to be so hard?"

Gavin stands still and slips his hands into his pockets. "Sometimes the best things in life can create the worst pain."

Stefani turns, faces him, and shakes her head. "I'm so confused, I don't know what to do."

He steps toward her with his hands still in his pockets. "Maybe I can help."

She snickers and then looks up at him. "I wish it were that easy."

"What do you mean?"

Stefani turns and faces the water. Gavin walks up behind her, his chest barely touching her. She presses back against him, and he wraps his arms around her. She covers his hands with hers and sighs heavily.

"Gavin, I don't know what to say."

"Just say what's on your mind."

"I can't."

He turns her to face him. "Stefani, since the day you entered my office and confronted me about the car, we have both been totally honest with each other. Now, I know we haven't been through any major situations and haven't been close for long, but it's been easy for me to express my feelings to you for the very simple reason … it's so easy for me to talk to you. Nothing feels more natural and comforting than talking to you. I have to pinch myself sometimes to remind me that for this very short time we've been together, it's real—not the dream I've imagined for so long."

Stefani laughs and falls against his chest. Gavin again wraps his arms around her and holds her tightly. "I want you to make me two promises, okay?"

She looks into his eyes. "Okay."

"Number one, always be honest with me and tell me the truth even if you think it will hurt me."

Stefani pinches her lips together and squints in a desperate attempt to hold back more tears. She nods and gasps as she inhales. Gavin gently wipes a tear from her cheek and smiles. "Number two … always do what's best for you."

She wipes her eyes with the tissue. "Gavin, that hardly seems fair."

"Stefani, that is totally fair."

Stefani steps backward and shakes her head in disagreement. "No … no it's not."

She turns and walks down the beach about ten yards. Gavin stays back, allowing her space. Suddenly she turns around and extends her arms out to the side with her palms facing up. "Gavin, how can that be remotely fair? If I stay in St. Michaels I have to relocate my sons, which means not only will they have to leave their school, but that may create a problem between them and me. What if they resent me because I take them away from their father? I don't think I could handle that. Then I have David to contend with. He'll want to see the boys, and I can't deny him that. Sharing time between here and there would be hard on the boys. If I go back to Charlotte, then I'm away from my parents."

Stefani shakes her head and takes a deep breath. "For some reason it took something substantial to happen in my life to make me remember what great parents I have. If I do go back to Charlotte I don't have a job, so I would be dependent on David, and right now that's not what I want, and based on the way I feel right now I'll never want … but it may be best for the boys."

She crosses her arms and shakes her head. "And if I go back to Charlotte …"

She turns and looks away as the tears flow down her cheeks. "I lose you."

Gavin slowly walks toward Stefani, but she continues to look away as her tears flow uncontrollably. He reaches up and gently puts his palms on her cheeks. She turns her head and closes her eyes as he wipes the tears with his thumbs. When she opens her eyes she can see him smiling. She looks back and forth at his eyes, finding a sense of comfort.

"Stefani, you will never lose me. I have loved you since the first time I saw you. I have never lied to you, and I'm not going to start now. Being with you has been the best thing in my life. Yes, it took years for me to get the chance to get close to you and tell you all the things I've held inside for so long, but that's okay because I love you. And it's because I love you I can live with the decisions you have to make. Whether you are here or in Charlotte, I'm not going to love you any less. And ... it's because I love you so much ... I can tell you honestly what I think is best."

"What's that?"

"You need to go back to Charlotte."

Stefani stands with her jaw hanging. "You want me to go back to Charlotte?"

Gavin steps back, slips his hands into his pockets, and looks down. "Yes."

"I can't believe you're saying this to me. After the time we've spent together, the talks we have had, and the feelings we've shared, you're telling me the best thing for me is to return to Charlotte? Are you serious?"

"Stefani, you just stood here and told me how hard things are. How uprooting your sons may be the worst thing you could do. How possibly it may be the best thing to do is return to Charlotte." He turns and slowly walks to a pile of rocks sitting off in the distance. He sits and stares at the open water.

She watches him for a moment and then joins him. She reaches down and takes hold of his hand. "Gavin, I'm sorry, I didn't mean to upset you."

Gavin puts his arm around her and pulls her tight. "You didn't upset me. The truth is, I don't want you to go. I want you to stay here with me. I want to meet your sons and be a part of their lives. I want you to meet my sons and be part of their lives. I want to share my life with you. I want to be there for you when you're hurting. I want to be there with you when you celebrate. I want what I've dreamed of for so many years."

He looks at her. "I want you." Then he turns and looks back out over the bay. "But I know it's not that easy. The reality is, as bad as I want your life to be my life, I know that it may never happen, and a part of me tells me not to let it happen."

Stefani pulls away. "Why?"

He clasps his hands and rests his elbows on his knees. He hesitates for a moment and then takes a deep breath and exhales slowly. "Stefani … I know what it's like to live half a life not truly happy. To be in a relationship or a situation you don't want to be in, but stay because you created it and it's the right thing to do. What it's like to wonder how differently things may have been had you made a different choice at some point in your life. It's because of this pain that I won't let you make the same mistakes I did."

Stefani reaches up and turns Gavin's head toward her. "I'm here now."

"Yes, you are, and those years were worth every second in exchange for the time we've had together. But I don't want you to feel the torment I felt for so long, because one day you may wake up and wonder 'what-if.' That not only applies to your situation with your sons but your husband as well. Stefani, I love you so much that I want you to be totally happy. No regrets, no second-guessing." Gavin stands, bends over, and picks up a rock. After rolling it around in his hand for a moment, he whips it into the water. "Even if that means losing you forever."

Stefani walks to Gavin and faces him. She looks him in the eyes. "Kiss me."

He leans forward, and slowly their lips touch. They stand totally still for a brief moment. When they separate, she puts her hand around the back of his neck and pulls him forward until their foreheads touch. She looks deeply into his eyes. "Gavin, I love you. I have never felt this way about anyone before. I want you to be the center of my life. You have taught me so much and made me think about things I've never thought about before. Before you, I could never had said this … Gavin, you are my soul mate. You were put on this earth just for me. I thought I had to leave home to find success in my work and in my personal life. I was totally wrong."

Gavin reaches up and covers Stefani's hands with his. "But you did find success away from here, success that made you happy, a world where you started a family and built a career. Would that have happened had you never left St. Michaels? Can you honestly say you know this for a fact?"

Stefani leans against his shoulder. "Yes, I did find success and what I thought was happiness, but sometimes you find out things are not what you thought. Gavin, if it weren't for my sons this would be a no-brainer."

"But, Stefani, you do have your sons, and they love you and need you. You love them, and you need them. What's it going to be like when they are with their father and not with you? What if one of your greatest fears comes to fruition, and they feel you're the reason they had to leave their home and only get to see their father occasionally? How will that make you feel? Stefani, you don't want to subject yourself to those possibilities … trust me."

"But I love you."

Gavin smiles weakly. "Then show me how much you love me by doing me a favor … go back to Charlotte."

Stefani stands frozen in confusion. She turns, walks toward the water, and stops, Gavin follows a few steps behind.

"Stefani, if I'm lucky enough to spend the rest of my life with you, I need to know that you have no doubts. That includes any reservations that may concern your children, your parents, your professional life, or your husband. I don't know any other way to put it."

She turns and crosses her arms. "Okay … how long do you want me to stay away?"

"Until you're sure."

"So you want me to go back to Charlotte, look for a job, and take care of my sons?"

"Yes."

"Gavin, I don't want to be with my husband. There is nothing there. After spending time with you, I now realize I don't love my husband anymore … I love you. So if I go back to Charlotte, I'm not going back to live with him. I'll have to find my own place."

"What about your sons?"

Stefani shakes her head. "Gavin, that's my only concern."

"And this is exactly what I'm talking about. I don't want to create tension or come between you and your sons. This is something you're going to have to work out with them. How can I be happy knowing you're here with me and your sons are unhappy? You know that would tear you apart."

Stefani closes her eyes and shakes her head.

Gavin sighs. "This is what I mean. Before we can move forward, we need to look back and make sure there are no issues that will create heartache for you. Like I said … I care too much for you to see you unhappy. You need to be able to leave Charlotte without looking back."

Stefani walks up to him and rests her forehead against his chest. "Come to Charlotte with me."

Gavin wraps his arms around her. "This is something you have to do on your own."

She looks up at him. "I mean move to Charlotte."

Gavin drops his hands down to his side and bows his head. Stefani looks up at him, but he slowly shakes his head. "I can't."

"Why?" He sits back on the rocks and stares at the water. Stefani remains standing and crosses her arms. "Gavin, why can't you move?"

"We are in a similar situation."

"I don't understand."

Gavin stands and faces her. "Stef, we basically did the same thing but in different locations. That doesn't make one of us right or one of us wrong. We did what we thought was best based on what we knew. You left the area to start a life and career. You did the right thing. I decided to stay here and make a life and a career, and fortunately it worked. I can't walk away from what I have here. My sons are close to me, I have my company here and we are doing well, and my home is here. If I left, I know I'd be happy being with you, but I would have another part of me hurting knowing what I left up here. That wouldn't be fair to you."

Stefani strolls from the rocks and faces away from Gavin. "So what you're telling me is, if I want to spend my life with you I have to leave Charlotte behind and potentially ruin my relationship with my sons."

Gavin walks up beside her and faces in the same direction. "What I'm saying is we both have complex lives and have to make sure we can live with the sacrifices we would have to make and have no regrets or second-guess our decisions."

"Gavin, no matter what decisions people make, there is always the chance they may second-guess themselves."

"Exactly ... and this is why you need to go a back to Charlotte. We aren't talking about minor decisions. We are talking about major choices that affect many people, people who are very important to both of us."

Stefani shakes her head and forces a smile. Gavin wraps his arms around her. "Stefani, don't give up. Trust me, this is hard for me as well. The time I've spent with you has been the best of my life. The thought of you leaving and not coming back tears a hole in my heart ... but ... I have waited so long to get to this point. If it takes a few weeks, months, or longer for everything to work out, it will be worth it."

Stefani reaches up and pulls his head down to meet hers. "Damn it, Gavin Thorne, why didn't you say something to me back then?"

Gavin grins and softly kisses her lips. "Because I am a stupid, stupid fool."

Chapter 22

The morning sun peeks through the bedroom window, hitting Stefani in the eyes. She has been awake for hours thinking about moving back to Charlotte, the boys, her parents, and of course Gavin. She sits up gingerly, feeling like she's hung over, and softly rests her feet on the hardwood floor. After a long pause she stands, slips on a pair of shorts and a T-shirt, and works her way down to the kitchen. Joanna is sitting in a chair reading the newspaper. Stefani slowly slides into the chair across from her.

Joanna looks up at Stefani. "Good morning, honey. I didn't hear you come down."

"I'm just feeling a little slow today, Mom."

"Do you feel bad?"

Stefani looks at her mother and shakes her head. "I'm not sick, but I have no idea who I am anymore or where I'm headed."

Joanna folds up the paper and clasps her hands together. "That is totally expected."

"Maybe ... but there is so much more going on, which makes me a total basket case."

"Should I ask or leave it alone?"

Stefani begins to fumble with a napkin on the table. "Mom ... do you think things happen for a reason?"

"Yes, I do, why?"

"Do you think maybe David cheating on me and me losing my job was meant to happen?"

Joanna winces and shrugs her shoulders. "Honey, let me ask you ... what do you think?"

"Mom, I think it was."

"What makes you so sure?"

Stefani snickers and shifts her weight in her chair. "Are you sure you want to hear this story?"

"I guess there's only one way to find out."

"You know that I've gotten to know Gavin pretty well."

Joanna nods her head.

"Mom, would you say Dad is your soul mate?"

"Absolutely."

"When did you realize that?"

Joanna thinks for a moment and then glances at Stefani, who forces a funny grin.

"Stefani …"

"I know it sounds absurd, and you're right … I've only gotten to know him over a very short time but, Mom … he's the one."

"Stefani, I think you need to seriously think about what you're saying."

"I have, and, trust me, I have tried to look at it from every angle and every possibility, but I always come back to the same place. Mom … I love him."

Joanna stares at Stefani and then reaches out to hold her hand. She smiles and says, "So what are you going to do?"

Stefani takes a deep breath and exhales hard. "Exactly what Gavin told me to do."

"What's that?"

"Go back to Charlotte."

Joanna snaps her head back and shakes it. "What?"

"Gavin told me to."

"He told you to go back to Charlotte?"

"Yep."

"So he doesn't feel the same way you do?"

"Quite the contrary, Mom … he wants to spend the rest of his life with me."

Joanna flops back in her chair and drops her jaw. "Sweetheart, I'm sorry to say this, but I am totally confused. He loves you, you love him, he wants to spend the rest of his life with you, but he wants you to go back home to Charlotte?"

"This is exactly why I love him, Mom. He puts me and the boys first. He wants me to go back and make sure there is nothing left between David and me. He wants to make sure the boys could handle a move back here and deal with seeing David on a limited basis. He wants me to make sure I won't miss the city life and can be happy in St. Michaels. Mom, he wants to make sure I'm happy and totally at peace with my decisions."

Joanna sits quietly for a moment and then shakes her head. "Well, I must say it's hard not to admire the man."

"Mom, he's the man I was meant to be with."

Joanna wipes her hands off in her apron. "So what are you going to do?"

"I'm going to pack up my stuff in a few days and drive back to Charlotte. I figure with the money Gavin gave me, I can stay with Tonya for a while, then get a nice apartment for the boys and me until I find a job, and go from there. At least this way I'm not dependent on David for anything."

"Do you plan to leave David?"

Stefani sighs. "Yes, I do. I've thought it over, and I would have done this regardless of whether or not Gavin was in the picture."

"Stefani, you know a divorce will be very expensive and hard on the boys as well as you."

"Yes, but in the long run I know it's the best for the boys and me. Things can never be the same between David and me."

"Do you think you'd be so sure if you hadn't met Gavin?"

"I do, Mom. I really do."

"Well, you know your father and I are behind you whichever way you choose to go. Just please be careful … for the boys' sake as well as yours."

Stefani stands up, walks over, and hugs her mother. "I promise. I love you, Mom."

"I love you too, sweetheart."

Stefani returns upstairs, takes a shower, and gets dressed. She looks over and sees the sweatshirt hanging on the chair. She slips on her shoes and heads out to the car. She drives into downtown St. Michaels and walks from shop to shop, trying to clear her head. As if being led by the hand, she enters a small antique store and browses through the many items on display. Slowly scanning the articles in a glass cases, she notices an interesting locket. She bends over and is examining it more closely when she is startled by an elderly woman standing on the other side of the display case.

"I'm sorry. I didn't mean to frighten you, dear."

Stefani laughs. "That's okay."

"I'm the owner of the shop," the woman says. "Is there something I can help you with?"

Stefani leans over the glass case again and looks at the necklace. "I can't help but look at this locket and chain."

"My dear, that locket has been in this shop for roughly twenty years. Strangely, no one ever seems to notice it, but it is the most interesting item in our store."

"Really? It's beautiful." Stefani continues to look closely through the glass. "What makes it so special? Is it gold?"

The woman unlocks the case and reaches in to pick up the locket. "Yes, it's gold, but that has nothing to do with what makes it so precious."

After the shop's owner lays the piece on a velvet cloth, Stefani reaches out and softly touches the locket. "What makes it so special?"

"My dear … I'm going to tell you the most beautiful story this old body has ever heard."

The lady smiles and begins to speak, her voice becoming passionate. "In the late 1800s there was a captain of a huge merchant ship. His name was Galen Triggs … the best man on the sea. He was born and grew up right here in St. Michaels and was revered as a man of great honor and integrity. Legend has it men would line up and fight for the opportunity to sail with him. Many times he was approached by the town fathers about coming off the sea and being president of the town council, but he respectfully declined and claimed his place was on the water. His ship made runs up and down the eastern seaboard and would bring goods up the Chesapeake Bay. The thing that made him so well respected was he always put his crew first and never put them in harm's way. He was very protective, and the people of the town all knew what a great man he was. He always made the right decisions, and his men took comfort knowing he was in control."

Stefani pulls her hand back, afraid to touch the locket.

"It's okay ... pick it up."

She picks up the locket and cradles it in her hand. "It's beautiful."

"Yes, it is."

Stefani looks up at the elderly woman. "So it's because it belonged to this captain that it's special?"

"Yes, but I haven't told you the best part yet."

Fascinated, Stefani says, "Please tell me."

"Much to the disappointment of all the single women in St. Michaels, Captain Triggs was spoken for. Although he wasn't married, he'd promised his heart to a beautiful woman who lived here in St. Michaels, and they planned to wed. When

RAINDROPS

he wasn't at sea he was with her constantly, and their love was without equal. She always told him she wished she could go with him on his voyages, but he would never permit it. So … she went and had a golden locket made and had a picture of her put inside. She gave it to him to wear while he was at sea so she would always be with him and close to his heart. The men who sailed with him knew he wore the locket around his neck but never mentioned it because they knew how much he loved her. Some men claimed every hour he would undo a button on his shirt, pull the locked out, open it, and look at her picture. Then he would gently put it back and close his shirt."

Stefani caresses the locket. "That's a beautiful story."

"Oh, there's more, but unfortunately the story takes a turn."

The lady props herself up on a stool and rests her hands on the glass display case. "Captain Triggs and his crew set out on a voyage like they had done so many times before, but tragically, on the second night, a fire broke out in one of the lower decks. The men tried frantically to put it out, but in no time the ship was overcome with flames. Captain Triggs ordered all of the men into the lifeboats but refused to leave the ship. After many pleas from the crew, Captain Triggs ordered the men to get away from the ship before it sank."

Stefani is now clutching the locket in her hand. "Oh my God, that is so sad."

"Yes, but there's more, and it confirms what a special man he was. Captain Triggs always sailed with the same first mate, who also was his best friend. They grew up together here in St. Michaels. Once Captain Triggs knew all of his men were safely off the ship he approached the last lifeboat, where he best friend was. He took the locket from around his neck and asked the man to return the locket to his fiancée. It was said, by one of the other sailors, Captain Triggs was seen writing a note and carefully tucking it into the locket before giving it to his friend. The man held the locket tightly as they rowed away from the ship. Many tell how Captain Triggs stood bravely on the deck as he watched his men paddle to safety. Then the skies went black as the ship finally went under with Captain Triggs. As asked, his best friend delivered the locket to his fiancée, but no one to this day knows what was written and tucked into the locket."

"What happened to his fiancée?"

"No one knows for sure. It is my understanding she left St. Michaels and never returned. Some speculate she moved away to avoid the constant reminder of Captain Triggs. Some of the older folks around say she was so depressed and lost that she walked out into the bay and drowned herself in an effort to be with him. Honestly, I don't think anyone really knows, but no one denies the love they had for one another."

"That is one of the best stories I've ever heard. Thank you for sharing that with me."

"Dear, it was my pleasure."

"I don't understand, considering the story, why the locket isn't in one of the museums here in town."

"I don't know. Like I said, it's been in this case for years."

"If I may ask ... how did you acquire it?"

"One day a man walked in with it. He told me he had been to an estate sale, and he bought a box full of trinkets and jewelry. He was disappointed that after having the contents appraised it wasn't worth what he paid for it. He told me he sold most of the stuff at yard sales, but no one wanted the locket. So I bought it and took it home and showed my husband. After looking at it, he suggested I take it to a local jeweler here in town. The jeweler was a man almost ninety years old. When he looked at it under a magnifying glass he sat quietly for a minute. I got concerned and asked if he was okay. He looked at me with an astonished expression and told me his great-grandfather made it. He showed me his great-grandfather's logo he put on everything he made, and if you look on the back you can barely make it out. Then when he saw the initials 'GT' on the locket he knew it was Galen Triggs' because he had seen the work order in his great-grandfather's records."

"Did he offer to buy it from you?"

"No ... he just handed it back to me and smiled."

"I can't believe no one wanted it."

"Sadly, like most things in life, the significance wears off. Unless there is a sizeable monetary value to something ... people don't care. Unfortunately it seems this is how the world is today. Everyone is so caught up in material things, they've lost the understanding of what is truly important. Money can buy a lot of things, but it will never buy or replace the kind of love Captain Triggs and his fiancée shared."

Stefani opens the locket and sees a small engraving.

My love, we shall never be apart

Stefani looks up at the woman, who smiles and says, "Certainly says it all."

"I can't believe anyone would sell this if they knew the story."

"Unfortunately most don't know what it is to love someone that much anymore. Everyone is so caught up in this fast-paced rat race we call life they miss out on the most beautiful things. Most will never be lucky enough to know that kind of love"

Stefani stands totally still, looking at the locket resting in her hand. She then looks up at the elderly lady. "I'm almost ashamed to ask you this … how much is it?"

Honey, I think it's priceless because of what it means, not because of what it's made of."

Stefani carefully sets the locket down on the velvet cloth and sighs. She looks up at the lady and smiles. The lady smiles back and then reaches out to softly touch her on the hand. "I can tell by your eyes you have the same love in your heart for someone … the same love that Captain Triggs's fiancée felt … this locket deserves that kind of passion." The owner winks at Stefani. "I'll sell it for what I paid for it twenty years ago."

Stefani swallows hard, knowing gold doesn't go cheaply. She slowly nods. "Okay."

"Fifty dollars."

Stefani's eyes widen, and her chin drops. "I don't want to sound out of line, but this is worth far more than fifty dollars."

"Dear, there is no monetary value that applies to matters of the heart. You give this locket a good home, and fifty dollars is plenty."

Stefani puckers her lips and then releases a huge grin. "I'll take it."

The owner wraps it up nicely, places it in a small box, and hands it to Stefani. As she takes the box, she says, "I don't know what to say ... thank you."

The lady grins. "Something tells me there is a very special someone who will be the new owner of this locket."

Stefani looks down for a moment and then looks up. "Ma'am, you are truly amazing."

Stefani returns to her car and sits for a moment, staring into the distance. Then she reaches into the bag and pulls out the small box. She removes the locket and softly runs her finger over the initials engraved on the back. "GT ... Galen Triggs ... GT ... Gavin Thorne."

She pops the locket open and reads the inscription again.

My love, we shall never be apart

"I couldn't have phrased it any better."

She places the locket on the console and then picks up her cell phone and positions it to take a picture of herself. After a few tries she finally has an image she likes. She drives to the nearest pharmacy and has a copy of the picture printed and then purchases wrapping paper, tissue, paper, scotch tape, a pair of scissors, a small ribbon, and a bow. She drives to the local park and places everything on a picnic table. First she carefully pulls the locket from the box and gently opens it. She trims the photo, places it inside the locket, and secures it. She smiles as she sees the inscription opposite the picture. She closes it and wraps it in tissue paper. She then gently places the locket back in the box and wraps it carefully. Finally she puts the ribbon and bow on. The package is beautiful, almost too magnificent to open. She throws all the wrapping materials in the trash can, returns to her car, and tucks the small box into the glove compartment.

After sitting for a moment she pulls out her cell phone and creates a text message. "Gavin, I need to see you."

"Sure. is everything okay?"

"Yes. I just want to see you."

"Okay. I have a meeting early this afternoon, but I can cancel it."

"No, that's alright. I was hoping tonight."

"I'd really like that. May I ask a favor?"

"Yes, anything."

"Can we do something a bit out of the ordinary tonight?"

Stefani grins. "Okay ... should I be concerned?"

"Oh, no. LOL. Nothing like that. Just one more thing I'd like to show you."

"Sounds great."

"May I pick you up at your parents' house?"

"Sure. what time?"

"8"

"That works for me."

"Okay, see you then."

Stefani starts the car and heads back to her parents' house. She walks in and finds a note on the table. Her parents have gone into town to do some grocery shopping, so she goes upstairs and lies across the bed. She runs all the scenarios through her head. After doing so she finally sells herself on returning to Charlotte in the next few days. She is going to give opportunity the chance with the boys as well as her professional life. Her marriage, however, is over and done with; she's going to file for divorce and custody of the boys. This will certainly create tension with her sons, but she knows they can pull through it and will be better off because of it. She rolls onto her back and begins to think of Gavin. The only reason she is giving Charlotte one last shot is because he asked her to. She knows he has requested this in her best interest, but thoughts continually race through her head. *What if I land a new job? How do I go into it knowing I plan to leave in a matter of months? How long does he expect me to stay before he is sure that I'm sure I know that my life is here and not in Charlotte?*

Stefani rolls onto her side and softly punches the pillow. "Why does everything have to be so damn hard?"

She sits up and grabs her cell phone. She scrolls through her contact list and hits send. Moments later Tonya answers.

"Hey, girl."

"Stefani! How are you?"

"I am doing well. How about you?"

"Not bad. This trying to figure out what you're going to do when you grow up thing is hard."

Stefani laughs. "I hear you. Hey, I have a very big favor to ask … I'm almost too embarrassed to even approach you with it."

"Stef, you know there is no favor too big to ask me."

"Okay … do you think you have enough room in your house to accommodate one—at times three—guests for a little while?"

"Stef, if you're talking about you and the boys, I will be seriously pissed off if you stay anywhere else."

"Tonya, it would be for weeks possibly. Are you sure?"

"I don't care if it's for a year. I have plenty of room and would love to have you and the boys here. Honestly, Stef, I want you here. Ever since Limp-Dick Michael moved out, the place seems eerily empty anyway."

"Tonya, what would I have done all these years without you to lean on?"

"Hey, Stef?"

"Yes?"

"Just get your ass down here."

Stefani flops back on the bed, laughing. "Okay. I'll be there in a few days."

"I'll put a spare key under the yard gnome in the flower bed. If I'm not here when you arrive, just help yourself."

"Tonya, I really appreciate this."

"No problem. I'll see you soon."

"Okay, bye."

Stefani ends the call and stretches out on the bed. She stares at the ceiling and then runs her hands through her hair. She begins to smile uncontrollably. *Gavin Thorne, you're driving me insane!*

She sits up and sees her reflection in the mirror. She puffs out her cheeks and then exhales hard. She grins as she shakes her head and says out loud, "Stefani Tanner, he's the one … no matter how long it takes.

Chapter 23

Eight o'clock rolls around, and Gavin pulls into the driveway. Stefani is already off the porch and halfway down the driveway before he gets out of the car. "I was going to come up."

"It's okay … you've got me curious about this different plan you have for tonight."

Gavin laughs. "I hope you aren't expecting anything spectacular, I just wanted to do something together that I have done for years by myself." He looks over at Stefani and blushes. "Ah … that didn't sound quite like I meant it to."

Stefani breaks out into rolling laughter as she climbs into the passenger side of the car. "You sure about that?"

He buckles his seat belt and starts the car. "Oh, I'm quite sure of that."

The two laugh as he pulls away from the driveway, and she looks at him with a beaming smile. Gavin glances at her and grins. "What?"

Stefani smiles harder and shakes her head. "Nothing."

"Nothing? You're looking at me and smiling, and … nothing?"

She reaches over and squeezes his hand. "Just another thing that makes me love you more."

Gavin gives her a rueful look. "Not exactly one of my prouder moments."

Stefani continues to hold his hand. "So where are we going?"

"It's a place I enjoy going to … but please don't expect much."

"Okay … should I guess?"

He laughs. "No, trust me, it's not even worth the guess. It's nothing really … just special to me."

"Well, I'm sure it will be special to me, too."

After a fifteen-minute drive he turns onto a dirt lane. Roughly a half mile later they reach a clearing. Gavin stops the car, and Stefani looks the area over. They're at a secluded beach surrounded by trees, with no houses in sight. The beach resembles a deserted island.

Stefani turns to Gavin. "So this is your special place?"

"Yes … are you disappointed?"

"No, not at all."

"Want to get out?"

"Okay."

Gavin gets out and pops the trunk open. He pulls out two blankets, two pillows, and a small cooler.

Stefani stands still. "If I didn't know better, I'd think you planned on taking advantage of me."

Gavin walks toward the beach. "That, my dear, is something you never have to worry about."

She watches as he spreads out the blanket, drops the two pillows, and sets the cooler beside the blanket. He turns and extends his hand. "Would you like to sit with me?"

"Yes, I would."

He reaches into the cooler and pulls out a bottle of wine and two glasses. He pours the wine and hands a glass to her.

Stefani puckers her lips and then grins. "Gavin, I thought you said you wouldn't try to take advantage of me."

Gavin takes a sip of his wine and then smiles. "Well ... not in the sense you're thinking of."

She quickly turns her head and sucks her lips in. "I see."

The sun has set, and stars are beginning to appear in the sky. Gavin pushes his glass down into the sand and lies on his side, propping himself up on his elbow. Stefani studies his every movement.

"So what makes this place so special?"

Gavin takes a deep breath. "I don't know if anyone other than me ever comes out here. But over years I have, and I've spent many hours here."

"Doing what?"

"Thinking."

Stefani turns, pushes her glass down into the sand, and then lies down on the blanket as Gavin's mirror image. "Thinking about what?"

He looks up and remains quiet for a few seconds. The sky is beaming brightly with stars. He fluffs a pillow, puts it under his head, and then lies flat on his back looking up in the sky. "Look."

She too fixes a pillow and lies beside Gavin to look up into the sky. "You think about the stars?"

Gavin reaches over, wraps his arm around her, and pulls her close. He pulls the other blanket over top of her. "Well, kind of."

"I don't understand."

He lies totally still. "Many years ago I named this place."

"What did you name it?"

Continuing to look up, he says quietly, "Stefani's Cove."

"Really? ... So what's the story behind this place?"

"I hope this doesn't sound ridiculous."

"Tell me."

"When you went away to college I used to come out here a lot. I came out here in the spring, summer, fall, and winter. I did exactly what we're doing now. I'd stare up into the sky and look at the stars."

Stefani lies still and looks at the sky. "It's beautiful."

"Yes, it is, but that's not why I would lie here for hours and look up."

"Why did you?"

Gavin pulls her closer. "I hope you don't think I'm weird."

"Please tell me. I want to know."

Gavin rubs his chin with his hand and then stares off into the sky. "I would lie here and think maybe you were possibly looking up at the stars at the same time I was. Even if for only a second, we might be looking at the same thing … almost like we were sharing a moment together. The thought somehow helped fill the emptiness I felt when you left. Over the years I came here fewer and fewer times until I stopped totally. I think it's because I finally accepted you were gone forever. Then, as if I was given a second chance, you were in the restaurant telling your story. That night I came out here for the first time in a long time. I imagined there was a chance you were sitting on your parents' porch thinking about what you had been through and looking at the stars. Once again I imagined we could be sharing a moment together. So many times I prayed for just that … a moment when just you and I shared the stars together. Like the entire sky belonged to only you and me."

Stefani rolls over onto Gavin's chest. Her guard is totally dropped as she looks him passionately in the eyes. "Gavin, I love you so much."

She slowly lets her head fall as their lips softly touch. When she lifts her head, she notices a sparkle in his eye.

"Stefani, I thought about this very moment for so long it hurt. Every time I would get up and go home I felt like a small part of me died. It was like I lost you over and over again."

"I promise you, Gavin … you will never feel that pain again."

"I remember the day I found out you were going away to college. I got in my car and just drove with no idea where I was headed. I eventually stumbled upon this beach. I had never been here before, nor did I know it even existed. I sat in my car and looked out over the water thinking of you leaving and how you were never coming back. I must have sat here for hours. The sun was setting, and it began to rain lightly. Then for some reason I began to focus on the raindrops as they hit the windshield. Each landed at random locations and would slowly trickle down. As they did, they would move back and forth, sometimes stop, then begin to fall again. It was as if they had no idea where they were going. Then I noticed two drops hit very closely to one another. Each one moved erratically, back and forth, coming close to one another but never touching. Then, as if drawn to one another, the two converged, making one big drop, and it raced in a straight line to the bottom of the windshield. Looking back on that I think the raindrops were a lot like us. Many times we traveled so close to one another but never joined. Then finally, by chance, we unite and become one big drop. The confusion of where to go and what to do is over, and we travel in a straight line together. The two drops traveled much faster as one, but I think when you're truly in love you become one, and because things are so wonderful … the time will seem to fly by. The journey is then perfect. I think we were two raindrops making our way through life and finally we are now one … we are complete."

Again she leans forward, and their lips meet. As their lips slowly separate, Gavin sighs intensely. "Stefani, you are the only love I've ever truly known. I have and always will love you with all my heart. You are everything to me."

Stefani smiles and softly kisses his lips once more. She lies down beside him again and looks up. "Let's make one of these stars ours. That way if we're ever apart we can look up at the same star and be together."

"I already picked one out."

"You did? When?"

"Oh... a little over twenty years ago."

She laughs. "Okay, which one?"

He points up into the sky. "See the Big Dipper? Now run a straight line through the two stars opposite the handle. See how it points to that one star?"

"Yes."

"That's Polaris, the North Star. That's our star."

"Why the North Star? It's not the brightest star in the sky."

"That's true, but many of the stars can only been seen during certain times of the year. No matter what time of year it is, I can always see the North Star. It is constant … always there … just like my feelings for you."

Stefani reaches over and gently turns Gavin's head to face her. "Gavin, I want you to do something for me."

"Anything."

She softly runs her finger across his lips. "Make love to me."

Stefani lies flat on her back as Gavin turns and stares into her eyes. He slowly leans forward to kiss her and then pauses. Stefani blinks as her body completely relaxes. She is totally at peace and is oblivious to everything but Gavin. Tenderly he kisses her lips and then her neck. She rubs the back of his head as her breathing intensifies. Her exhalations turn to soft moans when he reaches down and runs his fingertips on the inside of her thighs. He slowly undoes her belt and unbuttons her shorts, and then his hand slides down inside her shorts along her hip. Her shorts slip off with no resistance as they slide down her shaply toned thighs. He runs his hand up her side and then across her chest to the buttons on her blouse. With little effort he undoes each, and her blouse falls open. He undoes her bra and looks down at her soft breasts as he gently runs his hand across her firm nipples. Stefani has her eyes closed and arches her back as she moans softly. Gavin leans forward and covers her nipple with his lips as Stefani wraps her arms around his head and pulls him tight. He pulls away and rocks back on his shins. Stefani opens her eyes and watches his face as he takes off his shirt and then reaches down with both hands and bit by bit slips her panties off. Gently he rests his chest on her thighs putting most of his weight on his elbows. He runs his palms up across her flat stomach and over each breast. Again he rocks back onto his shins and undoes his belt and shorts and slips them off. Tenderly he lies on top of Stefani and stares into her eyes. He kisses her and then runs his lips down the center of her chest to her stomach. Stefani shivers and lets out a loud sigh as Gavin positions himself between her legs. She reaches down and grabs his lower back with both hands, momentarily opening her eyes to see their star. She closes her eyes and begins to breathe rapidly as he cradles her face with his hands and enters her with one gentle thrust. Stefani arches her back, releasing another cry of ecstasy. Gavin begins a slow, rhythmic motion while kissing her neck. The speed and intensity of his thrusts increase, causing Stefani to hyperventilate as she moans uncontrollably. She wraps her hands around Gavin's back and digs her fingernails into his skin. He pushes himself up and thrusts harder and deeper. Stefani is on the verge of passing out as she feels herself losing control. Her body is shivering intensely, and she cries out as she reaches the point of no return and climaxes. He simultaneously releases a cry as he explodes deeply within her and then collapses on top of her, totally spent and gasping for air.

He picks up his head and looks at her. She slowly opens her eyes as he lightly kisses her and whispers, "You are too good to be true."

Stefani reaches up and places her hand against the side of his face. "Gavin … I know I don't deserve you, but I'm never letting go of you. I never knew love could be such a powerful thing, and I have you to thank for showing me that."

He brushes a piece of hair from her forehead, and then he smiles. She tilts her head and grins. "What?"

"There were so many times I knew this would never happen. I resigned myself to the reality some things aren't meant to be. But for some reason I'm here with you, and I have confirmed one thing."

"What's that?"

"You, Stefani Tanner, were worth every second of the wait."

Stefani grins as she pops her head up and places a kiss on Gavin's nose.

He laughs. "But can you do me a favor?"

Stefani squints and turns her head slightly. "And that would be?"

"Please don't make me wait so long next time."

They both laugh, and then Gavin rolls over onto his back and sighs. Stefani turns onto her side and pulls his head next to hers. "That, Mr. Thorne, is a promise."

The two lay there holding each other while staring up at the stars. "Gavin, there is so much that I have ignored and left unnoticed. You have shown me more in the short time we have been together than I ever noticed in my entire life."

He turns his head and looks at her. "When are you leaving?"

She remains quiet for a moment and then turns and looks at him. "In a few days."

He turns his head back and looks at the sky. "That's good. You need to put everything in perspective so you know exactly what makes you happy."

"I know one thing that has made me happy."

He takes a deep breath. "Will I get to see you before you leave?"

"Gavin, I couldn't leave without seeing you."

Gavin turns and smiles. "I feel like I'm losing you all over again."

Stefani lightly touches his cheek. "Gavin, you will never lose me again. I love you, and I know I belong with you. Once I get everything in order, we will never have to feel this pain again."

"That's all I ever wanted."

She smiles and pulls him close. "Gavin, if it's okay I'd like to spend tomorrow with my parents. There are obviously some things I want to tell them, and I have to pack. That way I can leave early the following day."

"That sounds like a good idea."

"I'll come by and see you on my way out if it's okay?"

"Stefani, anytime you want to see me is okay."

She smiles and shakes her head. "Gavin, you'll never know how much I care for you."

Gavin winks. "I look forward to finding out."

Chapter 24

Stefani is packed and ready for the long drive to Charlotte. As she pulls away from her parents' house, a sense of sadness and guilt comes over her. While she drives she thinks about the time she spent home with her parent and with Gavin. It all seems so right, yet she has the boys to consider as well as the promise she made to Gavin. She parks next to his car and walks in.

Jean is sitting at her desk and smiles at Stefani. "Hello, Ms. Tanner. May I help you?"

"Yes ... is Mr. Thorne available?"

"I believe so. Let me check."

Jean picks up the phone and calls Gavin's office. She hangs up the phone and says, "Mr. Thorne will be right with you."

Moments later Gavin walks down the long corridor. Stefani looks up and smiles when he stops in front of her,

"Good morning, Ms. Tanner. How may I help you?"

Stefani stands and asks, "Is there any chance we can take a short walk?"

"Absolutely."

Gavin turns toward Jean. "Jean, I'll be unavailable for a little while."

"I understand, Mr. Thorne I'll hold your calls."

Gavin and Stefani walk out the large back door and stroll along the cobblestone walkway leading toward the water. Gavin slips his hands into his pockets while Stefani walks with her arms crossed. They stop at the end of the walk and look over the water. A slight breeze softly blows Stefani's hair away from her face. She's sure that Gavin can see the tears building in her eyes.

"Do you have everything you need?"

Stefani quickly wipes her eye and nods. Gavin looks down and scuffs his shoe across the cobblestones. She turns and forces a smile as she approaches him. She reaches out and straightens the knot on his tie. "You know, you really look nice in a suit."

"Think so?"

"Yes, I do."

He reaches up and wraps his hands around hers. "Stefani, please talk to me."

She quickly pulls out a tissue from her pocket and wipes her eyes. "I don't know what to say."

"Just tell me what you're thinking."

Stefani looks out over the water and then back at Gavin. "I'm thinking I'm standing in front of the man I want to be with, and I have to leave."

"I know ... but for now it's for the best." He lifts her chin with his fingers. "If and when you decide to come back ... I'll be here waiting."

Stefani smiles through the tears streaming down her cheeks. "Gavin, I want so badly to be mad at you for making me do this."

Gavin laughs as he pulls her tight and hugs her. "Trust me ... I'm mad at me enough for both of us."

She gently punches him in the chest. "I'm not so sure about that."

He takes her by the hand and leads her to a bench, where they both sit. Gavin puts his arm around her and rubs her arm. "Time sure is a funny thing."

"What do you mean?"

"Twenty years of wondering where you were, how you were, what you were doing seemed like an eternity. Then we are together for a short time, and in a flash those days are behind us. Now we are going to be apart again, and I'm sure it will feel like forever again."

Stefani leans into him and rests her head against his shoulder. "Hopefully not too long." She reaches into her bag and pulls out the small box. She holds it in her hands and slowly runs the ribbon between her fingers. "I got you something."

"Stefani, you didn't need to get me anything."

"Well, it's not much, but I saw it in an antique store. When the lady told me the story behind it, I knew it was meant for you."

Stefani hands Gavin the box. He holds it for a moment, looks out over the water, and clinches his lips. She is puzzled by his expression. "What's wrong?"

He slowly shakes his head. "Nothing … I was just …" He stops and looks off into the distance.

"Gavin?"

He takes a deep breath and sighs hard. "I'm afraid."

She reaches over and grabs his hand. "What are you afraid of?"

Gavin takes a moment to gather himself and then turns to her. "That you're not coming back."

Stefani slides closer to him and reaches up to softly touch his face. "Gavin, I'm coming back. I know this is meant to be. I know I have to work out the details with my sons and tie up things with David, but I'm coming back."

He looks down at the box and weakly smiles. "Stefani, are you sure that's fair to you?"

"Am I sure it's fair? Yes … why?"

"Because I'm making you leave a life you made for yourself and your family."

"Gavin, I'm coming back because I love you and want a life with you. It doesn't matter where it happens just as long as I'm with you."

Gavin looks down at the small package. He removes the wrapping paper and slowly pulls the lid off the box. He moves the tissue paper aside and lifts the locket. "Stefani, this is beautiful."

Stefani smiles. "Do you really like it?"

"Yes, I do … thank you."

"Before you open the locket, let me tell you about it."

"Okay."

"According to legend, a very well-known and respected sea captain promised his heart to a woman, a woman he planned to marry. Because they missed each other so much when he was on the water, the woman had this locket made for him so no matter where he was she was always with him … now open it."

Gavin pushes the small button on top of the locket, and it opens. He spreads it apart and sees the picture of Stefani and the inscription on the opposite side. He stares at it and smiles.

Stefani continues, "Once the captain put it around his neck, he never took it off. Every hour the captain would open the locket and look at her picture and read the inscription. He would then carefully close it and tuck it back into his shirt."

Gavin continues to hold the locket in his hand. "I can see why."

Stefani sighs. "On his last voyage the ship caught fire and sank. But before he went down with the ship, he tucked a note into the locket and gave it to the first mate, who was also his best friend, and told him to give it back to his fiancée."

"That's terrible … what did the note say?"

"No one knows … but I'm sure it was something very special. Legend has it his fiancée just faded away. After that it became just another piece of jewelry. Then years later someone figured they wanted to sell it. It's sad to think someone may have known the story behind the locket and sold it anyway."

Gavin leans over and gently kisses her on her cheek. "Thank you. This is the nicest thing anyone has ever given me."

Gavin puts it the locket around his neck and slips it under his collar. He positions it under his shirt in the center of his chest, and then he undoes the two middle buttons on his shirt and pulls the locket through and opens it. He smiles when he sees Stefani's picture, and then he reads the inscription aloud, "*My love, we shall never be apart.*" He closes the locket and looks at it more closely. "You had my initials engraved on it."

"No … those were the captain's initials as well. His name was Galen Triggs."

"Wow … that's kind of amazing."

"From what I was told he was an extraordinary man … so I think the initials fit."

Gavin tucks the locket in his shirt and redoes the buttons. He fixes his tie and turns to Stefani. "I will never take it off."

She smiles and leans toward him. They kiss and then touch foreheads for a moment.

Gavin grins. "Sweetheart, you better get on the road so you can get to Charlotte before dark."

"I know."

Gavin walks her to her car and opens the door. He watches her fasten her seat belt, and then he closes the door. She quickly starts the car and rolls down the window. She reaches out, holds his hand, and begins to tear up. "Gavin, I don't want to go."

"I know."

Gavin leans into the car and kisses her as she holds his head with both hands. As their lips separate, he smiles. "Be careful, and call me when you get there."

"Okay. You have Tonya's address, right?"

"Yes, I do."

"Just in case you get the urge to stop by."

Gavin laughs. "I'll always have that urge."

Stefani puts on her sunglasses. As she backs up she rolls up the window. She stops, drops the car into drive, and begins to pull away. She mouths "I love you" as the car rolls toward the lane. Gavin mouths the same in return and pats his chest where the locket is located. Stefani looks in the rearview mirror as Gavin waves. After she makes the first turn on the lane, he is out of sight.

Chapter 25

Two weeks later

Every morning Stefani is greeted with an early morning text message, and every evening she and Gavin share a heartwarming conversation. Although they stay in constant touch, the time apart gets more painful each day. After exchanging text messages with Gavin this morning, Stefani and Tonya decide they will attack the weed-filled flowerbeds out front. Certainly helping Tonya is of the utmost importance, but it will also help to keep Stefani's mind off the fact the boys are with David and Gavin is in St. Michaels.

As Stefani leans forward to tie her shoelaces, she hears a knock at the front door. Stefani leans forward to peek out of her bedroom door. Tonya left the house about fifteen minutes earlier to pick up some gloves and a six-pack of beer. Stefani stands and walks toward the door. She can see the silhouette of a man through the sheers that cover the large glass door. She walks over, peeks through, and finds a FedEx driver standing with a box. She opens the door. "Hello."

"Hello, ma'am. Are you Stefani Tanner?"

"Yes, I am."

"I have a package for you."

"Okay."

"Ma'am, if you'll just sign right here."

Stefani signs and thanks him. She holds the box and closes the door as she tries to read the label. She walks into the living room, sits down on the couch, and tucks her leg under her. She reaches over and picks up a letter opener off the end table and cuts the brown cardboard box open. After removing the packing material she pulls out a smaller box with an envelope attached. She frees the envelope from the box and opens it. It contains a small card.

> *Something to track the time until we're together.*
>
> *Love, Gavin.*

Stefani bites down on her thumbnail and smiles. She removes the wrapping paper and reveals a beautiful leather box. She rocks the hinged lid back and finds an exquisite Patek Philippe watch. "Oh, Gavin."

She takes it from the box and puts it on her wrist. She stares at it for a moment and begins to grin uncontrollably. She picks up her cell phone and creates a new text message. "Hope you're having a great day."

"It just got better."

"I knew it was time to text you."

"Oh?"

"Yes … I received a beautiful watch a few minutes ago."

"Do you like it?"

"Gavin, it's beautiful. I love it, but it's too expensive to wear."

"No, it's not. Know how I know this?"

"How?"

"I wear this priceless locket around my neck every day that is not only beautiful on the outside but twice as precious on the inside. I look forward to seeing the watch on you."

"Me, too." I miss you so much."

"I miss you, too."

"I'll talk to you soon."

"All my love."

Stefani sets the phone down, takes off the watch, and puts it into box. She takes it into her bedroom and tucks it safely into her dresser drawer. She hears Tonya enter the house with the gloves and beer. "Okay, Tonya, let's get to some yard work," she says as she returns to the living room.

"What do you say we take a break?"

Stefani laughs. "A break? We haven't started yet."

Tonya puts the gloves on the table, pulls a beer from the six-pack, and hands it to Stefani. She pulls another one and then puts the other four into the refrigerator. "Yeah … what do you say we talk?"

Stefani, somewhat confused, agrees. Both sit down on the couch. Tonya takes a huge swallow and then licks her lips dry. "Stef, obviously things aren't going well between you and David. What's the latest?"

Stefani smiles and then takes a sip. "Tonya, I'm leaving."

"Leaving? What do you mean leaving? You just got here."

Stefani takes a deep breath and lets her head fall backward against the couch. "I'm going to tie up the loose ends down here, and then I'm going home."

"Home as in …" When Stefani turns and smiles, Tonya grins back and nods. "Gavin."

Tonya lays her head back and smiles. "Stef … that's a good thing."

"I love him."

Tonya rests her beer on the end table and then rubs her eyes. "I knew something was up when you called and asked if you could stay here with me."

"Really? How could you tell?"

"Just the way you sounded on the phone and how happy you have been since you've been here. Although there seems to be a bit of sorrow thrown in, it doesn't seem to have anything to do with David."

"Geez, Tonya, am I really that easy to read?"

"Sometimes life has a funny way of treating a person, but for some reason this seems right."

"You really think so?"

"Yeah, I do."

"How can you be so sure?"

"Stef ... I've known you for a long time, and I love you like a sister, but ... you were never meant for this place."

"What's that supposed to mean?"

Tonya sits up. "Just wait before you get your thong in a knot." She turns and faces Stefani. "Sure, you are the most successful businesswoman I've ever known. You're a great mother, were a great wife to an absolute asshole, and a tremendous friend to everyone."

"You make that sound like a crime."

"No ... but, with the exception of your boys, you never really seemed happy here."

Stefani puts her beer on the coffee table and looks at her friend in surprise. "What do you mean I was never happy here?"

"Stef, you always made everyone around you happy … but yet there always seemed to be something missing. It's like there was a part of you that was locked up and dying to get out and couldn't. Maybe you were afraid to let that side of you show because you'd appear sensitive, and that would be unacceptable in the business world because you'd be perceived as weak or vulnerable."

Tonya picks her beer up and takes another swallow. "Personally, I think it's something else."

"And what might that be?"

"I don't think David ever had what it takes to reach that deeply into your soul."

Stefani pulls her legs up to her chest and rests her chin on her knees. Tonya smiles and finishes her beer. "But … Gavin obviously has been holding the key to that part of you. And, from what you tell me, he's patiently guarded that key for over twenty years. I see it in your eyes and see it in your smile. He's in your heart."

Stefani smiles and bows her head. "Tonya, you always knew how to make me feel good."

"As much as it hurts me to say this … I'm glad you're leaving."

Stefani looks up and gives her a questioning look, and Tonya quickly snaps her head to the side. "Stef, go back and let this man give you everything you and the boys deserve. Let him love you and make you happy."

Stefani wraps her arms around Tonya, who quickly clinches back. "Tonya, I love you."

"I know you do … I love you, too."

As the two separate, Stefani squeezes Tonya's hand. "You'll come visit me, right?"

Tonya smiles. "Girl, who do you think you're talking to? I'm going to be the maid of honor!"

"You're damn right you are."

Tonya stands and grabs her gloves. "Alright, let's go kick some weed-ass!"

Stefani breaks out into laughter. She pulls her phone from her pocket and enters a text to Gavin. "I love you."

Chapter 26

Three days have gone by with no text messages or calls from Gavin. Stefani picks up her phone and enters a new text message. "Hope things are okay."

She sits down on the couch and waits, muttering, "Why isn't he returning my messages?"

Stefani stands up, walks toward the deck, and begins to dial Gavin's office. Suddenly she stops. *I can't do that. Maybe he's been involved in a big meeting. Or maybe my phone isn't working.*

She starts to pace. "Damn it!"

Tonya enters the room. "Still nothing, huh?"

"No ... but I'm sure there's a good explanation."

As Stefani flops down in the chair, there's a knock at the door. She stands and sees the silhouette of a man through the shears.

"Gavin!"

Her heart begins to race as she jets to the door. She quickly opens the door and is dazed when she realizes the man standing in front of her is Duncan Davidson.

"Ms. Tanner, do you remember me?"

Stefani remains in her trance but then suddenly snaps out, "Yes … I'm sorry. You're Mr. Davidson from Perceptive Insight."

Duncan gives her a smile that doesn't reach his eyes. "Yes … may I talk to you?"

Stefani steps backward, confused. "Yes … please come in. This is my friend Tonya Conner."

"Hello, Ms. Conner, it's a pleasure to meet you."

Tonya shakes his hand. "Same here."

Stefani looks at Tonya and is totally baffled. "Mr. Davidson, may I get you something to drink?"

"No, I'm fine … thank you."

Tonya, obviously sensing the uneasiness, tries to break the tension. "Why don't you two go in and sit down?"

Duncan has a seat in a chair, and Stefani sits opposite him on the love seat. "How can I help you, Mr. Davidson?"

"Please call me Duncan."

"Okay."

"Are your sons here?"

"No, they're with their father."

Duncan flops back in the chair. "Ms. Tanner …"

"Please … Stefani."

"Stefani …" Duncan pauses as he stares at his hands resting in his lap. "Stefani, I have some bad news … some very bad news."

Tonya walks over and sits next to Stefani. Stefani's hands begin to tremble as she covers her lips with her fingers. "What is it?"

Duncan leans forward, rests his elbows on his knees, and clasps his hands. "Stefani, the day you left St. Michaels to return here was the worst day in Gavin's life. He went into his office and sat at his desk. He stared out the window for hours and never took a call or left his chair. Finally at six that evening, after everyone left, I walked in and asked him what was wrong. He told me how his heart fell apart as he watched you drive off and how he feared you weren't coming back. I told him everything would work out, but he just sat and stared out the window with the emptiest expression. Then he turned and looked at me and told me everything."

Duncan manages a weak smile. "That day he first saw you so many years ago. You could see the happiness in his eyes as he described you. He was totally overwhelmed by you. You were all he could think about. Then when he found out you were going away to college … he was crushed. He knew you were gone for good and he'd never get the chance to know you or get close to you."

Stefani pulls her legs up to her chest and wraps her arms around them. Tonya puts her arm around Stefani as Duncan's voice begins to weaken. "Then that wonderful day when he saw you in the restaurant. He felt guilty for listening in on your conversation but told me what you had been through. Even though he felt your pain, I saw a sparkle in his eye I had never seen before."

Duncan begins to tear up and pulls a handkerchief from his pocket to wipe his eye.

Stefani takes a deep breath. "Duncan, you're scaring me."

Duncan regains his composure and sighs. "The next morning Gavin arrived at the office. He called our attorney, and four days later we had a meeting. He told us how he'd been up nights thinking and finally realized there was nothing to think about, and he couldn't believe it took him that long to recognize the answer was so simple. He announced he was leaving St. Michaels. He was going to sell his home and move to Charlotte. His exact words were, 'I lost her once, and she came back. Now I've pushed her away. I'm not going to lose her again.' He contacted a real estate agent in the Charlotte area to find a condo and an office building. He was going to expand our company by opening an office down here."

Gavin takes a deep breath and folds his handkerchief.

"After the meeting he came into my office and told me he loved me and hoped I wasn't mad at him. I told him there was no way I could be mad at him and totally understood why he was leaving. He scheduled his pilot to fly him out three nights ago. I begged him to wait until the next morning because there was a terrible storm going through, but the pilot assured him they could fly out over the ocean and go around the storm and arrive in Charlotte safely. As he climbed into his car that evening to drive to the airport, he looked at me and smiled and said he wasn't going to wait another day to be with you."

Stefani is slowly rocking back and forth on the couch as tears stream down her face. Duncan again wipes his eyes and sighs heavily. "The last radio conversation between the tower in Easton and the pilot was the plane's electrical system had gone out … no one has any idea why. The gauges and instruments weren't functioning, so the pilot was totally disoriented and had no idea what direction he was flying. The tower tried to direct him on course, and he fought to keep the plane in the air for about ten minutes …"

Duncan bows his head and then slowly looks up with tears racing down his cheeks. "Then the plane disappeared off the radar."

Stefani gasps for breath. "What does that mean … off the radar?"

Duncan lets the tears flow down his cheeks. "The plane went down into the ocean."

Stefani begins to hyperventilate as she cries hysterically. She screams out and starts to fall onto her side. Tonya catches and holds her. Stefani grabs her hair with both hands. "No, God … please, no."

Duncan stands and walks over to help hold her. The two embrace her as she continues to cry. "Gavin, no … please, no."

Stefani lifts her head and looks at Duncan. "Please, Duncan, tell me this isn't true. Tell me he's okay. Please, Duncan, please!"

Duncan rests her head against his shoulder as tears run down his face. "Stefani, I'd give anything to make this not true,"

Stefani falls back against the couch. She turns to Tonya and in a broken voice whimpers, "Now I know why Gavin hasn't returned my text messages."

Tonya reaches out and grabs a box of tissue. Stefani takes a few and wipes her eyes. "Where is he now?"

Duncan leans back in the love seat and shakes his head. He looks at Stefani and squints his eyes in what looks like an attempt to keep the tears from running.

Stefani takes a deep breath and firmly repeats her question. "Duncan, where is Gavin now?"

He closes his eyes and then opens them slowly. "The impact was so intense … the plane disintegrated. Only parts of the plane were recovered. The Coast Guard combed the area for two days … There were search planes, helicopters, and divers … no bodies were found."

Stefani bows her head and begins to cry again. Duncan slides across from Stefani and sits on the coffee table.

Duncan takes a deep breath. "The Coast Guard did recover something."

Stefani slowly looks up. "What?"

He looks away but then turns back to her. "There was a flotation cushion with a strobe attached, the kind of thing a person would hold onto so they could be found in the water. It's actually what helped the Coast Guard locate the crash site about thirty miles off the coast of Chincoteague Island. Gavin's rain jacket was tied around it tightly by the sleeves. In the pocket was a note addressed to me. Somehow the pocket stayed sealed and kept the note dry."

Stefani works to breathe slowly and deeply. "What did it say?"

Duncan again begins to well up. He quickly collects himself and closes his eyes. "Duncan, please make sure Stefani gets this."

He reaches into his pocket and pulls out a folded-up cloth. He unfolds the cloth to reveal the locket. Stefani tilts her head backward and collapses against Tonya. "Oh, Gavin."

The two manage to get Stefani to her bedroom and lay her down on the bed. Duncan looks at Tonya. "What can I do?"

"I don't know."

Duncan nods. "Should I go?"

Tonya forces a weak smile. "Maybe for now."

"I'll be at the Hyatt if you need anything."

"Thanks."

Duncan hands Tonya the locket and leaves. Tonya sits beside Stefani and rubs her arm as she continues to sob uncontrollably. Tonya begins to tear up. "Stef, I'm so, so sorry. I don't know why things like this happen."

She places the locket beside Stefani's hand. "Stef, is there anything I can get you?"

Stefani pulls a pillow tightly against her chest. "No ... I just want to be alone."

Tonya leans over and kisses Stefani on the forehead. "I'll be right in the other room. If you need anything, call me."

Tonya closes the bedroom door. The room darkens, and Stefani buries her face into the pillow. She turns her head to the side and focuses on a patch of sunlight peeking through the curtains. "Gavin ... we had so much to do."

As she stares at the light, her body goes into shutdown, and she falls into a deep sleep.

Chapter 27

Stefani slowly wakens, still exhausted from the trauma thrown upon her. She lies motionless, running everything through her head. As she rolls onto her back, she slides her arm up to rub her eyes. As she does she bumps the locket. She slowly picks it up and briefly closes her eyes hard, trying to hold back the tears. She takes a deep breath and sighs as she pushes the button down, opening the locket. When she spreads the halves apart, a small piece of folded paper falls out onto her stomach. She reaches down, picks up the paper, and unfolds it.

My Love,

> *As I sit here knowing the end is near, I'm sure I understand what was going through the captain's mind. Stefani, your love has changed me in ways you'll never know. You touched my heart in ways no one ever has and made me feel alive. Because of you I know what love truly is. Although I know I'll never get to hold you or kiss you again, I want you to know my love for you will never weaken, and I will always be with you.*
>
> *All my love,*
> *Gavin*

Stefani covers her face with her hand and begins to cry as she slowly rolls onto her side. "Gavin, why … why did you leave me?"

Tonya enters the room. "Stefani?"

Stefani sits up and rests her back against the headboard of the bed. Oddly, she quickly gains control of her emotions. "Tonya, I don't understand. Why did this happen?"

"Honey, I wish I had an answer for you. I know how much he means to you."

Stefani looks at Tonya and hands her the note. Tonya takes the note and reads it. "Oh, Stef … I wish I knew what to say to make you feel better." She reaches out and hugs Stefani. "Tonya, I was going to marry him. We were going to share a life together … a life only a short time ago I never believed could be real. I thought people like Gavin only existed in fairy tales."

Stefani takes the note back from Tonya, carefully folds it, and closes it in the locket. "He was such a special person, so giving, so loving, so honest … he was my soul mate."

Tonya leans back and forces a smile as she fights back her own tears. "I know he was."

"Tonya, I'm going to St. Michaels."

"Are you sure you're ready for that?"

"Yes … I need to be there more than anything right now."

While Stefani packs, Tonya sits on the bed repeatedly begging to help, but she politely refuses and continues to arrange her clothes in her suitcase. She opens the top dresser drawer, stops, and stares at the leather watch box.

Tonya reaches out and touches Stefani's back. "Are you okay?"

Stefani nods and turns. "Yes."

She gently lifts the box from the drawer and hands it to Tonya. "Gavin sent me this a few days ago. It was so I could keep track of the time until we would be together again."

Tonya opens the box, revealing the watch. "Oh, Stef, it's beautiful."

Stefani smiles. "Yeah … I told him it was too beautiful to wear. Of course he disagreed."

Tonya slowly shuts the box and hands it back. Stefani stands still, closes her eyes, and begins to smile. "God, I swear it's like I can feel him here with me now. I can feel his breath on my face and the warmth of his body as he stands against me. I'm actually waiting to feel his arms wrap around me and hold me." She opens her eyes and shakes her head. "It just doesn't seem possible that he's gone."

She carefully packs the watch box into one of the smaller bags. She then crosses her arms and sits next to Tonya on the bed. "I love him so much."

Tonya reaches over and holds her hand. "Stef … think about how amazing you are."

"How amazing I am?"

"Yes."

"How do you figure?"

"Stefani, there was a man whose heart waited for you for over twenty years…twenty years! A man who loved you so much, yet at that time knew so little about you but knew you were the one God put on this earth for him. A man who loved you so much he was leaving everything behind to spend the rest of his life with you. Your happiness was—by far—the most important thing in his life."

Tonya reaches out and touches Stefani's hand that is holding the locket.

"Honey, the note he wrote you and tucked into the locket … that wasn't written by a man who was angry about dying or felt like he was being cheated. That note was written by a man whose heart was so full of love and thankfulness. Stefani, you showed that man what it felt like to live … to love … and to be loved. You did that. Stefani, I wish I could say I had that in me, but I know I don't. Very few women have it inside them to make a man feel like you made Gavin feel. You and Gavin knew more about love, in the short time you were together, than the rest of us will ever hope to know in a lifetime. Stefani, it takes two very special people to have that. We both know Gavin was special … you need to realize you are, too."

Stefani smiles, reaches over, and rubs Tonya's arm. "Tonya … I guess maybe that's why it hurts so much. Knowing we had so many things to do and time to spend together. Things I'll never get to do and feel."

"Stef … I would give anything to take away your pain."

"I know you would." Stefani reaches out and hugs Tonya. "I love you."

Stefani stands and lines her suitcases up. Tonya stands and slips her hands into her back pockets. "I wish you'd let me drive you home. I'm just not sure it's a good idea for you to drive that distance right now."

"It's probably the best thing I can do right now. It will give me time alone to get a grip on everything that has happened. Then I'll have Mom and Dad with me."

"What about the boys?"

"I'll call David and explain I have to go back to St. Michaels for a few days and will pick up the boys when camp is over."

"God, Stef, you've been through so much … are you sure you're okay?"

"Yep, I'm good."

Stefani reaches down and picks up a suitcase. Tonya quickly grabs the other two. "At least let me help you load your car."

Chapter 28

When Stefani pulls into her parents' driveway, she is quickly met by her parents. As soon as she gets out of the car, Joanna hugs her. "Hello, sweetheart. How are you?"

"Pretty good."

Jack reaches over and gives her a hug like he hasn't in years. "Hey, Tiger."

Stefani begins to tear up. "Hey, Dad."

Joanna grabs her by the hand as Craig gets her luggage. "Honey, let's go inside."

The three walk into the house. Craig carries the suitcases up to Stefani's room, and Joanna leads her to the kitchen, "Sit down, honey."

Joanna reaches out and grabs Stefani's hands. She has a small tear in her eye as she says, "Tonya called."

"Tonya called here?"

"Yes ... she told us everything."

Stefani's lower lip trembles as she squints, and tears fill her eyes. Joanna jumps up and hugs her as she lets her emotions go. She wraps her arms around her mother and continues to cry.

Jack quietly enters the kitchen and stands still as Joanna looks at him and begins to weep as well. He sits down beside Stefani and puts his arm around her. "Come here, Tiger."

Stefani turns and rests her face against his shoulder. He wraps his arms around her and holds her tightly. "Sweetheart, is there anything we can do?"

Stefani shakes her head. She lifts her head and wipes her eyes with a tissue. "I'm sorry."

Her father reaches up and gently wipes a tear from her cheek. "Honey, what are you sorry for?"

"For everything."

He lets out a comforting chuckle. "Tiger, you have nothing to be sorry for. Mom and I couldn't be prouder of you than we are right now."

Stefani looks up at her dad and frowns. "Why has this happened?"

"Tiger, the man upstairs has a plan for all of us. Many times it's beyond our ability to understand and often times very painful, but there's a reason for everything."

Joanna runs her hand through Stefani's hair. Stefani sits up, pinches her lips together, and then shakes her head. "Dad, I hear you, but right now I feel selfish. Maybe there is a plan, but I want Gavin here with me. He was the one that was meant for me, and now he's gone. I'm mad … I'm just so mad."

"We know, honey, and that's okay."

Stefani tilts her head and squeezes her eyes shut as she begins to cry again. "Mom, he was so special."

"Sweetheart, the way he touched you … we know he was."

Stefani sits back. "I know you two thought this was rebound thing from David, and at first maybe I thought so too. But this was real, and it was so right. I know everything happened so fast, but Gavin was like no man I've ever known."

Joanna smiles. "Sweetheart, I had a long conversation with Tonya, and she told me everything."

"I know. You told me that earlier."

"No, honey … she told me everything."

Stefani stares and her mother and then over at her father. He nods. "Mom told me, too."

Stefani bows her head. Joanna places her palm against Stefani's cheek. "You two hardly knew each other, yet somehow he knew what a wonderful person you were. People just don't feel that way toward each other anymore. Gavin was a man who lived today but had a heart from a time in the past when people really cared for one another. He had something special inside him that told him you were the one. And for him to refrain from approaching you years ago, because he felt it wasn't right, shows how much integrity he had. God only made so many men like that … Gavin and the old man sitting next to you are the only ones I know of."

Jack bows his head, and Stefani leans over and presses her forehead against his cheek. "I know."

Stefani turns and smiles at Joanna. "I love Gavin, Mom."

"I know you do. After seeing how much he has touched you and hearing Tonya's words … Dad and I love him, too."

"I just don't understand. Why did he have to leave me?"

Joanna and Jack sit and hold Stefani for a while. Jack leans back and rests his hand on the back of her head. "Tiger, why don't you go get some sleep. You've had a long, tough day."

Joanna stands and pulls Stefani by the hand. "Come on, honey. I'll help you."

The two enter Stefani's room, and Joanna helps her into bed. "Honey, if you need anything, you call me, okay?"

"I will."

Joanna turns and walks toward the door.

"Mom."

She turns. "Yes, sweetheart?"

"I love you, Mom."

"I love you too."

After Joanna closes the door, Stefani lies still for a moment and then reaches over to grab her handbag. She opens it and pulls out the cloth holding the locket. She opens the locket and reads Gavin's note again. She neatly folds the letter and then stares at her photo and the inscription. She closes the locket but tucks the note into a pocket in her bag. Moments later she is sound asleep.

Chapter 29

Just as the sun cuts through the blinds, Stefani gets up, dresses, and heads out to her car. She drives to Gavin's office building and arrives long before anyone is due in for work. She gets out and follows the long walk around the building that leads to the bench where she and Gavin sat together the last time she was with him. She sits and stares out over the water.

"Gavin, I know you can hear me."

A single tear rolls down her cheek as she continues to stare off into the distance. "I'm so sorry, Gavin. I should have stayed here and not gone back to Charlotte. You would have never gotten on that plane if I had stayed."

She reaches into her bag and pulls out the locket. She opens it and again looks at her photo and the inscription. She slowly closes it and softly caresses it. "Gavin, we had so much to do together. There were so many things I wanted to tell you and so many things I wanted us to share … why did you have to leave me?" Stefani takes in a deep breath and releases it slowly. "I want to hold you one more time … Gavin, come take me with you."

RAINDROPS

Stefani sits for a few more moments staring out over the water. Then she brushes a tear from her face and puts the locket back into her bag. She gets up and walks back to her car. As she opens the door, Duncan pulls up. Stefani closes the door and walks toward the back of her car. Duncan parks and gets out. "Hey, Stefani."

"Hello, Duncan … I'm sorry."

"Sorry? For what?"

"I wasn't snooping. I just needed to come by. The last time I was with Gavin, we sat on the bench in the back facing the water."

Duncan walks over to her. "Stefani, come in for a while."

"No, I don't want to be a bother."

"Stefani, please."

Stefani tilts her head and smiles. "Okay."

Once they are inside, Duncan turns to Stefani. "Follow me."

Duncan walks to Gavin's office door, pulls out a set of keys from his pocket, and unlocks the door. "Stefani, make yourself at home."

"Are you sure I should go in there?"

"Yeah, I am. I think being amongst his things may make you feel better."

She nods and rubs his arm. "Thanks."

Stefani enters the office, and Duncan closes the door behind her. She goes to the large bookcase and looks over the pictures of Gavin's sons and the other items neatly situated on each shelf. She then turns and walks over to his desk. She pulls the high-back leather chair out, sits down, and runs her fingers across the smooth oak desktop. She closes her eyes and leans back in the chair as if being held. She can faintly smell Gavin's aftershave lotion, causing her mind to drift to thoughts of her intimate times with him.

Suddenly she is startled by a knock on the door. "Stefani, are you okay?"

"Yes."

Duncan opens the door and walks in. He sits in a chair across from Stefani. "I've walked into this office and sat in this chair over a thousand times. I just can't get used to this. When I walk in, I expect to see Gavin sitting there either on the phone or working on his laptop … or pacing the floor. All this just doesn't seem possible."

Stefani nods. "I know. So many times I close my eyes, and I can feel him next to me. I keep waiting to wake up and find out this whole thing has been a terrible nightmare."

Duncan turns and looks out the window overlooking the water. "I miss him."

"Me too."

He turns back and looks at her. "You know, he has always loved you. He told me stories about seeing you or something you did, and it would light up his face."

Stefani crosses her arms and pulls them against her chest as if giving herself a hug. "I wish I knew this years ago. My life would have been so different."

Duncan stares at Stefani for a moment and then sighs. "Gavin showed me one of his most treasured belongings … it's in the center drawer of the desk."

"Here?"

"Yes."

Stefani looks down at the drawer and then up at Duncan. He smiles and says. "Pull the drawer out."

She pulls the drawer open. Lying there is a leather binder with a zipper enclosure. She looks at Duncan, and he nods and says, "That's it … take it out and open it."

Stefani's hands tremble as she lifts the binder and rests it on the desk. She slowly runs the zipper around the binder but then hesitates before opening it. Finally she opens it and turns it sideways. In front of her is a picture of the softball team Gavin coached and Stefani played for years ago. She sits and stares at it for a moment and then looks up at Duncan.

He softly grins. "He told me he would come out of a very intense meeting or if he had a rough day he'd pull the picture out and look at it for a while. No matter what was going on, it always made him feel better. He told me he'd always ask himself, 'Wonder where she is?' or 'Wonder if she's having a good day?' Then he would carefully close the binder and put it away. All the years I've known him, I never knew this. It was like something that was special and private. When he showed it to me that night we talked … it was the only time he smiled."

As Stefani softly runs her finger across Gavin's image in the photo, Duncan laughs quietly. "I remember he made the comment, 'Does this make me a stalker?' I told him, 'Maybe.' Then we both started to laugh."

Duncan's smile quickly leaves his face as he lowers his head. "He was never a stalker or anything close to it. He was the finest person I've ever known. If you needed something, he was always there to help. When we created this company, we agreed everything would be split down the middle … there was never a problem. He was one of a kind. I think it's magnificent how he knew you were the one for him from the first time he ever laid eyes on you. He never wavered from that."

Stefani stares at the picture and then looks up at Duncan. "So many years ago … yet it seems like it was yesterday. I wish so much he had said something to me back then."

She closes the binder and secures the zipper. She starts to slip it back into the drawer, but Duncan says, "Stefani … take that with you."

She pulls it back out and rests it on her lap. She runs her hands across the leather cover. "Thank you, Duncan."

The two stand, and Stefani walks around the desk. She reaches up and hugs Duncan. "Thank you for everything.

Duncan stands still as Stefani releases him. "No, Stefani. Thank you."

"Thank me ... for what?"

"Stefani, even though Gavin is gone, I know you made him the happiest he's ever been in his life. He was my best friend, and seeing him feel that way means the world to me. You did that, and I know in my heart, even if he could, he wouldn't change anything that's happened recently. I honestly believe if someone told him he had to trade his life for a short time with you ... he would have agreed."

Stefani and Duncan hug again.

"Thank you, Duncan."

Stefani turns and exits the building. She drives back to her parents' house and goes to her room. She lies on the bed and looks at the photo over and over again. She smiles, noticing how young she and Gavin look in the photo. Then she notices how close Gavin is standing to her but yet just beyond her reach. It's almost as if the photo prophesized how close they would come to each other but yet still be too far apart for anything long-term to develop. She zips the binder and carefully sets it on the nightstand. She pulls a blanket up over herself and quickly falls asleep.

Chapter 30

Stefani stirs from her sleep and then rolls over to look at the clock. She quickly sits up. "Oh my God ... it's six o'clock!"

She jumps up and races down the steps. When she enters the kitchen, her parents are sitting at the table. Joanna looks up and smiles. "Honey, are you okay?"

"Yes, Mom, but I've slept all day."

"Stefani, you're exhausted. You need the rest."

Her father reaches over and takes hold of her hand. "Here, Tiger, sit down and let Mom fix you something to eat."

Stefani sits down and takes a deep breath. "I can't believe I slept this late."

"Sweetheart, it's like Mom said, you need the rest. You've been through a lot."

"I guess."

Joanna puts a plate in front of Stefani. She picks at it with her fork but barely eats anything.

"Honey, you have to eat something."

"Mom, I just don't feel very hungry."

"Did you want me to make you something else?"

"No … I think I'll just go back upstairs, take a shower, and put my things away."

Joanna smiles as she rubs Stefani on the shoulder. "If you need any help call me."

"I will."

Stefani heads upstairs, showers, and dresses. She can tell the air has gotten cooler outside, and she reaches into her suitcase and pulls out her pink Bodie's sweatshirt. She slips it on and goes to close the suitcase. Seeing the edge of the watch box, she reaches down, picks up the box, and sits on the bed. She stares at the watch and then gets up and walks over to the window. Looking beyond the yard, she can see the water in the distance. She takes the watch from the box and puts it on. She softly slides the loose band up and down her wrist as she stares at the ornate face. Instead of putting the watch back in the box, she decides to wear it.

She walks downstairs and heads to the front porch. She wraps up in a blanket and sits down on the swing, oblivious to what is going on around her as she runs the last few weeks through her mind. Regardless of what she ponders, she always ends up thinking about Gavin and how he was taken away from her.

Jack opens the screen door and steps out onto the porch. "Hey, Tiger, can you use some company?"

She looks up and smiles. "Sure."

He sits down and sighs heavily. "Cool night."

"Yes, it is."

Jack puts his arm around her and begins to slowly rock the swing with one leg. Stefani leans her head against his shoulder. He smiles and rubs her arm. "Do you need anything?"

She shakes her head. "No, Dad … just sitting here thinking."

"Life is a strange thing … once you think you've gotten it figured out, everything changes."

"It sure does."

"Any idea what you're going to do?"

Stefani sits up straight and bites her lip. "Tomorrow I'm going to Chincoteague. The plane went down off the coast there. I guess I'm hoping to find some closure."

"Did you want me or Mom to go with you?"

She turns and looks at her dad. "No … I think this is something I need to do on my own."

"If you change your mind let us know. We will gladly go with you."

Stefani buries her head into his shoulder. "I know you would, Dad."

The two sit and rock as they both enjoy the silence. Stefani feels herself beginning to nod off, and then Jack glances over and says, "Hey, Tiger, why don't we call it a night? I think both of us can use the rest."

Stefani rubs her eyes and nods. "I think you're right."

Stefani slips into bed and pulls the covers up tightly. She begins to take the watch off and then stops. After staring at it, she reaches over and turns off the light on the nightstand. Moments later she is sound asleep.

The next morning Stefani makes the two-hour drive to Chincoteague Island. Although she grew up in St. Michaels and passed the turn to Chincoteague many times traveling to and from Charlotte via the Chesapeake Bay Bridge Tunnel, this is her first time on the island. Even though it is a vacation resort, it remind her of St. Michaels. Arriving at ten on an early summer morning, it turns out, isn't the best thing for someone who wants to be alone. People are walking the streets with hardly enough room to pass one another. The congestion rivals downtown Charlotte on a Monday morning.

Although the crowds somewhat annoy her, Stefani wanders in and out of the local shops throughout the day and picks up lunch and dinner to go. As the afternoon turns into early evening, she slowly walks toward a marina where a sightseeing boat is getting ready to take a small party out into the ocean for a sunset boat ride. Stefani quickly boards and sits completely in the back. As the boat pulls away from the dock, she is relieved that no one seems to pay any attention to her—actually, it's like she isn't there. The ocean breeze softly blows her hair back as she scans the open water. All she can see is an emptiness that seems to go on forever. Somewhere out there, the endless sea holds the love of her life.

She reaches into her handbag and pulls out a small glass container with a plastic threaded cap. Earlier in the day she had filled the bottle half full of sand. Slowly she slips the bottle into her pocket, and then she reaches up to the back of her neck and unclasps Gavin's locket. She opens it and reads the inscription one last time. She reaches into her other pocket and pulls out a small, neatly folded piece of paper. She slowly unfolds it and reads, one last time, the note she wrote earlier this morning.

> *My Dearest Gavin,*
>
> *I accept I must go forward, but I understand I'm never going to be alone. I know in my heart you are always with me. You are the only true love I know or will ever know, and I thank God every day for putting you in my life. Someday we will be together again, and I know you'll be waiting for me. I look forward to that day.*
>
> *All My Love,*
> *Stefani*

She carefully folds the note tightly and places it inside the locket. She glances at the wake the boat is making as they continue to head into deeper water. She carefully winds the chain around the locket and holds it in her palm. Then she once again reaches into her pocket with the same hand and grabs the bottle with her fingers. She pulls the bottle out and unscrews the lid. She gently pushes the locket into the sand inside the bottle and replaces the lid, twisting it tightly. As she holds the bottle in both hands, she can see the lights of Chincoteague in the far distance. She gently leans backward in the seat and extends her right arm out over the side of the boat, clutching the bottle in her hand. She can feel the water splash against her hand as if it is trying to pull the bottle from her. She closes her eyes and weakens her hold. She can feel the bottle begin to slip from her hand as her grip continues to fade.

I love you, Gavin.

Suddenly a large spray hits Stefani's hand, and the bottle plunges into the water. Stefani, little by little, pulls her arm back and opens her eyes. The sun has set, and the boat begins its journey back to the dock. After arriving, she slowly walks back to her car and begins the long ride home. Once again the painful feeling of emptiness overcomes her, and a tear falls down her cheek. The closure she is looking for continues to elude her. As she drives, she can feel the fatigue getting stronger, but her heart tells her she must go on ... there is something she is missing, something still unknown ... something she knows she owes Gavin.

Chapter 31

Stefani wakes and turns flat on her back. Unlike most days, this morning is overcast, and she can hear a light rain pelting the window. She'd had hopes of going for a run this morning, but the dreary weather quickly dampens that notion. She slowly makes her way into the bathroom and looks in the mirror. "God, I look terrible."

She turns on the shower and undresses. She looks down and notices her watch is still on her wrist. She gently undoes the band and places it on the sink. She showers, letting the hot water run down her body. She is completely exhausted from her journey to Chincoteague yesterday, and the rain isn't helping to boost her level of energy. She steps out of the shower and wraps in a robe. She picks up the watch, walks to her suitcase, and reaches for the watch box. As she stands, she is overcome with emotion. She slowly covers her face with her hand and begins to cry. She flops down on the bed and tightly holds on to the watch. After few moments she opens her eyes and takes a deep breath.

When she stands, she realizes the watch box has fallen from the bed. Reaching down to pick it up, she notices the lid is open slightly and the inner lining has come loose. She opens the lid fully and gently pulls the lining completely free. Taped to the back of the lining is a bright brass key. Confused, she pulls the key free. It is a strangely cut key with "First Bank of St. Michaels" pressed into the head. Carefully she puts the watch box back together and places the watch inside. After putting the box back in her suitcase, she quickly dresses and goes downstairs.

As she turns the corner, she sees Joanna working at the stove. "Hey, Mom."

"Hi, honey … you look tired. I think yesterday took a lot out of you."

"Yeah … me too."

Stefani opens her palm, revealing the key. "Mom, have you ever seen a key like this?"

Joanna walks over and squints through her glasses. She picks the key up from Stefani's palm and studies it more closely. "Can't say that I have, but it does say First Bank of St. Michaels on it. Where did you get it?"

Stefani quickly responds, "Oh … I found it yesterday on the road."

Joanna continues to study the key. "It looks important. One of us should run it down to the bank."

Stefani looks up and nods. "Yeah … I'll do it this morning."

Joanna turns back around and returns to her cooking. "You want some breakfast?"

"No … I … uh … have some things I need to get in town. I'll be home a little later."

"Okay. Lunch is at twelve sharp!"

"Gotcha."

Stefani turns and heads out to her car. Once belted in, she rolls the brass key in her hand. "Gavin … what does it mean?"

She drives straight to the bank. As she walks in the front door, she is met by an older woman. "Hello. May I help you?"

"Yes … I have this key."

The woman looks at the key. "Oh, you have a safety deposit box."

"Yes … yes, that's right."

The woman tells her, "Dear, you go downstairs and take as much time as you need."

"Thank you."

Stefani walks across the large room and down the flight of stairs. At the bottom is an elderly man sitting at a desk. "Good morning, Miss. May I help you?"

"Yes, I'm here to access my safety deposit box."

"Fine, I just need to see your identification."

Stefani sits down, pulls her driver's license from her wallet, and hands it to the man. He types her name into the computer. "Ms. Tanner, there you are. I see your associate Mr. Thorne and you just rented the box recently."

"Ah ... yes, that's correct."

The man smiles. "Please follow me."

The two walk into a large vault. The man puts his key into door number 100. He turns the key, and the door opens. He removes his key and slides a long box from the pocket. He sets it on the table in the center of the room. "If you need anything, just let me know."

"Yes, I will ... thank you."

The man leaves, and Stefani slowly sits in the chair beside the table. She is having a hard time catching her breath as she softly runs her hand across the top of the box. Nervously she takes her key and easily slides it into the lock on the box. With very little effort the key turns, and she hears a loud click. Her hands tremble as she lifts the lid. Inside, she can see a small box and a beige envelope. She picks up the envelope and turns it over. Written in bold on it is her first name. She sets the envelope on the table and places her fingertips against her lips. She then gently reaches out and picks up the small box. It is wrapped in gold foil paper. She carefully unwraps the package and places it on the table. It is a beautiful mahogany box trimmed in brass. She picks up the envelope and opens it. Inside is a folded piece of high-quality stationary. She unfolds it.

My Love,

For the longest time I was lost. So many times I would find myself dreaming of things that I thought would make me happy, make me whole. I searched and searched but always found myself in the same place ... hollow and alone. I had so much to be thankful for, yet something was missing. One day I decided this is my fate. I did my best to accept my life and promised myself I would never let anyone see my pain. Then one day everything changed. You came back into my life. You took an empty heart and made it overflow with nothing more than a smile. Your love filled a void in me and made me complete. My search was over ... I found what I was looking for. It was you. It was always you and forever will be you.

I know words will never express how much I love you and need you. My solemn wish is for this small gift to fill the one void that has caused suffering in your life. Your happiness is my purpose, and my love for you is eternal.

Happy first anniversary to my wife.
All my love,
Gavin

Stefani wipes the tears from her eyes and then carefully folds the letter and places it back in the envelope. She picks up the wooden box and tilts the top back on its hinges. Sitting inside on a beautiful blue velvet cushion is a Faberge Eternity brooch. Stefani squints her eyes and presses her lips together as she tilts her head to the side. Tears slowly stream down her cheeks while she holds her breath in an effort not to make a sound. She finally gasps for air and says shakily, "Oh, Gavin."

She carefully closes the box and puts it with the envelope into her bag. She replaces the lock box and returns to her car. Her drive home, although short, seems to take forever. Stefani walks into the house and makes her way to the kitchen.

Joanna is sitting at the table and looks up. When she sees Stefani's face, she says, "Oh, honey, you've been crying. Please sit down. Are you okay?"

Stefani sits and nods. She begins to weep again, and Joanna reaches out and holds her hand. "It's okay, sweetheart. It's okay."

"Mom, I lied to you."

Her mother raises her eyebrows. "When?"

"Earlier today about the key from the bank."

"Oh?"

"Yes ... I found it hidden in a watch box Gavin sent me, but I'm pretty sure I wasn't supposed to find it until Gavin told me to look for it."

"Oh? How can you be sure?"

"I accidentally dropped the box this morning, and the lining in the lid came loose. The key was taped to the back of the lining. It's a key to a lockbox."

"And you went and found the box."

"Yes." Stefani pulls out the envelope and slides it over to Joanna.

Her mother pulls the letter from the envelope, glances up at Stefani, and then begins to read. Within moments tears are running down her cheeks. After reading it, she folds it up and carefully puts it back in the envelope. "Honey, that's beautiful … He had a heart full of love for you."

Stefani's lip quivers. "Mom, I told him the story about Grandma's brooch and how much pain losing it caused her, you, and me. I told him how I loved to walk through antique shops and had the foolish hope that one day I would stumble upon a replacement to fill the void in our hearts."

Joanna sits back and presses her trembling fingers against her lips. Tears begin to race down Stefani's cheeks as she slides the wooden box across the table to her mother. Joanna follows the box with her eyes and then looks up at Stefani. Stefani nods for her to open it. Joanna reaches out with shaking hands and opens the box. "Oh, my God."

She looks up.

Stefani stands, steps around the table, and hugs Joanna. Both cry uncontrollably. Stefani manages to mumble, "I miss him so much."

"I know you do, sweetheart … I know you do."

Later that evening Stefani is sitting on the front porch swing wrapped in an afghan. Joanna walks out and sits beside her. "How are you?"

"Brokenhearted."

"I know you are. I don't know why things happen the way they do."

Stefani sits up straight and continues to look off into the distance. "Mom, I use to think I was in total control of my life. I was absolutely sure nothing happened by chance and my life was what I made it … my education, my job, and my marriage. Then all at once I was in control of nothing. David's betrayal, losing my job … no matter how hard I tried, there was nothing I could do about anything. For the first time in my life, I was afraid. I had never been in a situation like this before. Then when things seemed the darkest and I had no idea where to turn, a man reenters my life. He made me realize that I had it all wrong. He made me a better person … a person who now knows success isn't a job title but the people in your life. I'm ashamed to say that, before Gavin, I was too insincere and obtuse to understand."

Stefani shakes her head as she looks down. "Mom, too many people have it all wrong. Somewhere people lost sight of what is important and replaced it with what they perceive is important. I know this … I was one of those people. Gavin helped me wake up and appreciate Dad, you, and the boys.

He loved me for who I am, not what I am or who I thought I was."

Stefani turns to Joanna and gently smiles. "Mom, Gavin was so genuine…He truly was one of a kind."

Joanna tilts her head to the side. "Yes, he most certainly was."

Stefani slowly nods her head and releases and weak smile.

"I know this sounds selfish, because he meant so much to so many, but I believe Gavin was an angel put here for me."

Stefani looks up and out into the distance again. "Mom, he knew he loved me the first time he saw me and waited endlessly for me. When I thought all was lost, he picked me up, showed me limitless love, and made me a better person. Once he did that … his time here was complete, and he was taken to a better place. Now I know he watches over me continuously … he is always with me and will always take care of me."

Stefani turns and grins at Joanna. "God does some amazing things."

Joanna reaches up with her hand and runs her fingers though Stefani's hair. "He sure does, honey … he sure does."

Chapter 32

Stefani wakes the next morning and notices her room seems darker than usual. She climbs out of bed and makes her way to the window. As she separates the sheers, she can see the overcast skies blocking the sun. The gloomy weather makes her misery worse, and it takes every ounce of energy to climb into the shower and dress for the day. Eventually she drags herself down the stairs and into the kitchen.

Joanna is busy making cookies and takes a few minutes to notice that Stefani has slid into a chair. "Hi, sweetheart ... I didn't hear you come in."

"Just moving kinda slow today."

"Would you like something to eat?"

Stefani shakes her head and looks out the window. "No ... just not hungry."

"Stefani, you have to eat to keep your strength up."

"I know, but just not right now."

Joanna goes back to placing the dough balls onto the cookie sheet. "So what do you plan to do today?"

Stefani tilts her head down. "Mom ... I have no idea. I just don't feel like doing much of anything."

"Well, if you need anything ..."

"I know."

Stefani stands and heads back upstairs to her room. She sits on the bed and pulls out the leather binder containing the photo of the softball team. She softly runs her finger across Gavin's image and smiles as she studies his much younger appearance. Quickly her smile disappears, and she slowly zips the binder shut. She stands and again stares out the bedroom window, looking over the water in the distance.

"Gavin, I know you can hear me ... I miss you so much."

A single tear runs down her cheek. "I just wish somehow I knew you were okay and happy."

Moments later she brushes the tear from her face and heads back downstairs. As she passes the kitchen, she sticks her head in the doorway. "Mom, I'm going for a ride."

"Are you okay?"

"Yes ... I just need ... some time."

"If you need anything, you call me."

"I will."

Stefani climbs into the Range Rover and begins to drive with no destination in mind. She drives through St. Michaels, to Oxford, and past Gavin's office building and the entrance lane to his house. Finally she finds herself heading down the lane that leads to Gavin's beach. She stops the car just short of the spot where they made love. She places the car in park and turns the engine off. She recalls the night they spent together on the blanket. How they talked, laughed, and made love under the star-filled sky. How Gavin described the way he chose their star and told her he loved her with all his heart. Somehow the dark, overcast sky seems to embody her inability to be with Gavin. The heavy clouds blanket the sky and would prevent the stars from shining through, blocking any attempt to unite with what she wants most.

After staring into the distance Stefani sinks into the seat and closes her eyes. She tilts her head back as her reminiscing weakens her, and she begins to quietly weep. "Gavin … where are you? I need you so much … I'm totally lost without you. I need to hear from you and know you are here with me."

Stefani's head falls forward. "Please, Gavin … talk to me."

She sits motionless. There is total silence, and the only thing she can hear is her own breathing. Just as she is drift into a doze she hears a soft tap on the windshield. She opens her eyes and slowly raises her head. Directly in front of her on the windshield is one single raindrop. Bit by bit it begins to fall, hesitating … then moving again. It continues its descent, moving back and forth erratically. Suddenly a second drop lands beside the first. It too struggles to maintain a course as it heads for the base of the windshield. Then, as if drawn toward one another, the two drops touch and become one large drop. It immediately races in a straight line to the bottom of the windshield and disappears. Stefani begins breathing heavily and quickly throws her door open. She jumps out, takes a few steps away from the car, and looks up at the sky. All at once rain pours down, saturating her hair and clothes. Stefani extends her arms out to her side with her palms up and closes her eyes. She stands in awe for a moment, and then a magnificent smile crosses her face.

"I love you, Gavin!"

Made in the USA
Middletown, DE
07 August 2016